Praise for *Shi...*

"North, of course, is a man with a broken moral compass. He is a man who protects himself avidly, crouching behind surliness or dutiful charm. . . . The soulless man is Begley's stock-in-trade, and . . . Begley's prose is masterful."

—*Newsday*

"All cheating husbands should be so worthy of sympathy."

—*Entertainment Weekly*

"Begley is a major talent. . . . He is totally in command here, and we can only marvel at his portraiture. . . . *Shipwreck* is a novel of skill, insight, and authority."

—*The Sunday Star-Ledger*

"With this beautiful, haunting novel, Begley has given us an exquisite record of one captain's internal strife as his ship looks poised to go down."

—*The Columbus Dispatch*

"[A] chilly, wonderfully controlled tale."

—*St. Louis Today*

"Swimming sometimes in a sea of sex, *Shipwreck* is at once title, interleaved metaphor, and plot propulsion. Its first page shows John North, the book's narrator, accosting a solitary stranger in a Manhattan bar. . . . The novel is an incongruous admixture, braided as it is with broodings on the problems of the creative process as well as one's literary reputation. . . . Begley provides plunder enough for a whole shipload of readers."

—East Hampton Star

"[A] spellbinding story . . . Begley has again written a novel that fully demonstrates his impeccable talent and his deep comprehension of the human condition."

—National Jewish Post & Opinion

"The story of a personal moral disaster compellingly and compulsively told . . . [with a] vivid sense of detail."

—Los Angeles Times

"This glimpse into the world of international high class and culture is intriguing and provocative."

—Rocky Mountain News

SHIPWRECK

Shipwreck

LOUIS BEGLEY

BALLANTINE BOOKS • NEW YORK

A BALLANTINE BOOK

PUBLISHED BY THE RANDOM HOUSE PUBLISHING GROUP

In memoriam Siegfried Unseld

"Shh, shh," you said,
"I want to put my legs around your head."

DONALD HALL, "Conversation's Afterplay"

SHIPWRECK

I was smoking a cigarette at the bar, an empty glass before me, wondering whether I should have another or leave, when I felt a hand on my shoulder. A rather deep, pleasant voice said, Let me treat you to a whiskey. I don't like drinking alone. I bet you don't either.

There was no reason to refuse. It wasn't as though I were expected elsewhere. I nodded and followed him to a table. Seeing a waiter lounge unoccupied within hailing distance, he ordered a bottle of whiskey, ice, and soda water. We were served with surly efficiency. With a sigh of what I took to be satisfaction, he crossed and recrossed the ankles of the long, thin legs stretched out before him, and looked about. I too once more took in the flickering lights, the grouping of shadows at other tables, and the murmur of voices. After a moment, he broke the silence: I should introduce myself. North. I am John North.

I bowed slightly and reciprocated the politeness.

Abruptly, he spoke again, this man so like me in appearance and demeanor, from the crown of his neatly barbered head to the tips of his brogues, well worn but beautifully polished.

Listen, he said. Listen. I will tell you a story I have never told before. If you hear me out, you will see why. I would have been a fool to tell it. With you, somehow I feel secure. Call it instinct or impulse or fate—your choice. Besides, could it possibly matter what I say to you over a pleasant drink here, at L'Entre Deux Mondes?

Something in what he had said or had failed to say must have amused him hugely. He laughed to the point of tears. It was a moment before he got hold of himself and was able to continue. Is not this benighted place the perfect no-man's-land? he asked.

I made no comment.

Well, speak up, said North, with a touch of irritation. Can it possibly matter what I say to you here?

I am by nature shy and uncommunicative. This intimacy that nothing justified and that I had done nothing to encourage put me on my guard. At the same time, I did not wish to rebuff out of hand what might turn out to be a harmless conversational gambit. It seemed best to say nothing.

North nodded, perhaps to indicate that in the end my silence didn't matter either. I suppose it will strike you as droll, he said, that my story should begin at a café. A café in Paris that you may know. By the way, are you familiar with my work? I mean my novels.

Seeing what was no doubt my blank expression, he laughed and said, Don't worry, I much prefer honesty to polite lies I see through immediately. It doesn't matter, please don't protest. I will simply assume that you haven't read a word of mine. Take it on faith though that for many years I have been a writer of considerable literary reputation and reasonable commercial success. When this story begins, my then most recent novel,

The Anthill, had been out for a little over six months, having been published in the States in the fall of the previous year. The French translation had just appeared. It was displayed in the windows of most bookstores in Paris, and you could find it even at the newsstands at Roissy and Orly, which normally carry only French best-sellers and foreign trash. I have always had the same publisher in France. He published *The Anthill* and all my earlier novels. His name is Xavier Roche, and over the years he has become a friend. I was in Paris at his invitation. It wasn't exactly a book tour. Nothing of real importance in literary life happens in the French provinces anyway. Rather, the idea was to spend a week or so in Paris and be interviewed by print journalists. If I was very lucky, I would appear on *Apostrophes,* a television show about books that has a huge influence on sales, as well as literary opinion. But that didn't happen. Mind you, I had some things going for me. All my novels were available in French, I have always had good reviews in France, and my spoken French is almost native, altogether an unusual profile for an American writer. Xavier hoped to exploit these advantages, especially since he had nothing by a "name" French author to bring out that year.

So it happened that I found myself in May, on a gray afternoon of the sort that makes you want to curl up and go to sleep, at the Café Flore, being interviewed by a young woman for a feature on me to appear in French *Vogue.* No, I'm not that kind of novelist, I assure you; but when there is a "peg" they can use, the glossies sometimes do profiles of serious writers, and even run a competent review. What was the peg here? My modest celebrity in the States and in France, the various storied adventures of my parents, who in their day cut a wide swath here and there, and especially in Paris, and the fact that I had lived in Paris myself. Whatever the reason, the article had been assigned, and there was a possibility that American and British *Vogue* would pick it up in translation. A photo session was to follow directly. When the journalist—I really mean to say the girl, since I couldn't help thinking of her as such, not because she was juvenile, I guessed her age was somewhere between twenty-five and thirty, probably closer to thirty, but because something in her looks and in her chipper professional manner made me think of the "girl reporter" type in movies of the 1940s. Anyway, when the girl asked whether I would like to have a cup of coffee while the photographer and his assistant set up, I accepted. I was pleased with the interview. She had read my work carefully and also knew much of what had been written about me. Her questions were intelligent.

As soon as I said yes, she led me to a table on the other side of the café away from where we had sat during the interview. I supposed that she wanted to avoid our being disturbed by the photographer. Or overheard.

Thank you for everything, she said. For your books and this interview. You were really eloquent. The new book is wonderful. I think it will be very well received.

The coffee and the scotch I had ordered for myself presented a distraction that allowed me not to answer right away. I drank the coffee quickly, while it was scalding hot, which is my habit, and asked for another. Then I worked on my drink, stirring the ice cubes in the glass. Of course, I knew I had been eloquent. She might as well have said brilliant. And the prospects for my book? At home, the reviews in the news-papers and magazines that count had been favorable, leaving aside the few cranks who always go after me for personal or ideological reasons. There had been some raves as well. All the same, in a split second, the girl had soured my mood. It wasn't only my ingrained dread of optimism and premature congrat-ulations, although there is much to be said for this particular superstition, one of many that I am mostly proud of. For instance, when we drive from the city to our place on Long Island, near the property of my wife's parents, I always plead with her not to tell me, before we have as much as crossed the Triborough Bridge, that the traffic is moving well. Without exception, every time she says it, immediately we get stuck in a jam behind an overturned truck or the like. It's guaranteed. No, it wasn't what the girl had said that bothered me. She spoke the inevitable truth: *The Anthill* would get good reviews followed by anemic sales. But Xavier couldn't blame me or my book for that. It's simply the fate of ninety-nine percent of translated novels in the French market. I knew the roots of my sudden disquiet. They were different and sank deeper than her well-meant comment, way down to a discovery I had made recently while Lydia—my wife—was away in Hawaii, attending a congress on kidney disease in infants and very young children, a subject on which she is a great authority.

I was alone in New York and idle. The new project I had in mind was too unformed for me to start writing. At most, I could have taken notes on what I might do later, but I didn't, taking notes and making outlines being forms of activity I ordinarily eschew. I didn't especially want to see friends, and I was too impatient—nervous, really—to do any serious reading. Usually I welcome this state of wary inertia into which my mind drifts between books. It makes me receptive to impressions that I would otherwise miss or seize incompletely, and yet these are the very impressions that later nourish my work. So it was without my having intended it, by accident—but I think it was the sort of inevitable accident that waits for you—that I found myself sitting in judgment on my novels. I had been to a movie I found annoying because of a cruel streak that ran through it, rather at odds with the banal and fundamentally cheerful plot. The screenwriter or the director had spoiled it by putting on airs. Afterward, I had a plate of pasta at the only restaurant in my neighborhood that serves real food after eleven. My first thought, when I got home, was to go straight to bed. But I was too tense and irritated, so I poured myself a drink and took it into the library. There are things you do only when you are alone. I sauntered over to the shelves reserved for the first editions of my novels and their translations and stroked the familiar spines. Then, as though under a compulsion I was unable to resist, I took down first the new book and later all the others and looked at certain passages. I was to remain in my armchair the whole night and the next day, and most of the night that followed, with hardly any pause, although I suspected that I had a fever. I reread my production. At a certain point, entire sentences I had written seemed to disintegrate like figures in a kaleidoscope when you turn the tube, only my words did not regroup and coalesce as new wonders of color and design. They lay on the page like so many vulgar, odious pieces of shattered glass. The conclusion I reached came down to this: none of my books, neither the new novel nor any I had written before, was very good. Certainly, none possessed the literary merit that critical opinion ascribed to them. Not even my second novel, the one that won all the prizes and was said to confirm my standing as an important novelist. No, they all belonged to the same dreary breed of unneeded books. Novels that are not embarrassingly bad but lead you to wonder why the author had bothered. Unless, of course, he had only a small ambition: to earn a modest sum of money and short-lived renown. You can see how these feelings, unknown to the girl, had turned her innocent bit of flattery into a *faux pas*.

North refilled our glasses and looked at me brightly. There is a reason, he said, for telling you about this somber little epiphany, although in itself it may not interest you. It's a part of the setting. Without it, you might not be able to judge fairly what followed.

I mumbled assent. The whiskeys I had drunk had induced in me a sort of hypnagogic state. Time no longer mattered.

And what should one think of a man who writes such books, he continued, where does he belong if not to the race of trimmers, men who live without infamy and without praise, envious of any other fate?

He did not wait for me to answer this question, which I took anyway to be rhetorical. Instead, he resumed his monologue: Always be alert among such men to their capacity for envy, even if it's not center stage! Actually, trimmers of my kind do get praise, but it's never enough. There is always old Joe or old

Max who got more and better praise although he is less deserving. Yes, it came upon me painfully that I had wasted my time writing the stuff. Those enthusiastic reviews that had greeted my new novel in the American and English press, and still continued to straggle in from the odd magazines, the praise that had made me blush with pleasure and had delighted Lydia, should have reddened me with shame. Sitting there with the girl at the Flore, thinking about my discovery, I recalled especially the review faxed by my agent, which I had read at breakfast that very day. Somehow, I had misled, in fact duped, the reviewer who wrote it, an astute and immensely scrupulous woman whom I admire, duped her, like so many of her colleagues, into finding in my work qualities that I, with my eyes newly open, knowing my work as only the author can, every sentence and paragraph, could certify were entirely absent. Such articles, which moved my agent, my editor, and my writer friends to telephone or write with congratulations, didn't they in the end serve only to enlarge the con game? And now this girl, with her chatter, and the profile with which I was brazenly collaborating, was going to add to the scandal, and to the vast accumulation of my shame.

North paused, evidently upset. He rubbed his eyes. The gesture seemed to be a tic of which he was aware. After a while he continued.

I had drunk my baby whiskey, so I asked the girl if she would reconsider and join me while I had a second larger drink. No, but she would have another coffee. She wanted to continue reviewing her notes. That was all right with me; no is no. Meanwhile, since she had really launched me into orbit, I continued my own review of my monstrous predicament. There was no doubt that I had become a novelist honestly, thinking there was a world of stories in my head waiting to be told, and that I knew how to tell them. Writing novels had become my trade when I was very young, straight out of college; my only trade. I was qualified to do nothing else: not to sell insurance or manage a restaurant or trade commodities futures or perform any of the other tasks requiring no hard physical labor but still deemed useful and worth paying for. Only a preposterous public recantation could purge the fraud. I knew of one writer who had so rejected his work, but the disavowal had coincided in his case with his new conviction, almost religious in nature, that he had found a different way to write that was worthy. I had nothing like that up my sleeve. Perhaps the only honorable solution was to scrap the book I had just begun and forever after keep my peace.

All of a sudden, the girl spoke up. Mr. North, she said, when we were discussing the sources of your new book, I wrote in my notes: "Come back to this. Don't let him dance around the question." Do you remember when I asked you whether *The Anthill* is autobiographical, perhaps even more so than your other novels? You went dead on me. Were you offended? Could we talk about that?

There was some whiskey left in my glass. I studied the girl's face through the yellow liquid. The eyeglasses she wore were surprisingly thick. I decided she must be extraordinarily myopic, and too much the girl journalist to wear contact lenses at work. Maybe contacts weren't much good for reading. Her skin was smooth, almost buttery, and her nose very small. Should I quit right now, I asked myself, tell the girl I want to go back to my hotel, and refuse to do anything more to promote my book and myself?

North stopped and stared at me. Speak, man, he said. You look as though you want to say: Why didn't you?

I didn't answer.

He raised his eyebrows and continued. Let me tell you, it's not so easy. The only point in giving an interview in this hard and cruel world is to get the journalist to say something favorable about you and your book. For that to happen, you must make yourself liked. I knew that if I antagonized the girl, there was a good chance she'd get right back at me. How? There are so many ways—the simplest would be to intimate that I was conceited and fundamentally uninteresting. I decided to play it safe, and even tried a smile. In truth, I hadn't yet tested my new conviction that my value as a writer was close to zero. In my shame and cowardice, I had not even spoken about it to Lydia. That was something I would do when I returned to New York. No, this didn't seem to be the time or place for a proclamation.

Look, I said to the girl, I'm sorry if I was brusque. Each time I am asked this particular question or one like it I begin to feel that I am suffering from metal fatigue. As though some important structural support inside me were going to crack. Or my arms were going to fall off. Because there isn't an interviewer who hasn't asked it. You'd think it mattered, but believe me, it doesn't; it's a dead end. So I have perfected a standard answer I am quite resigned to giving. I didn't give it to you because I thought you deserved better, but I am not sure I have anything better to say. So, if you want the standard speech, go right ahead and turn on your tape recorder.

That won't be necessary, was her answer. She opened her notebook, found a clean page, switched to a high-tech ballpoint pen, and waited.

All right, I said. But first I'll have another whiskey. It's outrageous how little liquor they put in a drink in these St. Germain des Prés cafés.

The waiter brought my drink and, after a large sip, I began: It is a given that a novelist of my sort finds his material principally in his own life. The memory of places he has lived in or has visited and the events in which he has been caught up, even if he was completely passive. He uses his nightmares, fears and sorrows, ambitions and disappointments. Of course, he draws on his joys too. I don't mean to suggest that only unhappy memories go into the work, although that often seems to be the case. Oh, yes, he also uses everything he has read and has not forgotten, and tales and anecdotes told to him by others. When he is dining out, for instance, like Henry James.

The look on the girl's face made clear that we had failed to connect; James was not to be found in the French lycée curriculum. I didn't let that detail slow me down.

All sorts of stuff gets stored inside a novelist, I said, including stuff he doesn't know is there until he begins to write. Was it the effect of the drink or of listening to my own words? I found myself wanting to impress the girl and pushed on with more brio.

Once the novelist has found, I said—stumbled upon, would

be more accurate in most cases—once he has found a subject that attracts him, and makes him want to start a book, he shapes these odds and ends until they become useful material and can be hung like laundry on the line of his story. Garments of words, fashioned word by word and sentence by sentence. This is hard work, and most would give anything to avoid it if only there were some other way a novel could be written. But there isn't. Not sure that I hadn't lost the girl again, I tapped my fingers on the table. Forgive the digression, I said. What I hope you will accept as true is that my new novel, just like its brothers and sisters, is autobiographical in only one sense: it's made out of stuff that life has deposited inside me. But my novels aren't about me, and none of them is the story of my life.

The girl wrote busily, put away her pen, and said, This is just what I needed. Thank you again!

She smiled joyously, displaying regular, strong, and very white teeth. I have always liked women with good teeth. I have to admit that altogether I like the new kind of French. I like their healthy looks. So different from the sallow kids I knew when I was a kid myself, with their passion for politics and their yellow teeth that melted in plain sight as they drank their scotch. Better pediatricians and dentists, a good diet, and vacations given over to strenuous sports, that's what made the difference. I am constantly astonished to see how the young French get to do everything. Ski the high Alps, sail off the coast of Australia, walk across China—the wonder is they can afford it. Perhaps forgetting about politics has helped too. When I think of what the war in Algeria and May '68 meant for the French of our generation, I feel like a goddamn museum piece. If there is any great political or social cause like that

that could quicken the pulse of this girl or her friends, I assure you that I have not found it. Not even after I got to know her very well.

But to go back to the interview, North said, I certainly wanted to be fair. You can sympathize with that. So I told the girl: I've warned you. When you get ready to put these pronouncements into your article, please remember that this is not the first time I have made them. But, however often repeated, they are what I think. Honest to God.

Another joyous smile was my recompense.

It doesn't matter, she said. I'm not worried about your interviews with other magazines. This one is for our readers.

I was tempted to ask the girl why she assumed that her readers read only *Vogue,* but I forbore. We had already talked enough. For that same reason I didn't tell her there was a follow-up question she should ask: Why is the one story I hadn't told, and seemed to have no desire to tell, in place of the bits and pieces of it mixed with other bric-a-brac, the story of my life? Had she asked, I might have told her what, at the time, I believed quite strongly: that such need as I had to confess was more than satisfied by the bits and pieces—the occasional allusions tucked into my novels to that unconfessed life. Do these occult messages, to the confection of which I think I have devoted far too much time, have addressees? Lydia is the principal one, of course. There is always the possibility of some other ideal and preternaturally sympathetic reader, too shy to have made himself known or not yet born. It doesn't matter. Do my messages have a purpose? I used to think of them as minor acts of defiance, like clues that a murderer convinced of having committed the perfect crime feels compelled to leave behind him. In truth, however, I believe that I make up these messages mainly to have fun, which may also hold for the murderer.

North paused here, his composure perhaps not so complete as it had been. The unexpected silence gave me an opening. I took advantage of it and asked why he hadn't had the desire to tell it all, to write a memoir. He looked at me queerly and asked, in turn, Don't you think that the chat we're having is quite enough? Seeing that I had no ready answer, he extracted a case from the inside pocket of his blazer, opened it, and offered me a cigar. I declined. He took one himself, clipped the end with a penknife, and, once it was drawing satisfactorily, continued his tale.

At last the photographer was ready. Now I sat on the banquette, across the table from him. As he clicked his way through a series of frames that had me turning away from the lens, I stared at the girl, at first because you have to look at something, but soon with growing interest. She was taller, I realized, than she had seemed when I first saw her rise from a table on the terrace of the Flore, a copy of *The Anthill* held aloft so I could identify her. I noted the expensive-looking jeans, the lipstick that gave her a Marilyn Monroe mouth, and the shock of dark blond wavy hair through which she kept running her fingers. She had told me her name: Léa Morini. Jewish, perhaps, though I knew that in France it wasn't only Jews who might choose that name for a daughter, and there was nothing particularly Jewish about the girl's features, or her bold, almost rambunctious manner. But, as you know, among the French it is difficult to draw any conclusions from physical type except in extreme cases. The family name, Morini, told me nothing: it could just as easily have been of Corsican as of Sephardic origin. So I pursued thoughts of a different order. Were her parents the sort who would knowingly burden an innocent infant with a biblical tag that might not suit her, or were they *tout bêtement* ignorant of how Laban's tender-eyed daughter was never the sister Jacob preferred, no matter how hard she tried? Either hypothesis was plausible. After all, little girls are called Gilda, Cordelia, and Judith all the time, as if those names told no story, and also Felicity, perhaps to give the child a push in the direction of happiness, without taking into account the possibility that the child might have to pay for the parental presumption.

We're losing you, Monsieur North, said the photographer. You're somewhere in the clouds.

Sorry, I replied. Let's try it again.

I collected myself, and even offered to put on my reading glasses or to hold them in any one of the gestures I have practiced in the course of hamming it up for many shoots. You know the secret? Always channel energy into your eyes. Otherwise, the camera betrays you. It captures your flaccid face and empty stare.

We finished. I shook hands all around and offered my thanks. Then I remembered my usual injunction to journalists who interview me. There is just one thing, I told the girl, I will have to check any direct quotes you want to use. Not to censor the article; I only want to make sure that I don't seem incoherent. You know where to find me.

You'll have the quotes tomorrow, she replied and gave me her card.

I read the home address. Rue de l'Abbaye de St. Germain.

How nice, I said, just around the corner, nestled against the church.

It is wonderful. My studio is on the top floor. There is no reason you should know it, but I have two careers. I'm also a painter.

Although it was drizzling, I decided to walk up the boulevard St. Germain to the hotel in the rue du Bac, where Xavier had as usual arranged for me to stay. There was no message from Lydia. My old friend Pierre Lalonde, my best friend in France, had telephoned again. I had not had the chance to return his first call. This time he left a message. He and Marianne were expecting me for dinner at eight-thirty. Would I please confirm? Why Pierre should think that I might have forgotten or changed my mind was puzzling. I have always been meticulous about keeping appointments and arriving on time–something that one could not have said about him. The girl had left a message too. Just to say that she was very grateful. No need to call her back. I have always liked the sort of good manners you can still take for granted in France even if, as in this case, they seem utterly perfunctory, the result of being on automatic pilot in these matters. Obviously, there was no other reason to thank me again by telephone after having thanked me in person less than half an hour earlier. Long ago someone had taught her that this sort of *coup de fil* was the polite thing to do, and therefore she went ahead and left her telephoned thank-you note without considering whether the act made sense. And perhaps in some way it did, because the gesture turned out to be quite welcome. I received it like a cup of steaming hot tea offered at the end of that dreary afternoon.

It also moved me to call Pierre and assure him there was no misunderstanding. *Calme-toi.* I won't stand you up.

I knew that, with the rain, traffic was going to be bad at the dinner hour when all of Paris is on the move. Even so, there was no reason to deprive myself of a drink or a bath. The drink, I thought, must come first. I decided to have it in the hotel bar. Do you know that bar?

I shook my head.

Really? It's in the basement, a long space furnished to replicate some Frenchman's idea of an English club. Left Bank editors and publishers have made it their headquarters since the beginning of time. That's where they meet their writers, and, I bet even more important, their partners in adultery. Discretion is supposed to be guaranteed by the dimness of the light. That is, of course, pure nonsense, a *blague.* As one look around this place will teach you, eyes adjust to darkness rather quickly. For my taste, it was carried too far, like all farces. I am thinking of a dashing editor I know with a remarkable stable of Latin American writers. Hot properties in France, and in Germany as well. He used to have lunch there, every day, weekends excepted, always at the same table, with his mistress, who was not in publishing. She happened to be married to a man who had been two years behind me at college. Three lovely children, house near Fontainebleau, and so forth. At the other end of the room, but not more than forty-five feet away, was the table at which this dashing editor's wife lunched, also every workday of the week, with one of her husband's colleagues, a specialist in Central European literature at the very same publishing house. The wife of the Central

European expert worked in publishing as well, in publicity, but at another house. Tact, sadism, or plain carelessness? You tell me. In theory, face was saved, because the first couple arrived invariably at one o'clock, and the other, just as methodically, after one-fifteen. I remember being shocked not merely by the fact of adultery but by the casual acceptance of it by each of the four. Whether my college friend and the publicist wife were *au courant* is another matter. I hope they were blind and naive. How much heartache and bitterness lay behind these arrangements, I have no idea. The fact is that they clashed violently with my own sense of acceptable behavior.

Anyway, at the end of that afternoon in May there was no one in the bar whom I recognized, which was just as well. The interview with the girl at the Flore had worn me out, and I knew that there would be more than enough conversation later. I found a table away from the crowd, settled down in one of those club chairs with which the place was furnished, and ordered a drink—scotch, out of caution, in preference to gin— and a smoked-salmon sandwich to line my stomach: father's prescription for getting through a round of diplomatic parties with flying colors. There would be plenty of drinking at Pierre's as well. You may be surprised, seeing me guzzle here, to hear that I had given any thought to how much I would drink that evening. I hope it won't disappoint you to learn that my consumption of alcohol is ordinarily quite unremarkable— hardly above the level that my doctor, a very reasonable fellow to be sure, finds acceptable. No, I wasn't hitting the bottle at the time when these events took place. The dinner was certain to begin and to end late. There was nothing to be done about that. With luck, if there were no other guests, I would get away before midnight, right after coffee. In that case I might catch Lydia at home, after the hospital and before she went out to dinner. I supposed that she would be going out to her sister's or her brother's, in which case, if I missed her, I could call at home, first thing in the morning her time. Trying to get through at the hospital was a time-consuming and irritating nuisance to be avoided whenever possible. Or, indeed, I could ask to use the telephone at Pierre's. Leaving his party early, before the last guest had kissed Marianne's hand, before that old reprobate and I had had a last whiskey or, if he happened to be in touch with a good, small producer, a calvados, invariably struck Pierre as preposterous As did my confessing that I felt tired. We had always loved our private *tours d'horizon* at the end of the evening, which covered everything from his business through the wonders being accomplished by his two daughters—the elder was studying composition at the Paris Conservatoire; the younger, my goddaughter Mélanie, was a star at her lycée—all the way to the book I had most recently finished or was writing. But Pierre's gallery on avenue de Matignon did not open before eleven. The deals that made him rich were rarely consummated there anyway; and his presence in the office upstairs, where he did the serious dealing, connected to the gallery by a spiral staircase, was not regulated by any schedule. The gallery served to impress clients by its serious chic and to show the work of artists Pierre was trying to move to a higher commercial plateau by means of the exquisitely mounted and researched exhibitions for which he had become famous. No wonder he was still able to carry on exactly as in the days when he and I could never find a cabaret that stayed open late enough, until the sky had turned into a gray smudge, and Paris, a city that sleeps late, was beginning to stir. By that hour, the women with us, whether we had started the evening with them or found them along our way, were generally ready to give up on us as lovers. All they wanted was a lift home and a chance to go to bed—alone! But not much later in life, I discovered that my writing was best done in the morning—after at least five and a half hours of sleep. That means going to bed before midnight. An unpleasant thought interrupted these lazy, pointless ruminations. Wouldn't my new perception of my work soon require me to decide whether those hours of work were still necessary? Would I ever want to write again? And at the cost of what sort of sacrifice? I wondered whether it all depended on Lydia, on what she would say or, more important, on how she felt after I had told her how deeply I feared that all I had accomplished was empty and devoid of significance. For the moment, I thought, there could be no answer. I had to stay on course.

Will you have something to eat? North asked all of a sudden. Shall we tell that man with sideburns to bring us some canapés?

I confessed to the stirrings of hunger.

Good! The memory of the sandwich I had just begun to eat at the bar of the old Pont Royal when the bellhop brought me my faxes has made me ravenous. There were three of them: I laid them out on the table. One was from Lydia. It may strike you as odd, but I have before my eyes even now, quite distinctly, her angular, beautifully disciplined script, and the words I read:

> The parents have struck again! Mom telephoned to say they couldn't understand why we haven't told them our plans for the Memorial Day weekend. That's this coming weekend, in case you've lost track of your native calendar. They count on us at the beach because Harriet and her gang are coming, and so are Ralph and his brood. Maud isn't. What could be her excuse?
>
> Since you said you might not be back, I accepted.
>
> So once more you are off the hook, darling John. Stay in your lovely Paris but think of me with every wild strawberry you eat, every scrumptious melon, and certainly every bite of foie gras.

That message was a liberation to be thankful for. My in-laws are called Frank, and the Frank family festivities—at any of the senior Mr. and Mrs. Frank's residences, and for that matter at the residences of Lydia's brother and sisters—have a quality of ponderous self-satisfied good cheer I used to find unbearably oppressive. Lydia claimed that exposure to the Franks at Thanksgiving, Christmas, and so forth awakened the monster in me. What kind of monster? So long as they put it down to my misanthropy, I didn't mind being teased. I don't mind it being known that I am not overly fond of my fellowmen. But I knew that the sour stirrings I felt inside me, like the taste of bile after you have retched your heart out, were those of the monster envy, of all my vices the one that fills me with greatest shame, the one that I wanted to conceal from Lydia. Have I succeeded? There is no telling. She sees through everything and doesn't always say what she has seen or, I believe, admit to herself how far she has penetrated. Otherwise, I am certain she would have taken more care not to let me think then, as at certain other times, that she was arranging to exclude me, whether or not she was. I reread the fax. Almost the entire family was to be there, at that gathering in East Hampton from which I was to be absent. The monster writhed. Of course, when I called later in the evening, I could ask Lydia to tell her parents that I would be there after all; I could leave for New York in the morning. The truth was, though, that neither seeing her action as a reflection of her judgment about my character, nor the judgment of my better self that I should grow up and go to the Franks' cheerfully and in good faith, nor even my envy of those who were to participate in these festivities that I fundamentally disliked, were sufficient to change the fact that deep down I wanted to stay in Paris. I preferred not to spend the Memorial Day weekend among my assembled in-laws. I didn't like the figure I cut among them, and I thought it was just possible that Lydia didn't much like it either. So why go there, against my will, and make trouble? I asked myself, feeling more comfortable. I should add that I am not sure about Lydia's judgment of my character; and I am never sure that I interpret correctly her motives and actions when it comes to her family. Seeing that the other faxes were only from my agent, I stuffed them into my pocket. They could wait. I finished my drink and the sandwich.

Apropos, North said, pointing to my empty glass. Don't you think we should have another?

I gave my assent. Nodding approval, he resumed the narrative.

In the taxi I read the faxes from my agent. In one he asked me to be on the alert for a message I was likely to receive after midnight Paris time announcing that I had been awarded the biggest of American literary prizes for my new novel. He gave me the names of the other two finalists. In his judgment, there was no way I could lose against them. In the second fax, he submitted an offer from a major studio to buy the film rights to *The Anthill.* The price made me gasp. There are bound to be issues we would normally raise when we see the contract, he warned me, but the price is so generous that we won't break the deal over them. Celebrate, and feel proud of yourself, was his conclusion.

No doubt I would celebrate, especially the sale and the prospect of a large inflow of cash. But the immediate question was whether I should tell Lydia right away or wait until the fatal fax, when I would know one way or the other about the prize. I decided to wait. If I did really win, that would be splendid news to give her, and if I didn't, news of the movie contract would be like having a ready antidote. If I lost without mentioning it, she would see what had happened in the *Times,* when it published the winner and short list, without having been prepared. That was a disadvantage, but it couldn't be helped. As you might imagine, all the while, prize or no prize, the judgment I had reached about my work had to remain unchanged, and that was bitter. But I have to admit that I felt less depressed than I had following the interview with the girl at the Flore. The prize was new evidence of sorts, perhaps sufficient to justify a new trial. I liked the thought that, at least while news of the prize was still fresh in their minds, the Franks would have to hold both my work and me in somewhat higher esteem. You see, I had pretty much decided that the jury would vote for me.

The ride was interminable. I fell asleep and woke with a start when we stopped at Pierre's address, in the rue de la Faisanderie. Perhaps you know that street in Passy. If it were wider, and not so aggressively residential, you might mistake Pierre's apartment house for a bank, a smaller version of the Crédit Lyonnais building on the boulevard des Italiens. It certainly would have been convenient for Pierre to live directly above a bank: each time he and Marianne were to be away from Paris, they could have taken the paintings off the walls of their foyer, living room, dining room, and library and carried them to a vault a couple of floors down. But the building is, in fact, only a discreet redoubt of *haute bourgeoisie,* and I suppose that Pierre had to resort to all the ingenious devices that Parisians use to fortify their apartments and town houses against the burglaries one hears about every time one goes out to dinner. To my knowledge, the Lalondes had no live-in staff, which made the problem acute. At most, some lady who cleaned and cooked, and at night tucked herself away in the servants' quarters under the roof. I began to think though that there might have been a change. The manservant who greeted me at the door and led me to the salon did not seem to have been sent by a caterer, nor did the canapés he was passing. I quickly catalogued other novelties since my last visit. Gone was the strangely prescient Cézanne of a clearing in the forest of Chantilly, as well as Picasso's portrait of Olga and both Renoirs. A full-length Klimt of an Oriental dancer and other works of Austrian and German expressionists had taken their place. The comings and goings of those and other masterpieces seemed to be the subject of brisk conversation among Pierre and Marianne and an American couple in their late fifties.

Jim and Edith Cleary, from Oregon, said Marianne.

Pierre embraced me and added the significant missing information. You have before you two very eminent collectors, he said. Extraordinary knowledge and taste! So far they have concentrated on contemporary works by American artists. The quality of what they own is astonishing: not a single painting that isn't first class. Now they feel ready to expand into modern and impressionist masters. Jim and Edith already know you, John, through your novels. A famous novelist never needs an introduction, he added with the sort of grating joviality that usually accompanies such remarks.

Once the word "collectors" had been uttered, I realized that I knew about this couple. More than once, my father-in-law had spoken of them and their collection with respect. Their being from Oregon should have been sufficient to identify them. So these were the Clearys of Portland and of the vast forest products fortune founded by the Cleary grandfather. The son had increased it enormously and, so far, the grandson had kept it intact and entirely private. Pierre's theory, I also realized, must be that they were fans and would like to meet me. That was why he had wanted to make one hundred percent sure that I made it to this dinner and was more or less on time.

In fact, I was ten minutes late, but that's good form in France. It gives the hosts a chance to stop bickering. But did Pierre know that they had heard about the novelist John North? Or had he taken my celebrity for granted? Without false modesty, I can say that I have never made such a leap of faith. I was even more curious to know whether Pierre had announced in advance that I was coming or only when the Clearys had arrived, the way in a smart restaurant the maître d'hôtel announces a surprise side dish offered by the chef only when it is served. He seldom left important matters to chance; I would have bet that he had used me to lure them here. The answer to my question was given immediately. Pierre did know that the Clearys professed to admire my books. I was the bait. They weren't at all sure that they should go out to dinner, Edith announced, they were so jet-lagged, but once they heard the author of *Green Island* would be there, they decided that having dinner in their suite was out of the question. It would have been like being in Paris and not visiting Malmaison! Did I think, she asked, that *Green Island* was my best? By the way, *Green Island* is my first novel, not that it matters very much. Without thinking, I fired back my standard rejoinder: I don't talk about that. Then, because I wanted to be polite, I added that one can't say that sort of thing about a book any more than about children. A good father, I continued, isn't supposed to say which child he loves most. Immediately she allowed that I was so right, they would never rank their three boys and two girls, all of whom they adored, and, anyway, weren't comparisons odious? Could I imagine how much fun they had with their brood? She hoped our children gave my wife and me as much joy.

Yes, I could imagine it. It did not seem necessary to tell Edith that Lydia and I had no children. Lydia had wanted them, and the subject came up as soon as we seriously discussed marriage. We returned to it over and over. I was quite direct and open about my reluctance, and eventually she said she understood my conviction that children have little place in a writer's life. You see, said North, I had been telling her that my books were my real children, and my first duty was to them. All the time and energy I had were to go into writing and trying to be a good husband. If we had children, I maintained, those human children would find in me at best a sort of benevolent uncle or godfather. I would be happy to see them, provided they didn't interfere with my work, I would be ready to advise them, and would give them money so long as I had it. Beyond that, I droned on, she would be pretty much on her own as a parent. I also talked, even more fatuously, about a writer's need for freedom to travel, to seek new experiences, and to avoid commitments. I kept this up with even greater vigor after we got married. Always, she would grow very serious. That is how I liked to characterize the effect of my speeches, although I knew that her "seriousness" in reality was nothing more than a mask for bottomless regret and sadness that overcame her when she heard those pronouncements. As for me, mouthing them put me in high spirits. I must have thought I was clever. At first, she used to reply that we could have children on my terms; she would manage. When she said that, I believed her. My respect for her strength and capability continued to grow. I thought she could manage anything. And since, thanks to her grandparents and parents, we had plenty of money, I took the view that there was no reason that we shouldn't get properly organized for the job. You know, hire the right nannies, a good cook or housekeeper, and so forth and later make sure the children go to the right schools. But she was thinking more deeply, the way she always does, and one day—I think we must have been married for three years by then, and I believe she hadn't been on the pill—she said that in the end she agreed with my view of things. We wouldn't have children. The only way to do it right on my terms would be for her to give up patients altogether. She couldn't, as a single parent, do clinical work and research and still be a good mother. Not alone. And she wasn't able, she said, to give up an indispensable part of her work. The subject was closed, so far as she was concerned, although I knew she was saying these things only as a sacrifice to me, to our marriage. She had talked herself into believing that the children would come between us—her and my monumental selfishness. Except that she wouldn't have even thought it selfishness; she would have scrupulously thought of John, John the artist, John the man she loved. In fact, we didn't return to the subject for many years. I had no interest in reopening it. But Lydia is older than I. Almost exactly five years before the dinner at Pierre's, when she was thirty-nine, she told me in bed, after we had finished making love and were lying very quietly, with our arms around each other, that she had been thinking again about having a child and how this was her last chance; she would make whatever adjustments in her work were required. It's difficult to make a child on command when you are her age, after years and years of contraception. Our first years of marriage gave little reason to hope for instant success. But we beat the odds.

Lydia was pregnant within two months, quite naturally, without any treatments. Her happiness was so complete and so candid that I began to feel a participatory joy. Then, in the sixth month, she miscarried. The child—a little girl, to be precise—was stillborn. Do not even think of trying again, was the advice of the doctors. As though in a Greek tragedy, we were left on a bare stage, with our regret and self-reproach as the chorus.

I had wandered into this minefield, North said, by talking too much without thinking, it was my fault and nobody else's, so I kept up the literary act with the Clearys, repeating large chunks of what I had said to the girl that afternoon. That seemed fair enough, the questions being almost identical. I know of no rules against self-plagiarism. I saw Marianne watching me, as though I were a man on a high wire. She understood. At last, I was able to direct the conversation back to collecting, whereupon the art historical and art market twaddle began to flow with no interruption except Marianne's increasingly anguished musings about the lateness of her other two guests, and whether she should just give up on them and ask that dinner be served. Meanwhile, as the manservant, with pleasant assiduity, continued to refill my glass, my thoughts turned to the Franks. How was it that I felt so diminished by the Franks and envious of them? The question and answers were old, but that did not stop their gnawing at me. They belonged, no doubt, to those matters that Dr. Czarny, the analyst on whose couch I had many years ago explored my underworld, identified as deserving treatment someday. That day never came. Instead, I reformed my life and married

Lydia. My parents were still flying high then. When they had time to speak to me about my marriage, which was not very often, they invariably said Lydia was a gift from heaven to me and them. But I knew they could not repress a certain polite amusement, never revealed to Lydia, at my having married "one of those Franks." Oh, they respected the way that the Franks' real estate fortune had financed good works at every school and college any member of the family had ever attended, and at various museums and hospitals in New York that they had showered with money, and the decency, industry, and unity with which members of the clan conducted their lives and business. But why, sighed my parents, must the Franks be so self-satisfied, as if they were really the first to have given generously to charity X, Y, or Z, or to have bought old and new masters to hang on their walls, or, the most central but unspoken question, to have so much money and no debt? Clearly the Franks were far richer than my parents and, more to the point, had more money than any of our long-nosed and watery-blue-eyed distinguished ancestors had ever dreamed of accumulating, back when in my family one made money instead of just spending it. That did not put my parents off their pace. Not really. Money meant less to them than to many other people. And it is true that if you talked to the senior Franks—to the adorable Bernard, known to his family, myself included, as Bunny, or to Judy—you were bound to hear, whether you appeared interested or not, all about the academic degrees and successes of all their children and grandchildren and nephews and nieces of school age. Did that make my parents feel envious, considering my sister Ellen's and my

modest attainments? I don't believe that it did. They were too
sure of themselves and, alas, too stylish. For them, as for so
many of their class and age, the school and university you had
attended, the teams you had played on, and the clubs you had
joined were more important than scholarly prowess. So my
parents simply kept smiling at the wonderfully fit Franks, so
tanned and so well preserved—give or take a few hip or knee
replacements. Then suddenly everything went dark for this
elegant and ironic pair. They declined more or less in tandem,
as though they had made some pact and the agreed signal had
been given: both had moments of increasing frequency and
length at first of confusion and then quite obvious lack of
awareness of where they were or to whom they were speaking.
Within a bewilderingly short time, my sister Ellen and I found
ourselves the guardians of an equally demented mother and
father, both still lodged at their gorgeous Federal house in
Georgetown but now cared for by relays of nurses and other
specialized helpers. As soon as we understood how it would be,
we sold the apartment in Paris and, after a tussle between
Ellen and me, the house in Aspen as well, which she and
her husband had wanted to keep, being passionate skiers. I
insisted on putting it on the market because it was clear to me
how that luxury nursing home for two we had organized would
devour our family money. So you see, it did not require too
much intelligence or an unusual habit of introspection for me
to figure out that the Franks saw me as barely acceptable. They
hadn't expected their beautiful daughter, who was a star, to
marry a scribbler of the sort of good family that has seen
its best days, a perfectly decent fellow but not to be taken

seriously compared, for instance, with the husbands of the other two sisters. One of those husbands was a partner in his father's private investment bank on Wall Street, and the other issued from a rival real estate dynasty. As it happened, the relations between the two clans were exceptionally amicable, by reasons of intermarriage and a shared struggle to climb to the top. Otherwise, that son-in-law might have been as welcome to the Franks as a Montague to the Capulets. That leaves Ralph, the son. Well, he was the heir, and that would have sufficed even without his rough good sense, hard work at the family office, and superior ability as sailor, golfer, and fund-raiser for the United Jewish Appeal and allied causes. In fact, my well-bred modesty aside, I thought the Franks' picture of me wasn't entirely fair. It undervalued my work—not for its aesthetic merit, because *entre nous* the Franks valued that aspect of it more highly than I did, but, especially as of late, for its public standing. Then there was that more mysterious asset, my personal standing in a world that both counted and didn't count for them. It was as if they couldn't understand the abiding distinction of my family, or accept in me the heir to an American tradition tested on battlefields, in both chambers of Congress, and in finance when the foundations of our country's industrial strength were laid. Forgive me, I know I am pompous just now, but these feelings are quite strong in me. It doesn't matter. Whatever it was, they had their picture of me before their eyes, and so I was weighed on the family scales.

At last the door leading from the foyer into the living room opened to admit the tardy couple, a man unknown to me, evidently French, and roughly my age, and, of all people, the girl–Léa Morini. She favored me with one of her smiles and said to Marianne that we had already met, that very afternoon. The man and I were introduced: Jacques Robineau, the second-in-command of a state-owned bank. That told me that he had been one of those students who flash like a comet through the French system of *grandes écoles* and competitive examinations, become by the time they are thirty high civil servants, move upward through a series of ministers' cabinets, and by the time they reach forty are placed by their elders, who preceded them at the same schools, near the top of just such a bank or state-owned industrial establishment. So he would have just arrived, on time, at his scheduled career stop. I thought his friendship with our hosts must be recent; otherwise I would have met him before. Since the Clearys spoke no French, his fluent English was likely the reason he had been invited–and told to bring a friend, if he had one who spoke English well. But perhaps Pierre and Marianne knew the girl, and knew she was the friend he would bring. I supposed that the nature of the friendship between her and Robineau was obvious, but somehow I preferred to treat it for the moment as a subject for eventual investigation.

I was, as I had expected, placed at table between Marianne and Edith Cleary, and therefore planned to speak with the girl after we returned to the living room for coffee. In fact, it was she who took the initiative. As soon as I was installed in the Louis XIII chair toward which Marianne had pointed, Léa sat down on the floor beside it. The way she managed it, turning her torso toward me and stretching her legs behind her on the floor, gave me a full view of her legs. She wore a black angora turtleneck. Her stockings were also black. The short red skirt had ridden up to the middle of her thighs. I could smell her perfume, heavy and, it seemed to me, old-fashioned. The girl-at-work spectacles were gone. Apparently she wore contacts when she was out on the town. At the Flore, I had taken stock of her skin, nose, and pouting lips. Now with her opulent blond mane so close to my face, as I stared at those fabulous legs and imagined the shape and heft of her breasts, I became aroused. There was no doubt about it: she was truly beautiful. And seductive beyond what I had imagined. That Robineau was sleeping with her was indeed not open to question–to judge by the complicity I sensed, rather than anything specific that I could overhear at table. As she chattered, I began to pic-ture for myself her gestures, the positions her body assumed, and how his large hands moved over it when they made love. Would I have wanted to take his place? You bet. I could not really concentrate on anything else. Meanwhile Léa told me that she had managed to spend a solid couple of hours on the article and that she hoped to have a complete draft ready by noon the next day. She believed she was coming up with exactly the piece her editor wanted and she hoped I would also approve. If I was willing to take the time to read it, she would like to show me the full text, not only the direct quotations.

All the while, I wanted to call Lydia, but feared that I would be unable to conceal my erection if I got up. Even worse, Léa was unlikely to remain crouching on the floor next to an empty chair. I would lose her for the rest of the evening. That was a chance I didn't want to take. It seemed far better anyway to call Lydia from the hotel, after I had taken a bath and the trance had passed. If by that time she had left the house, I would leave a message. Or send a fax. As it happened, in a short moment, the party ended. The Clearys told me that their car was waiting; they offered to drop me off at my hotel. I said they mustn't think of any such thing, the rue du Bac was out of their way. In fact, I had it in mind that if Robineau heard me refuse, he would have to offer me a lift. I was right. He had a low-slung English car. Getting into it, the girl revealed even more of her thigh. From the backseat I answered the questions that Robineau, grown very voluble, was putting to me, first about my work, and then about Broadway plays I would recommend for his next visit. The French presidential election was the number one subject of conversation in Paris, the moneyed French contemplating with horror life under a Socialist regime. In fact, political coverage of the campaign had put an annoying crimp into some aspect of the launch of *The Anthill*. To keep up my end I remarked that France was strong enough and rich enough to permit herself a fling with François Mitterrand. Like a true member of his political class, he snorted contemptuously. Undeterred, I said that I had met Mitterrand in New York a few years back, in '76 or '77, and had had the feeling that I was in the presence of a great man, a view that made Robineau observe that it was easy to have such lofty ideas if one was lucky enough to be American. Leaning toward him and Léa from the backseat, I observed how his hand moved up and down her thigh—a thigh that had begun to obsess me—squeezing it on the inside every second downstroke or so. The girl was silent until we reached my hotel. They got out to say goodbye. *À demain,* she muttered, and offered me her cheeks to kiss, instead of her hand.

And what do you think happened next? asked North after

we had prepared and lit our cigars. His eyes were bright and I sensed that he was eager to keep talking. I replied that I had an idea or two, but, rather than guess, I preferred to hear the story from him.

He nodded, recrossed his ankles, and continued.

Lydia was at home when I telephoned, directly after I had read the fax from the president of the prize jury. She kept on saying, You see I was right, I was right. They had to give the prize to you, how can you think that your books aren't wonderful when I keep on telling you that they are? I saw that she had understood the doubts and worries that finally overflowed during the night in New York that I have described to you, although until that very night I had not admitted to myself their force, and certainly hadn't revealed them consciously to her. Not as I had really felt them even before the nocturnal epiphany. When she spoke tenderly like that her voice changed, and she made, quite involuntarily, I believe, a cooing noise that enchanted me.

I was struck by it the very first time we met, at a buffet dinner in New York that went on until all hours, given by an old flame of mine who had married a cousin of Lydia's—a man unlike the other Franks I know—working then as a staff writer for *The New Yorker.* My old flame has been my friend forever. I really mean forever: we attended the same kindergarten. You see, I have always parted from girlfriends on very good terms, and often I became, I suppose because I seemed so vulnerable before I married Lydia, a sort of pet for both the husband and wife. In fact, I have thought that my meeting Lydia at their house was not much of an accident. I can remember how each

made sure we had been introduced, and that we found ourselves placed at the same end of a sofa after the usual scramble
at such parties for a place to sit down and eat that doesn't
expose you to your worst enemy or a bore. I saw at once that
Lydia was brilliant: one of those doctors whose conversation is
particularly captivating, more than that of other profession-
als, because they have an interesting sort of specialty and are
able to talk about it with such clarity that you begin to think
you understand what they do. It isn't unusual for their general
culture to be at a high level as well. Lydia is prodigiously culti-
vated. There isn't a great museum she hasn't visited, and her
visual memory is such that she can discuss with striking accu-
racy works of art she has seen a long time ago. Her knowledge
of music is equally remarkable, even though her piano lessons
ended when she was still a schoolgirl. And she has read and
remembers every novel worth reading in English and French,
as well as a good deal of German literature. Her maternal
grandmother, who was born in Germany, spoke German to
her children and tried to speak it to her grandchildren. Lydia
was the only one willing to learn, I suppose because she vener-
ated her grandmother. The result is that her German is excellent—as is her French.

We talked until the other guests had departed and our hosts
had gone quietly to bed, leaving us in the care of the caterers'
people, who were still busy cleaning up. Lydia told me that she
lived in a small apartment, split off from a very large one, on
the mansard floor of the Dakota. It had a great advantage: all
the rooms, even the kitchen, looked out on the park. When
the taxi arrived in front of the building, she invited me up for a

nightcap. I was intrigued by Lydia and accepted. She proposed champagne. We drank it standing by an open window, looking at Central Park as though from an enormous tree house. She said that she had read all my books–only three had been published by then–and explained very precisely and unpretentiously what she liked in them. I was relieved that she was not one of those readers who undertake to give a writer critical comments. Nothing is dumber or more infuriating. A new novel of mine was making its way through the publishing machine. Although I am usually very reluctant to show unpublished work to anyone who is not professionally involved with the process, I asked whether she would like a bound galley. She would love it, she told me. By that time, it was dawn. We shook hands, and I really believe it was only then that I became fully conscious that she was a great beauty, whose features, coloring, and regal bearing recalled Klimt's rich Viennese enchantresses. You smile, said North, because you do not think it possible that I would have paid so little attention to Lydia's looks before. Of course, I had noticed in a general way that she was tall, handsome, and very elegant. But this was really the first time–no, surely the only time–in my life that I listened so hard to what a woman was saying that I did not think about her lips, breasts, thighs, etc.

That was a digression, North told me after a moment of silence. Let's return to my telephone conversation with Lydia.

And your worries, she said, that you weren't earning enough, don't you see that they were silly too? The studio is paying you a fortune. Just think what it will be when they add to it the usual bonuses. I couldn't argue about the money, but I defended my negative view of my work. The prize is just the whim of the jury while my concerns are fundamental and very serious, I said, whereupon, after a cascade of her laughter, she said that we could have a colloquium on John North and the art of the novel as soon as I returned. If I liked, and the weather was good, we could go to the Vineyard for the weekend. It would be just us, we wouldn't see anyone else at all, and we could talk literature nonstop for two days. Then she said it had just occurred to her that her parents and brother and sisters should be told at once and, of course, my sister, Ellen. Shouldn't she call everybody? I thanked her, but was at the same time almost disconcerted by how fast she was moving. Couldn't I speak at least to Ellen, in my own way? I wondered, without saying anything, because it wasn't worth the trouble and risk of seeming ungrateful. She was always ahead of me by a step or two. I thought we were about to say goodbye when she asked—perhaps she had meant to since the beginning of the conversation—whether I wouldn't like to come to East Hampton after all, to celebrate with the whole family. I reminded her how bad I am at dealing with congratulations and the inevitable toasts and teasing. Beyond that, I said, it was a bad moment to leave Paris. I had begun to do some real work on the new book and should probably continue for a few days without interruption. I wanted to get the characters of the husband and wife more clearly defined. The truth was very different. Since dinner, I had not been able to stop thinking about Léa. I had decided I must sleep with her. That was my project; not my book. It filled me with shame and dismay to have Lydia speak to me with all that sweetness and good cheer and clear concern for my well-being while my mind was full of the girl and the urge to possess her, to do with her whatever Robineau had done, and more if more was possible. It seemed a worse crime than a violent, lethal assault against Lydia. I was violating her unquestioning trust. The strange truth is I had not been unfaithful to her before. You shake your head and wonder how that could be. I don't think it is all that surprising. My life before I fell in love with Lydia had been turbulent enough. Until the events I am describing took place, I had felt no urgent curiosity about what could be done with another woman and no temptation to find out. There were to be no more voyages of exploration. Lydia was the serene harbor in which I was content to have at last found a mooring.

I was really determined to possess the girl, North told me after a prolonged silence. Filling her would not be enough. The scene changed and changed again as I replayed it in my imagination, but always it led to a gigantic climax in which I literally made her overflow. Next morning, as soon as I woke up, I dialed the Lalondes' number. Marianne came to the telephone. I thanked her for dinner and told her about my new good fortune. She may not have fully understood the significance of the prize, but being herself a busy and successful scriptwriter she knew more than most people about film rights, and certainly more than I. There was nothing I could tell her about the studio's intentions other than the amount of money I would be paid—I had been friends with her and Pierre for so long that I would have told them even if I hadn't been quite sure that the sum would be reported in *Variety* if not more generally—and that the producer had made clear to my agent he wanted me to be available during filming, even though the adaptation would be written by someone else, as yet unnamed. She said that was most unusual, producers being normally willing to go to any length to keep the author away—even to pay more money for the rights if necessary. I explained that Joe Bain, the producer, had been at school with me, and apparently had thought up this idea out of pure friendship. He's a sentimental fellow, I said, quite unlike me. Ah, in that case, replied Marianne, anything becomes possible. I added that the intention was to shoot on location, whenever conditions permitted. That meant Paris, where much of the action in *The Anthill* takes place. It will be like old times, she exclaimed. Then she said that she would give Pierre the news when he called from Geneva. He had gone there with the Clearys to look at a private collection. Two works in it that might be perfect for them were for sale. She thought that I should be able to use his aunt Viviane's apartment on avenue Gabriel. Pierre would find out whether the aunt minded. Of course, I was welcome to stay with them, but Viviane's apartment was ideal: so centrally located. Pierre will be *fou de joie*! You will be completely independent, but who knows what Lydia will think of that! A stroke of genius, I replied, but no more independence than in a hotel. After I had finished thanking her, repeating how much I had enjoyed the dinner party, I brought up Jacques Robineau. It's funny, I told her, I'm not sure you heard me say it, you were so busy with Edith Cleary, but I actually spent a good part of the afternoon with the other half of that couple, at the Flore of all places, being interviewed by her for a piece in *Vogue*.

She told me she didn't think they were really a couple, that in principle, Robineau was with Françoise Lecomte, another journalist, who was in Rome on assignment. That was why he brought Léa instead.

Oh, I said, I thought I detected a sort of intimacy between them. Certainly in the car, when they were taking me to my hotel.

Marianne laughed at that. She said she hadn't meant to suggest that Jacques didn't go to bed with her after dropping me off; he had slept with half the women in Paris. Actually, *la petite* Morini also has someone else, she added. Pierre can tell you all about it.

But she had just told me everything I needed to know. What did it mean, though, I wondered, that Robineau was in principle "with" another lady journalist, and the girl "has" someone else, if Marianne took it so casually for granted that Robineau was sleeping with her? Certainly it meant that Léa wasn't uniformly faithful to her principal *monsieur.* That favored my designs, provided that letting Robineau fuck her wasn't a lapse attributable to his special qualities—for instance great sexual attractiveness, not always evident to other men, even when it acts very strongly on women, or his reputation as a master stud. The more general implications of these arrangements and Marianne's matter-of-fact acceptance of them also intrigued me as a subject for future reflection.

I think that North noticed the expression of surprise that passed over my face, because he said quickly: Please forgive the vulgarity. "Fuck" is the word I have used in my thoughts in relation to Léa when it seemed appropriate. Euphemisms do not come near to giving a just measure of how I thought about her.

After a pause that may have been intended to give me a chance to protest, North continued. Yes, Léa's willingness to stray had to be seen as encouraging. On the other hand, if she turned out to be truly promiscuous, *une Marie couche-toi,* would I know how to go about the business at hand with the requisite nonchalance? It's locker-room wisdom that with a girl who lets the whole swim team lay her you don't need the "Say It with Flowers" stuff. You don't talk about love, you don't say you'll die if she doesn't let you. Instead, you get your hand on the old crotch and stick your fingers up her pussy. Such maxims learned during my last year at school rattled in my head, ready for application, as did the unfortunate memory of a girl from the Main Line a couple of years older than the other girls in her class at Radcliffe, who wouldn't let me near her, although she had given blow jobs and more to just about everybody I knew and was reputed to smell so bad that guys who had scored held their noses whenever her name was mentioned. I'm no longer sure, but I think that her name was Lilly. Lilly Leffingwell? I really don't remember. It was one of those Philadelphia names. Once I got up my courage and asked her, Why all the others but not me? Without batting an eye, she said: Just lay me. Cut out the speeches.

You want to hear something funny? North continued. I decided to take her advice. I told her I knew a meadow not far from town where we could have a picnic. Afterward we'd fuck. It was a perfect spring day, during the reading period. Final exams must have been a week away. We drove out there and walked around. She liked the spot, so we sat down in the shade of a tree. I was putting my arm around her as a prelude to getting my free hand under her skirt and into the center of the universe when she screamed. What's the matter? I asked. Horror of horrors: my arm had brushed against her nose. She'd had it fixed a month before, and it was still extremely tender. Or so she claimed. That was the end of Lilly and me. With those thoughts in the background, can you see now how the prospect of putting the make on Léa, if she was another Lilly, terrified me? Because it was possible that Marianne meant to imply that Léa screwed right and left. In that case the courtly Mr. North, in his accustomed role of distinguished author, propositioning a young journalist ever so subtly, in accordance with his overly polite habits, would expose himself to hoots of laughter and, on top of that, being skewered by that same journalist in an article she was writing for *Vogue.* Not that she'd come out and tell how I made this pass at her that I imagined romantic while I really showed myself to be *un vieux con,* but there were many less crude and perfectly effective ways she could get me.

North had gotten himself into such a lather that I felt an urge to laugh. He understood me before I had opened my mouth.

I know, he said. My concern about how an interview will turn out. The utter implausibility of my having been so timid. All right. Don't forget the long years of my marriage to Lydia. I was seriously out of practice. Besides, I was too busy to think clearly. The press release about the prize was out. Had I been in New York, he continued, my editor or one of the publicists would have taken many of the calls from the media asking for a telephone comment or an interview with me. Alone in Paris, and not having thought to ask Xavier for help in fending off at least the French journalists, I had to deal with the calls myself, although, in fact, I was waiting for only one—from the girl. I supposed she had probably tried, maybe more than once, and had been told my line was busy. I was right. A message was finally brought to my room. She wanted to know whether she could come over. The article was ready. Ha! Could she come over? Yes, but not before I had made arrangements to change hotels. I was fond of the Pont Royal, where Xavier always put me up, fond enough to use it also whenever Lydia and I came to Paris on our own. All the staff knew us. That was a reason to remain, but also to leave if there was going to be anything for them to gossip about. The money from Hollywood gave me an inspiration: a long weekend at the Ritz. I made a reservation for arrival that very afternoon. While I was at it, I also booked a table for dinner at the restaurant. How would I explain the move to Lydia? I would say that the Pont Royal couldn't keep me through the weekend. Ah, so you went to the Ritz all by yourself! A voice of mild regret. Sweetie, all of Paris is like the Pont Royal, full of tourists. It was a stroke of luck that the Ritz could take me. We'll stay there together next time.

Yes, I was like the man preparing to commit murder. Fully concentrated, he assembles the necessary paraphernalia and checks them off against a list. After he has finished, he will put a lighted match to it. Latex gloves, passkey, duct tape, syringe and vial of morphine, and a Solingen dagger, because one can't be too careful. They're all there. In the same cheap black attaché case, he packs his passport and an envelope thick with cash. Some twenties and tens; the rest are used fifties and hundreds. He snaps the case shut, checks the fuel gauge of his car, and makes sure he has the necessary roadmaps. There is no turning back. Nothing will stop him.

Murder of whom? a listener less subtle than you might ask, added North. Isn't it all too clear? Murder of my adored Lydia.

As though exhausted by the tension of his own story, North fell into a reverie. I too was thinking. Could it be true that he really took to heart, *au tragique,* as he might say, an infidelity that was so wretchedly banal? A man who likes women, who has known many women, is away from home on a business trip, in another country. A sexy young thing is planted in his path. She flatters him. There is reason to think she is available. If he tries his luck and succeeds, where is the harm, so long as he goes on loving his wife? I would have liked to put the question to him, but decided not to. He was a novelist, he might be spinning a yarn he would write someday. Why should I interfere? One way or the other, it was his story. I concluded I would let him tell it as he thought best.

I asked her to come to lunch, North resumed, at the bar of the Pont Royal. I had a strange yearning, which amused her when I confessed it, for a club sandwich washed down by a gin martini. At the time, you could get both, of excellent quality, at that bar. All through the meal, I behaved very correctly. To be sure, I was busy at first reading her text, and then, after a request of such diffidence and modesty that it made me melt, I answered some questions she had written out about the prize: what it meant, who were my predecessors, and so forth. Of course, she wanted to know about the film too. Toward the end of the lunch, she became oddly flustered. She said she intended right after lunch to add to the article what I had just told her. Could I possibly review the revised version? She didn't want to inconvenience me, but her deadline was the next day. She hoped I knew that magazine deadlines are very rigid. I laughed, because she had just given me the opening I wanted. Look, I told her, nice things have happened to me and it seems wrong not to celebrate in some minor way. Would she like to have a dinner with me? A good dinner, on the pompous side. Dining alone isn't much of a party. Oh yes, she replied, nothing could make her happier, she would come to the hotel and bring her papers with her, but could it be on the late side? Perhaps around nine? I was to learn only gradually, over subsequent dinners and lunches, the meaning to Léa of "around" nine or any other hour. So I said that would be perfect; nothing could make me happier either. I told her to come to the Ritz, not the Pont Royal, and to look for me in the bar on the rue Cambon side. I gave her the same reason for the move as I had given to Lydia. I didn't see how I could tell her the truth, and I thought that she would look down on me if I said that I had upgraded my hotel because I had won a prize and was coming into some money.

I took possession of my quarters at the Ritz after lunch, and decided they would do except for one detail: there were no flowers in the room. That was, I supposed, because I had never stayed at the hotel before, although I was certainly an old patron of the bar. I had been drinking there with great enthusiasm ever since my father first brought me, and was, in fact, treated as a friend by the august bartender, to whom, when I began to be published, I never failed to send inscribed copies of the French translations of my books. There was a new wave of telephone calls and messages. I was too feverish to deal with them well and took advantage of the first pause to hurry to the nearby florist in the rue de Castiglione and get bouquets of spring flowers for the tiny living room and the bedroom. The latter, I had been happy to note, was ample in its proportions. I might have spared myself the trouble and expense. Léa noticed flowers only in their natural setting. In hotel rooms they were invisible to her; she judged a hotel's standing mainly by the quality and quantity of chocolates provided by the management—she consumed large numbers of them on the spot and took away the rest to eat at home. Her lithe and perfectly muscled body seemed impervious to the huge intake of sweets, bread, cheese, pasta, and wine of which she was capable. Soap, shampoo, and skin unguents weighed in her judgment as well. She liked large cakes of soap and pouted if I unwrapped a large soap. It's a waste, she would tell me, you won't be here long enough to use up even the smallest soap. And if you do, the chambermaid will bring another one. Léa would pack the loot in her huge pocketbook, which, if she was to spend the night with me and then go directly to the magazine, contained, in addition to her address book, a full-size desk calendar, hairbrush, and comb, as well as jeans and a black turtleneck sweater to take the place of the white crêpe de chine blouse with plunging neckline and the tiny black velvet or silk skirt she would have worn to dinner.

I took a short nap late that afternoon. Afterward, I went

down to the bar. Resisting the blandishments of my friend the bartender, I had only one martini. Having finished the drink, I asked him to hold a corner table. I also checked on the restaurant. The table was all right; we would sit side by side on a banquette. Normally, I dislike that arrangement, preferring to look at the person I am talking to—even if it is a young woman—over real or imagined physical intimacies. But not that evening. Then I went back to my room and gave an unaccustomed amount of thought to what I would wear. This would be what Lydia called a grown-up dinner, which meant I shouldn't dress like an artist. That ruled out the ratty tweed jacket she had already seen me wear three times in a row. Fortunately, I had packed what the occasion called for: a pin-striped suit. It fit me well and didn't need to be pressed. I had the right necktie to go with it, and a cream-colored shirt that also fit, I suppose because it dated from the days before I began, in the interest of economy, to have my shirts made in Hong Kong. Incidentally, the first generation of those shirts was just fine and I would have recommended the shop to you. It was only later, without my having lost weight, that they began to hang on me as though on a scarecrow. Just look at the one I have on right now. It's loose at the neck and too full across the chest. That is why it wrinkles in this bizarre way. You might ask why I haven't had the pattern adjusted by the Hong Kong fellow. It's a good question. I suppose I prefer to leave bad enough alone. The Chinaman might take revenge by making up shirts that are tight, and I detest that, or with sleeves that are too short. Sleeves that are too short are somewhere near the top of my list of *bêtes noires*. What else is on the list? So much that if I were to tell you, there wouldn't be enough time left for my story.

North laughed at his own joke. I managed a smile.

To get on with the story, said North, my toilette finished, I took a stroll around the place Vendôme. The days were already long and the sky had not yet turned dark, but a three-quarter moon peeked from behind high clouds like an old cocotte. Worries about Lydia, misgivings, impatience with the time—to say nothing of the money—that I was wasting on a silly adventure with this girl had begun to oppress me, as did the thought that instead of having dinner with her and whatever tasteless proceedings might follow, I could be seeing *Bérénice* performed practically next door, at the Comédie Française. Perhaps under the influence of the beauty and grandeur all around me, these thoughts gradually gave way to exhilaration. This is a prank, I told myself, a harmless prank, just the sort of escapade you need. When you begin to think that your books are pointless exercises of a certain skill you happen to have, you are allowing your critical judgment to be distorted by boredom, by your stale bourgeois routine. Up at seven-thirty, because Lydia must get to the hospital and you had better get to your writing table and squeeze some pages out of your poor head, lunch at the Chinese restaurant down the street from your office or, if Lydia can get away for three-quarters of an hour, at the delicatessen two blocks from the hospital, after lunch read and answer the absolutely important letters or write three more pages of text, most nights late dinner with Lydia at home, and then to bed. With Lydia. Make love to Lydia. Unless the roof has fallen in at the hospital, you spend the weekend in East Hampton. Alone with Lydia. Drive home to the city on Sunday night with Lydia, and *da capo*. The boredom may be affecting your work as well. When do you break out of your routine? Rarely, and then Lydia does everything she can to be with you, which is very nice but keeps you from real contact with anything outside this world made for two. Perhaps whatever comes of this girl will be the shock you need to restart your system. It's true that you can't go to see *Bérénice* any night you please, but you can read Racine tomorrow morning and every day of every week. Can you fuck Léa any night you please? No. Does one need to see *Bérénice* onstage? Not if one has seen it performed at least once, with a decent cast, which you have. In that case, the little theater in the head can serve quite nicely as you sit in your chair and read the immortal lines. Is it necessary that you fuck Léa? No again, but, however it goes with this girl, you will have a memory to nourish and revisit. How long has it been since you had a secret memory like that?

The voice of temptation was persuasive. I rushed back to the hotel, emptied myself, and inspected the bedroom. The chambermaids had put out those odious terry-cloth slippers that I take to be a monstrous amenity intended for Japanese guests. Why they have to be inflicted on the rest of us I do not know. I threw them into the closet along with mint chocolates and the weather forecast that had been placed on the pillows. Even the breakfast menu seemed to strike a jarring note: it spoke of an orderly and unromantic progress to bed. Such as an old married couple might enjoy. Or lovers so accustomed to their trysts that ordering breakfast is the first thing they think of when they enter the bedroom. I stuck it into the desk drawer.

She was not very late that evening. A mere fifteen minutes. She explained that she had hurried so as to be on time, but imagining that I would want her to change for dinner she went home from the magazine and then, of course, there were no taxis, not even in front of the Lipp. Did I like what she had on? Yes, I did. It was a skirt as short and as tight as the one she had worn when I saw her at the Lalondes', but it was black, the color I decided went best with her skin and her hair, and one of those crêpe de chine tops I have already mentioned. A long string of beads filled her cleavage. I was sure that her breasts were hard, but even so she wore one of those bras that push them up. Perhaps it was really intended to cover her nipples, which would have otherwise shown through the fabric like large brown buttons. She gave me her new draft and, while she drank a glass of champagne, I read it attentively. I had realized that she was very serious about her writing and that my comments had better be precise. I read slowly, because she was looking over my shoulder and I liked the warmth of her arm against mine and the smell of her perfume, which oddly enough was not the same as the one she wore the night before. I thought I recognized lilies of the valley. When I asked, just to see whether a personal question would anger her, she said, with a smile I found encouraging, that she varied her perfume according to the occasion. The other perfume made her feel old.

I was relieved to find that the article was really very good. I told her so, and added that the excessive praise of my work was a matter to be resolved between the writer and her editor. I wasn't going to complain. But she's your biggest fan, Léa blurted out and blushed. As we talked over dinner, the impression I had formed at the Flore, that she was intelligent, was solidified. I noticed, however, an oddity in her speech: When she talked about her work as a journalist, she was articulate and enunciated words clearly. As soon as she began to speak about personal matters—for instance, in the next sentence, when she was telling me about her studio, which I must visit, and her paintings about which she wanted to know my opinion—she became nearly incoherent. Words were half swallowed or mumbled. Often I simply didn't understand what she was saying. It occurred to me that perhaps she had overcome a speech defect, but only in certain contexts, in this case, her job, the way a stutterer can learn to make a toast without stumbling but has trouble asking you to pass the salt. I wasn't sure, and it didn't matter. My desire seemed to grow with every oddity I discovered.

She was not a picky eater; in fact, we both found the menu of the restaurant at the Ritz a touch too newfangled. The desserts consoled her, as did the wine, of which she drank more than I. I listened intently as she mumbled about vacations and her brilliant older brothers, and spoke with great authority about Georges Perec, only one of whose books I don't detest. All the while, I worried about my next move, which had to come soon, since we were about to be served coffee. I did not dare to say anything on the order of, Look, I want you, what do you think, shall we go to my room? So I tried what must be the oldest trick, of the sort that proved to Lilly Leffingwell that I was a jerk. I had kept a chaste distance from her on our banquette, and, contrary to habit, gesticulated with my right hand to emphasize whatever idiotic statement I was making. While she replied, I would let my hand rest peacefully on the plush between us. During a moment of quiet I felt her hand touch mine. I did not stir. Instead I asked whether she would like a cognac. Oh yes, she would, she told me and, as though to confirm her enthusiasm for the decision she had just made, allowed her hand to cover mine and to caress it. This called for a new initiative. I touched her knee with mine, and to make sure she understood the contact was intentional, I pressed harder and turned my face toward her when I noted that her knee had not withdrawn. She responded with a look that I read as submissive.

What followed, after more coffee and another glass of cognac, was not the orderly seduction I had anticipated, based on my ancient exploits, and which is the sort of thing you would have found all too often in my novels if you had read them: The lady is shy and nervous about anyone–particularly the concierge and his minions–seeing her go upstairs with the protagonist. They negotiate that perilous passage safely. In the elevator, mindful of surveillance devices, they stand side by side, but stiffly and not too near each other. He doesn't even hold her hand. The elevator door opens. It's his floor. Immense relief! No cart loaded with towels, sheets, and toilet paper warns of a housekeeper's imminent appearance, not a chambermaid or bellhop anywhere in sight. Now they hold hands; still holding her hand, he raises his so that he feels the outline of her breast. They reach the room. He takes the purse and the shimmering evening shawl from her trembling hands and puts them on an armchair. They kiss. She opens her mouth and moans. As the kisses grow more passionate, she bites his lip. Hard. He dislikes being marked, so he breaks the kiss and begins to fondle her breasts, at first delicately through the silk of her blouse, as if only to learn their shape and heft, and then, when he has lifted them out of the bra, almost brutally. Her narrow skirt is a hindrance. He drops to his knees. She leans back against the armchair and, with a sigh, opens her legs just wide enough for his right hand to explore her while the left hand is busy with the nipple of her right breast. Another moment, and he has pushed her skirt up over her hips so it is no longer in the way, her panties and stockings are at her ankles, she thrusts her pubis at his fingers, lips, and tongue. He undresses her. Waiting, face pressed against the pillows, she curls up on the bed. Her behind, white unlike the rest of her suntanned body, is a provocation. He bends over it and finds he is welcome. In great haste, he throws his clothes on the floor and returns to her fully opened body.

Did you enjoy that description? North asked me abruptly. Yes, I replied, but I guess hardly as much as you.

He nodded.

Well, it wasn't quite like that with Léa, he said. With her, I entered the world of new sex. A good world. Perhaps the graybeards are right to claim that her generation differs from ours in ways that ours does not differ from that of our parents. You see, to use my sometimes old-fashioned vocabulary, I had decided to seduce her. Therefore, so far as I was concerned, I was the stage manager of the seduction scene. It was supposed to be just as described. The truth is that she took over. No sooner had the elevator door shut behind us than she jumped me—quite literally, causing me to lose my balance and stagger against the wall. She took possession of my mouth, and straightaway began to knead the front of my trousers. Her fingers inserted themselves between the buttons of my fly, and then went for the fly of my shorts. It wasn't a long elevator ride to the third floor, but she was a fast worker. Fortunately, I had a respectable hard-on, so that these imperious, marauding fingers found what they wanted. I fumbled with the key. She took it from me and opened the door of the suite. The accommodation, the box of chocolates, and the assorted soaps passed muster. With a triumphant *Youpi*—which soon became as familiar to me as the war cry of the daughters of Wotan—she hopped on the bed, pulled me on top of her, wiggled her pelvis so that one of my legs lodged between her legs, and began to writhe. I said, Léa, I want to see you and touch you, let's take our clothes off. She shook her head vehemently. I got the point. She wanted a dry fuck. I think that's what these simulations were called when I was a freshman in college, and perhaps they are today, if anybody still bothers. At the time, the point was that so long as the fellow kept his pants on and his pecker inside them the girl was safe. He wouldn't knock her up.

We carried on with increasing vigor, our mouths fastened together, my hands hooking her armpits, her crotch rubbing against my leg, my crotch working up and down her thigh. She made a lot of noise, some of which could have meant that she was coming. Later, when I knew her better, I learned that

shrieks were not to be trusted. I had to wait for the sudden
silence followed by a sort of whine and a spasm that couldn't be
faked—not that she ever faked anything. Very soon, it no
longer mattered to me at what station she was on the way to
orgasm. I lost control and came like a fountain. That, by the
way, used to be the added benefit of dry fucking from the girl's
point of view: the guy would get his load off without her having
to give him a hand job, which some of those *demi-vierges*
claimed to find revolting. I felt the stain spreading over my
trousers. I couldn't even try to pretend it hadn't happened.
The cat was out of the bag.

I thought she'd say something to console me and acknowl-
edge that we had both become too excited playing around, but
I was wrong. She got up from bed without a word, smoothed
her clothes, pulled a hairbrush out of her huge pocketbook,
and disappeared in the bathroom. Meanwhile, I surveyed the
damage. The stain would come out in dry-cleaning, and I had
better take care of it while I was still in this good hotel, even
though some claim it's advisable to wash it at once with cold
water. The last thing I needed was to have our housekeeper see
it when I got home. She might sniff at the stain to confirm her
suspicion. Here, I could call for dry-cleaning service and leave
the trousers on the bed just as I was going out. I would be
spared the embarrassment of watching the valet examine the
problem and draw his own conclusion. There was also, I
noticed, more serious damage to my suit jacket: during our
contortions the middle button had been torn out, with its
roots, as it were. In its place was a small hole in the fabric
through which showed the beige horsehair tailors insert to

stiffen the front of the suit and the lapels. I found the button on the floor and cursed. Not on account of the hole–I was pretty sure that no magic weaving would be required; with a bit of care the chambermaid should be able to conceal it when she sewed on the button–but because, no longer feeling either sexual desire or the effect of the wine, I saw in the damage to my clothes a crude but apt demonstration of my stupidity. This young journalist had produced as good an article on my book and me as I could have wished for, and would have become a useful ally. I turned our meeting into a wrestling match with an incontinent satyr. She would remember me with contempt, and in the future I would have to avoid her. And who was to say that she wouldn't talk? She might give an account of our evening to her friend Jacques Robineau, who would, in turn, say something about "those Americans" to Pierre or Marianne. Just enough for them to get the point. That would demote Lydia, in their eyes, to the rank of wives whose husbands cheat on them. I realized, of course, that a husband's or a wife's infidelity hardly impressed the Lalondes, not even as an amusing subject for gossip, but it mattered for Lydia. That was something they understood. Therefore, they also understood that, if she were to discover not only what had happened but also that they were aware of it, she would feel doubly humiliated: by my disloyalty and by her loss of dignity. She had always treated the Lalondes with confidence and affection, not because they were her sort but because they were my old friends. She would never want to see them again–even if she didn't leave me. My childishness did not stop there. Suddenly I was sickened by the callousness of having so frivolously deprived her of something nice, a pleasure she so clearly deserved: the fun of watching the fuss that the media, my publisher, my agent, and our friends would have made over my book and the prize if I had, as my duty dictated, returned on the first plane to New York to receive their plaudits. I also withheld the pleasure she might have had of parading me before her normally condescending family. Interest in a literary prize is short-lived; the author has to be there to catch the wave and ride it. It might have been all right to turn my back on the hoopla if I had done so out of modesty or pride. But I had done so for the sake of tawdry adventure. I too had been humiliated by this girl, but the punishment was insufficient.

It seemed to me that, for someone presumably brushing her hair and putting on makeup in preparation for storming out of my room, Léa was taking a great deal of time in the bathroom. But perhaps there were other necessities of nature to which she needed to attend. It made no difference. I went into the living room, contemplated my spring bouquet on the coffee table—more grandiose and more absurd with each minute that passed—and lit a cigarette. Night had fallen. I opened the window and stared at the great square below, so empty at this hour, wishing "the scene with the girl"—that is how I had begun to think of it—to be over. As soon as she left, I would take one of the sleeping pills an Israeli doctor friend of Lydia's had given me, the kind that knock you out like a baseball bat. So it was with a feeling of relief that I heard her knock on the door between the bedroom and the living room, which I had in fact left open. I turned toward it. *Coucou,* she called out, are you surprised? Indeed, I was. She was naked and shaking with laughter. Come on, she continued, stop looking so grim. I want it now, so I'm giving you another chance.

Lest you jump to the conclusion that she was forgiving in such matters, I must confess that during our subsequent copulations, often preceded by bouts of foreplay that drove me wild by reason of their duration, the marvels of her body, and her inventiveness, she was never to overlook an occasion—they were, alas, too frequent—when I didn't manage to stay the course. She took to calling me by the initials P.E. (for this purpose she used the English term and pronunciation), told me to practice, and compared my lack of self-control with the power of some of her other friends, who were able to carry on indefinitely. Whether such supermen in fact existed, without some compensatory complications in their libido or performance, I had previously doubted, but Léa's testimony was difficult to disregard. She was an objective observer, and certainly knew the field.

As the night went on I was to learn that, in addition to the daring and knowledge of a high-class whore, Léa had a whore's gift for making a man feel that each thrust into her, and each surrender of her body to a new demand, was the willing sacrifice of a barely nubile virgin, a part of mysteries one imagined to have been performed at a temple in Greek Asia. This is just for you, she would murmur. I would whisper back, Why? Why for me? It's to show that I belong to you, was the unvarying murmured reply. And her complaisant body was beautiful beyond anything I had imagined: she was a maiden of Sparta painted by Renoir after a mural by Puvis de Chavannes. Her small imperfections thrilled me. For instance, the feet that

were a trifle fat, with chubby little toes, the long dark hairs sur-
rounding the aureoles of her nipples, the ears that stuck out.
At times she would ask me to stop moving. It hurts now, she
would say, or, I want to think about how it was so I can remember when you start again, or, I am going to sleep now, take me
while I am asleep. She slept profoundly but, if I entered her,
she either awakened at once or, from some zone of other consciousness that I couldn't define, offered herself even more
fully. I could not deny that I had fallen in love.

And what of Lydia and my remorse? Had it been only a
movement of pique and wounded self-esteem? I don't think so.
Lying by Léa's side, watching the night sky turn pink and then
gray again—I had opened the curtains to let in more air—it
seemed to me, as I thought about Lydia, that I had been split in
two. One half was Lydia's husband, whose limitless and unre-
served love for her was like a vital organ of his body. The other
was an unserious man, besotted by this girl's body and what
she was willing to do with it, and, to be just, by her startling
charm. Why couldn't these men coexist, I asked myself, so
long as I kept them apart, so long as Lydia never found out
about Léa, and I succeeded in shielding Lydia even from the
abstract humiliation of having others know? Coexist for a
while, is what I really meant, because it was clear to me that,
however irresistible I found Léa, our affair—what else was I to
call it?—must have a limited term and limited importance.
There were those other men, about whom I had not yet asked;
there was her age, which made children her natural goal and
marriage to me, even if I were free, questionable; there was my
own selfish nature, which had always put me to flight from

time-consuming unnecessary complications. I was sure that last consideration alone would keep me from wasting time which I needed for my work, or dividing what little of it was left over between a wife, whom I would not rob of her due, and a mistress. I have always admired Henry James's Prince in *The Golden Bowl*; for a goodly period of time he was able to keep two women quite content. But the system broke down when he allowed the mistress to push him into an indiscretion that humiliated his wife. I would not allow that to happen to me.

She left me at seven, her mouth full of chocolates, her teeth brushed with my toothbrush. She would walk to her studio, she told me, and change into work clothes before going to the office. I stood at the window and watched her traverse with long strides the place Vendôme in the direction of the Tuileries. Perhaps I should have gone with her, across the garden, where the sand was still wet from the soft rain that had fallen during the night, over the passerelle de Solférino and down the rue Jacob until she reached St. Germain des Prés. She had already taken a shower in my bathroom. Changing at her apartment would be a matter of five minutes before she raced up the boulevard St. Germain to the place du Palais Bourbon. Unless, of course, she had telephone calls to make from home: to her real *monsieur,* to Robineau, or to her brothers, of whom I had learned she had two, both graduates of the Polytechnique. The elder had been working in the cabinet of the prime minister and the younger in the cabinet of the minister of industry. Their assignments in the new regime were uncertain. There must exist parents of these siblings as well, leading a very correct bourgeois existence somewhere or other, but she hadn't mentioned them. How opaque her life seemed! For a moment I thought that I didn't even have her telephone number. Then I remembered that it was on the business card she handed to me at the Flore. It had to be in the pocket of my tweed jacket.

We were to meet that evening for dinner at the Balzar. She said she liked bistro food better than the food served in the great restaurants I proposed, but rejected my suggestion of the Lipp, because she said everyone she knew was always there, checking on who would walk in with whom. She refused to have lunch with me. The reason she gave was that we would have to eat near the office—she had so much work—and wherever we went in the neighborhood we would run into her colleagues. She didn't want people to gossip about her and a married American. Quite obviously, I was a trophy for a young journalist trying to specialize in cultural reporting and book reviews. That she didn't want to show me off seemed an excellent sign. Paradoxically, I was also reassured by the identity of her principal *monsieur,* which she had revealed to me in bed during a pause. If a man of his standing had confidence in her keeping their secret, why shouldn't I? It did not occur to me to take warning from this particular breach of confidence, or to ask myself how many other such breaches there had been. The revelation had come in a roundabout way. I said that Marianne had spoken of a lover she had other than Robineau, whose name she didn't know, although it was known to Pierre.

Not at all, Léa protested, at most he knows there is someone in my life more important than Jacques. Probably Jacques told him. He can't keep his mouth shut. I let Jacques fuck me from time to time, when Françoise is away, that's all. Probably I shouldn't, because he is—she hesitated before using the English expression—a son of a bitch. Is that what you say? I mean a *salaud.* You won't believe it. For a long time last year he was after me to get my older brother to speak to Raymond Barre about making him the number one at the bank. Otherwise he'd stop sleeping with me. Naturally, I wasn't going to do it, and anyway my brother wouldn't have listened to me or would have pointed out that, after a request like that, the prime minister would show him the door. At the same time, this *salaud* says I'm the best lay in Paris! Do you think he's right?

I don't know, I said, I haven't done the research. But you're good enough for me.

You know, I only sleep with Jacques because my great love is a married man like you, and we can't be together very often.

And who is your great love? I inquired.

She made a face and said she couldn't tell me. Then she changed her mind. Because it was I who had asked, she would tell me after all; it would be like the things we were doing—a sign that she belonged to me.

And what about him, your great love, I asked, still not knowing who he was, don't you belong to him?

I do, she replied, but there is a difference: the me that I've given to you is not the same as the me that belongs to him.

I saw that she subscribed to my new theory of split beings, and had herself developed it considerably. It had not occurred to me that I could offer my body, still mine but quite chaste, to Lydia.

He is a French academician, she informed me, and pronounced the name of a celebrated winner of the Nobel Prize in physics. He'll never leave his wife. Anyway, I wouldn't want him to, he's much too old for me to marry.

And what about me, I asked, what plans do you have for me?

You could have been my great love, she told me, but I met you too late. I don't think you will ever leave your Lydia. You can be my lover and best friend and dance with me at my wedding.

Seeing that I was shaking my head at his narration, North stopped; he looked at me thoughtfully and said, At least you aren't laughing at me to my face. You have every right to do so. All of this was foolish nonsense, but for the moment I believed it, and in fact continued believing it longer than should have been possible. But let me return to the rest of the stay in Paris. As I said, we were to meet at the Balzar. At nine-thirty, she specified. I should note that during the time I knew her, the hours at which we met grew progressively later. She blamed it on deadlines at the magazine, and also parties, plays, or the opera performances she was obliged to attend. Nine-thirty was all right with me, even ten. I like dining late. I was glad to be able to fill an additional hour or two with work or a drink with Pierre, and I told myself that Léa's habits went very well with mine. By the way, so do Lydia's: no lunch or dinner could ever be late enough for her, and a lifetime of hospital emergencies has made her very understanding of those times when a book was going badly and I wanted to stay at home and wrestle with it instead of going to a movie or when it was going so well that I could not bear to leave my desk. But the Balzar! That particular evening Léa arrived forty-five minutes late, at a quarter past ten. By then I had drunk two and a half whiskeys instead of the usual one drink before dinner, and kicked myself for not having brought a book to read. Even though the clientele of Balzar is less boring for a student of physiognomies than that of most restaurants, it was too much time to devote to the faces of my fellow diners, too much time during which to brood about my conversation with Lydia. I had called her in East Hampton and caught her, as I had expected, just as she arrived from New York. To invent what I had done the previous evening and what I would do during the evening that stretched before me was child's play. I told her I had managed to buy a ticket for the Racine the previous evening. Not having seen the play did not interfere with the account I gave of it. This evening I would have dinner with my publisher. I chose him, because there was little chance that the subject would come up, even if Lydia and I saw Xavier together when we next came to Paris. Of course, I was working on my book, but I hoped to get to the Louvre. Perhaps even the Musée Guimet. It was not these lies, inconsequential in themselves, that broke my heart, but the contrast between my shabby behavior and Lydia's unvarying goodness.

Do you find that I am succumbing to Victorian mawkishness? North asked abruptly.

I shook my head.

Apparently this didn't satisfy him. He looked at me sternly and said, Be careful, my dear fellow. We are all in danger of succumbing to an excess of sophistication. Goodness of character and probity of conduct are precious and rare. Altogether too many of us—both writers and upright citizens like you—

avoid naming them, so as not to seem naive. We shouldn't: they deserve to be proclaimed from rooftops. Lydia, you see, had things to tell me that were about me and only me and she was so eager about them: the stories she had clipped from New York papers about the prize and the movie sale, other clippings that my agent and the publishing house had sent, people who had called to congratulate, what my sister and each member of her family had said, how her father had the *New York Times* article blown up and pasted on a board and planned to display it during the Memorial Day lunch when they would toast me with vintage Krug, how I had made her very proud. It was only at the end of the conversation that I succeeded in worming out of her, through direct questions, that something far more important had happened concerning her career. The control-group study had been completed, proving beyond any question the validity of the treatment she had pioneered for infants fewer than eighteen months old. The *New England Journal of Medicine* was going to carry her paper. She put her success down to the simple power of inductive reasoning correctly applied and tested by the most commonplace scientific procedures. Not precisely proof of her creativity, she told me. I dwell on this instance of her modesty not only for its own beauty but to let you see how absorbed she was by my achievements and my happiness. She is the only person I have known whose wishing me well—always—I have never thought to doubt. Alas, as soon as Léa appeared in the door of the Balzar, my remorse receded. Where? Into that part of my brain—I suppose it would be more poetic to call it my heart—where I store my shame and the rest of the stuff I harangued Léa about, of which I make my books. How could it be otherwise? She was so immensely desirable, and I knew that after the two hours at most it would take to eat dinner and get out of the restaurant, her naked and obedient body would be in my hands. We'll sleep at my place, she told me. I want to show it to you, and I want you to see my work. I am a painter, remember? Not only your whore. She was full of talk. About the magazine—everyone loved the piece about me, there would be one or two cuts, no other changes—about her best friend to whom she had described me as her new lover and perhaps a candidate for her new great love, and about her *monsieur,* who didn't much like the news of my arrival on the scene, but too bad, what could he expect if he could see her only once a week, and about the opening at the opera the following week. It was *Pelléas et Mélisande.* She had two tickets, could I stay until Tuesday and go with her? I reminded her that I was leaving for New York, and forbore from confessing my dislike for that work. Then, perhaps thinking of the sublime fidelity of the incestuous lovers, she said that she would go on sleeping with the great physicist but would give up Robineau, whom she found more and more loathsome, *puant.* What about me, she wanted to know, did I have anyone else in New York? Or elsewhere? I reminded her of what I had said: she was my only adventure, and I expected to have no others. She agreed I had said that, but she meant to ask how I would manage when I wasn't seeing her—when I wasn't in Paris. It seemed ludicrous to have to say it, but I explained: I sleep with Lydia, I said. I like to sleep with my wife. Léa considered this information, and said, My great love doesn't sleep with his wife. Really, I replied, even though they aren't very old? Oh, perhaps I am mistaken about that, she replied, and then reassured me. They do it maybe once a year, on her birthday! And with you, I asked, once a week is enough for him? She told me it seemed to be, the great man wasn't oversexed like her. Then she asked how often I slept with Lydia. When I told her that usually it was every night, she looked troubled. After a moment she said it was a real pity, because that made it impossible for me to become her great love, even if she were to leave the physicist.

It really doesn't matter, I said to her. You need to get married to a man you love, and live with him. Have children, if you can. I don't need to get married to have children, she corrected me. Perhaps the first child could be from you? Think about it.

Her studio looked out on the street, a northern exposure. The bedroom was in the back and had a small terrace. We made love right away, at first standing up, Léa with her back to me, leaning against a chest of drawers. Afterward, she asked whether I wanted to look at some of her work. When I said I did, and started to pull on my trousers, she whispered, No, stay just as you are, so that we went into the studio naked. She wanted to show me only her new work, oils on stretched canvas. The paintings were in a storage bin. She went through the familiar routine of studio visits: the canvases out of the bin, set on easels so they can be seen at the proper height, other paintings lined up against the wall, and so forth. I think that the combination of the very bright light in the studio and our nudity—especially hers, as she performed tasks one associates with stocky men in work smocks, the naked girl crouching and lifting, and thus showing off the strength of her arms, back, buttocks, and thighs—added to the unease her work caused me. I suppose I might have had a similar feeling if I had found myself unexpectedly on the set of a blue movie. Her paintings were quite large, all of them two meters by one fifty, mostly horizontal, and, to my surprise, because I supposed, for no special reason, that she was an abstract painter, figurative and realistic. They were landscapes—various views of what I was quite sure was the same garden—with male and female figures whose stiffness of bearing made me think of the Amish, scantily dressed in old-fashioned clothes. Some of them displayed their sexual organs. Not ostentatiously or aggressively. The organs were simply there, rendered with great precision. No contact among the figures. Their eyes were directed neither at the viewer nor at their companions. If they weren't blind, they were looking at something away from me and away from the painted scene. The vegetation was tame: the sort of plants and flowers you would find in any suburban garden near Paris and for that matter New York. Among the plants, however, there were large insects of species unknown to me, very meticulously portrayed. The insects gave the impression that they were staring at you.

You will doubtless conclude that my pal Léa had been studying Balthus, and you will be right. I thought though that her paintings were less flat and, somehow, in spite of the isolation and rigidity of the human figures, more exuberant. Had she not told me that they were her work, I might have guessed that they were paintings not only from a different time but also from a different continent. Although the vegetation seemed to be, as I said, European and quite banal, and the figures were pale skinned, the overall impression was of tropical excess. Something I might have found less disturbing in the work of a Latin American painter. I knew that I should say something, and that she expected me to speak, but I was troubled. You should never allow yourself to sound like an art critic when an artist invites you to his studio and shows you his work, and obviously, I had to be especially careful with Léa. So I remained silent until she asked what I thought.

Your work is very strong, I told her, overpowering. You are gifted–and skillful. It's all a wonderful surprise. Especially your technique.

She made a face and said that I must have been surprised because I thought she was only good at screwing–and maybe writing flattering magazine pieces about me. Then, abruptly, she turned out the lights and pulled me to the bedroom.

We had breakfast on the terrace the following morning and afterward returned to the studio. I looked at the paintings again, in part to please her but also in order to understand them better. You should buy one, she said. I'll charge you half the gallery price and throw in a special discount. Do you know why you should have one of my paintings? So that you will have a reason to invite me to dinner at your apartment when I come to New York. You will tell Lydia I want to see how you have hung it. And she gave her cry: *Youpi!* Obviously, when she offered to sell me one of her paintings, the only answer I could give was that I would be happy to own one, particularly a work that she chose for me. She pointed to a painting of three female figures. I thought that one of them perhaps had some-thing of Léa about her face. Certainly the pubis, visible through a slit in that figure's long skirt, was shaved like Léa's, the razor having spared on the delta a narrow vertical strip of hair, like the brush one sometimes sees in a Western School painting on the head of an Indian brave. The other two figures were not exposing themselves.

That's perfect, I said, exactly the one I would have picked myself. Then I said I would pay in cash. I realize now that I was already unconsciously acting in accordance with the rule I was to adopt somewhat later, that I must never let Léa have anything from me in writing, unless it was a professional communication, such as a note thanking her for the article in *Vogue*. A check, constituting nothing more than the means of payment in a business transaction, should have also qualified as an exception to the rule. I didn't think of that and, in the end, it was probably just as well that I gave her cash. A check on an American bank takes forever to clear in France. And cash was certainly more convenient than a check if she didn't intend to declare the income to the tax inspector, which is the normal French modus operandi.

The sale of the painting having been successfully concluded, Léa said that she had to go to the opening of a sculptor friend that evening. She wasn't asking me to come with her because both her physicist *monsieur* and Jacques Robineau would be there, in addition to *le tout Paris,* in other terms altogether too many people she fucked gathered in a rather small space. Let's have dinner late, she said, in your room. I would invite you to dinner here, but I have to be in the office in the afternoon, and then there is that *vernissage,* so I won't have time to cook. Please order something good. I will be starved.

It was another beautiful day. I walked from her studio to the hotel, and worked on my book until noon. Then I had lunch at the counter of the café on the Maxim's side of rue Royale that is always full of tourists—these days more of them Japanese than American. It serves superior ham and Gruyère sandwiches on buttered baguettes. I had coffee afterward and then went shopping for Lydia and Léa. To buy a present for Lydia was easy, in theory. I know her taste and size so well that I rarely need to ask a saleswoman of the same build as she to try on the dress or jacket or top that has caught my eye. But like all questing knights in moral trouble, I dawdled and took a great deal of time shuttling back and forth among the three shops I like best on the rue du Faubourg St. Honoré until I found what I wanted for her. It was a crêpe de chine blouse, cut exactly like the one that Léa wore on our first evening, but in ivory rather than white. I thought it would go better with Lydia's skin, which is as white as rice powder. An image came to mind: when she put it on—which she would want to do as soon as she opened the package—I would plunge my hand into her cleavage. We would make love at once, without waiting until I had unpacked or shaved or even bathed. She would be grateful for my impetuosity—far more than for the present. I was certain of our shared, triumphant climax. Thinking about Lydia that way aroused me powerfully, although had I been questioned before I bought that garment I would have surely said that the night with Léa had left me sated. Now, on the contrary, I felt tormented by desire. I wanted to fuck. I looked at the saleswomen with the eyes and instincts of a male on the prowl, appraising their breasts and mouths, their legs and their buttocks, asking myself how this one or the other among them would respond if I propositioned her. For instance: Yes, I will take this *chemisier* and also the other one, which is more in your colors than the one I am buying for my wife. They should be wrapped as separate gifts. You see, the second one is for you. Here is my card. The Ritz–room 307. From six o'clock. That's where I will give you your present. Please don't keep me waiting.

The chances of success? Better than fifty-fifty, I would say. I am reasonably attractive; I have known women to fall for just such a mixture of surprise and disrespect. And what could be more exciting than to get one of those high-style salesladies to come to my room, laughing to cover her confusion, accepting the glass of champagne I handed her and the invitation to try on the garment that I would have taken out of its wrapping and draped over the back of an armchair?

People are most often wrong about sex. As you have probably guessed, I opened this parenthesis, which I will soon close, to demonstrate that, contrary to ignorant middle-class prejudice, which holds that men become "fucked out," intense and inventive lovemaking with any woman who is a great lay–to borrow Robineau's *mot juste* for the girl we both happened to be humping–redounds to the sexual benefit of the wife. The husband's interest in women, and in the unbeatable pleasure to be found in fornication, rises sky-high. When he thinks of what he did with that woman during an illicit encounter in the afternoon, he wants to improve on it, or at least match it, in the evening with the woman to whom he is married. On condition, of course, that he loves his wife or, at the very least, is well disposed toward her. I loved Lydia. No, the injury to the wife is deep, but of quite a different nature.

I shook myself out of the erotic daydream and, with Lydia's package under my arm, concentrated on what I would get for Léa. My heart wasn't in the business of finding her something to wear. Really, the crêpe de chine blouse was her one garment the elegance of which I completely understood–and knew where to find. Her other clothes, which I liked on her, seemed to derive their chic from the way she put together the elements of her costume. For instance, her jeans, belt, and boots. They were not individually what I would choose. This was true of her pocketbook, for instance, which resembled an overnight bag and often served as one. Her style was, I thought, particular to young women of her precise generation and milieu, so that even at the best and most expensive shop, an accessory that I thought corresponded essentially to something I had seen her wear would, if I bought it, most likely turn out to be a gaffe, because, in fact, the one she actually owned and others truly like it could only be found by the initiated, after hours of research, in a little shop off the boulevard Richard Lenoir that I would have never noticed for many reasons, including my rarely venturing into that part of Paris. Pushing forward with my own search, I saw, in the window of an antique dealer in the rue St. Honoré, a pin in the shape of a lily made of gold and enamel that I recognized to be a good turn-of-the-century piece just right for Lydia. As for giving it to Léa, I understood her well enough to realize that she would thank me for it with a big kiss, because she would have understood that it was valu-able and in very good taste, stick it in a drawer, and never wear it–unless the fashion she followed changed radically. On the other hand, the sort of hard-edged silver ornaments I saw her wear, most of which I thought could be acquired from Hermès, or wherever counterfeit Hermès products were distributed, were so clearly not to my taste as to be, coming from me, an absurd present. Besides, how was I to choose the one that was right among the clunky wristwatches, chain bracelets, and rings that looked like brass knuckles? The same antique dealer sold picture frames. I found one that was Viennese, made of silver like the Hermès ornaments. Encrusted in it was a sphinxlike feminine face carved in ivory that Art Nouveau favored. Léa's paintings led me to think that she might like it. The price was more than what I had intended to spend, but I was celebrating the sale of my film rights–as well as the prize. I told the dealer I was taking it. A murmur of protest somewhere deep in my psyche made me understand that Lydia was entitled to compensation, by way of an equal or greater extravagance. I bought the lily pin for her.

It was understood that I would stop by Pierre's gallery for a cup of coffee. But a thought that had been germinating since I finished work and put away my manuscript that morning seemed to be putting out new shoots. I was at that early phase of the composition of the novel I eventually called *Loss* when the closest and most tender attention must be paid to each such growth. Unless you examine it promptly, turn it into words, and actually put them down on paper, the danger is great that by the next day it will have disappeared or become unrecognizable and useless. I called Pierre from the shop and asked whether we might have a drink instead that evening, and hurried back to the hotel. It was already too late. I reread what I had written in the morning–two double-spaced pages, a

decent output at the early stage of a novel–made the necessary
corrections, and was unable to move forward. There was, alas,
no reason to alter the judgment I had reached about my work. I
was describing a love scene between a couple in their early
middle age: a wife and the husband whom she is leaving. Why?
She thinks that he has not gone far enough in his career or his
personal development, disappointing her legitimate expectations, that he doesn't have a strong sense of who he is and what
is due him, that he demeans and denatures her by yielding to
her whims. To a degree I intended this to sound plainly crazy.
One might also look at their case and reasonably conclude that
while in the past she found him moderately amusing, now he
bores her. People change. She has met a man who seems to
have more élan and is just enough of a son of a bitch. So, for old
times' sake, she lets her husband do one more time the things
they used to do in the past, and she throws in for good measure
the new stuff she has learned from the s.o.b. Her orgasms are
rare, so the fact that she doesn't come this time is not a big
deal; the proceedings are pleasant enough and, anyway, they
satisfy her need to feel generous. But, paradoxically, the husband, who had begged to sleep with her, is devastated. The
gestures, the mounting excitement, the ejaculation, all utterly
meaningless. Because he hadn't accomplished what he knew
most probably couldn't be accomplished. As I corrected those
pages, I couldn't deny that I had gotten it exactly right. You
can find much worse stuff in almost any book by one of my
colleagues or–I suppose, if such a thing exists–in an anthol-
ogy of great American prose. Yet my pages left me cold. Was
there any value in them if such was their effect on me? Quite

honestly, I didn't know. At the same time, having just been engaged in a round of scribbling, I had to admit that this activity gives me more pleasure than any other. Except for fornication, in certain cases.

So what do you make of that? North asked point-blank, and fixed me with a menacing glare.

I shrugged.

A dreadful and vulgar form of reply, said North. I am surprised to see you resort to it. It means, I take it, that you have no point of view you care to express. What a pity! Allow me to inform you that, when the scene I have described was formed in my mind, and when I wrote it, I was thinking of the farewell visit—in fact the only visit—Madame Arnoux pays to Frédéric in Flaubert's *L'Éducation Sentimentale,* the greatest novel ever written, according to Franz Kafka and me. The two scenes have nothing in common. Frédéric had never slept with Madame Arnoux, whom he loved to the limit of his powers, and he doesn't sleep with her now, although she as much as offers herself. The reason, apart from the fact that he has the temperament of a wilted lettuce leaf, is that he fears the disappointment. She has aged, and so has he. What will he find when she disrobes? Isn't it better to live with old disappointments than with a new ones? So they part, she foolishly deluding herself into thinking that he did not take her because of his generosity and refinement of soul, he full of bitterness that engulfs his entire wasted life. Why was I thinking of Frédéric and Madame Arnoux when I described my hapless married couple? There are various parallels: the corrosive sadness of irretrievable opportunities, the failure of the senses. You expect a rush of pleasure that takes hold of you like a huge roller in a heavy surf—but nothing happens. The most important link, though, is me. I realized that the events I was describing moved me in the same way as my memory of that last meeting between Frédéric and Marthe—Marthe is Madame Arnoux's given name, by which she authorizes him much too late to call her. You might say that I was dedicating those pages to Flaubert, an homage he would have scorned. But we were talking about pleasure. As you may have guessed, I did not carry out my brilliant scheme and invite one of those ladies from rue du Faubourg St. Honoré to call on me at the hotel. I was tired after my shopping and even more tired after rewriting my pages. It's exhausting work. It was hours before I would see Léa and I did not need to hurry because I was meeting Pierre at the bar of the Ritz. I undressed, got into bed, and masturbated thinking of Léa and Lydia. Masturbating while on the television screen some hairless ape sodomizes a floozy with bad skin, and then whacks his phallus over her face until at last he gets his shot off and wets her with semen, has never been my road to heavenly peace. I am left feeling exploited. The flicks I can see with my eyes closed are higher class and more effective, and they cost nothing. I have a lifetime supply. So it was this time. I would have been hard put to say which of my two leading ladies had more power over me.

North paused and smiled. I fear I have shocked you, he said.

Not at all, I replied. Do go on, please.

I somehow think I have, said North. But I prefer to be wrong in this case, and to go on with my story. Over drinks, Pierre told me that he thought Marianne was seeing someone. He wasn't sure of it; he had noticed, though, that she was treating him with a sort of bemused detachment, which was new in their relations. Also, she had announced that she would spend a week in London in June, alone, to see the new plays. It is true, he told me, that he doesn't like the theater all that much, certainly not in English, which he can't always follow, whereas she is passionate about it, so that it wasn't unreasonable in principle for her to go to London without him. But she had never done such a thing before. He couldn't help thinking there might be a link between the London expedition and her new attitude. On the other hand, if she was seeing someone, she didn't need to leave town for that purpose. Both she and Pierre had such unpredictable work hours that she could manage any sort of tryst right here in Paris without lies and pretexts. But, he said, in these five-to-seven romances, there always comes a point when one party starts complaining about never getting to spend the night together. That could explain London, because to be in Paris and not come home for the night would be the same as declaring that she was having an affair and didn't care whether he and Mélanie and her sister knew it.

That Mélanie was in danger of being hurt saddened me especially. You see, North said, as Mélanie's godfather, I almost always think of some treat for her when I'm in Paris, something we can do together. This time I hadn't. I asked Pierre how she was doing. She regretted, Pierre told me, not having been at home when I came to dinner, but she had promised her current best friend, whose parents were away, to sleep over at her apartment. He went on to tell me that Mélanie was very proud of her godfather. She was continuing to do well at school, and was beginning to go out with boys. That made another problem, he told me. Marianne and he had to enforce rules about whom she could go out with, where she could go on dates, curfews, and so forth. None of this would be any easier if Marianne's mind were on other things, or if she took to setting a bad example by her own conduct.

I realized that Pierre was more upset than he let on, and that upset me too. He had married Marianne two years before I married Lydia; I was a witness at the wedding, on his grandparents' property near Bordeaux. They had lived together for two or three years before that. I liked being with Marianne and Pierre. But when the wedding date was set, I could not help wondering what marriage to Pierre might imply for Marianne, by way of sacrifices she would have to make. Pierre, you must understand, had a very precise idea of the way a bourgeois household should be kept: exactly like his parents' and grandparents'. It wasn't clear to me how Marianne, the hyperactive television producer, was going to combine her professional ambitions with the duties attendant upon being Madame Lalonde. But, as I observed their marriage, it became clear that she managed it without stumbling. Her example, in fact, encouraged me when I began to think of marrying my hyperactive and incomparably gifted research doctor. Not that my ideas of how we should live were as elevated as Pierre's! Our very much *comme il faut* existence all came from the Frank side of the family. So, as you can imagine, quite apart from my feelings for those two, which ran deep, the possibility that Marianne had wearied of Pierre, who was more handsome and ebullient than ever, and a spectacular success, having evolved from a specialist in eighteenth-century furniture with no money and no backing into a very prosperous and important dealer in modern art, might have a significant impact on my view of the characters in the new novel. Marianne's own evolution into a hot screenwriter might have such an impact as well. She had gone further than could have been expected.

I asked Pierre whether the marriage still suited him. Perfectly, he told me. You know that I'm not a saint, and I haven't become a prude like you. I have had little flings, all meaningless. A matter of having lunch with a girl at a hotel restaurant and then going upstairs to a room I had reserved beforehand. Or I might invite some young thing to come with me on a business trip to Geneva. For instance, that Morini girl, who came to dinner the other evening. It's something that happened and was almost immediately forgotten. Sometimes when I see her I am at first not completely sure that I have slept with her, although I know perfectly well that I have. I haven't anybody just now. In fact, these days I have no time to think about it.

I said I hoped he was wrong about Marianne, and that I would call him at the office to check in, once I got back to New York. Fortunately, we would be seeing much more of each other when I came to Paris to work on the filming of *The Anthill.* Ah yes, that reminds me, he said, the apartment on avenue Gabriel. It's yours if you want it. My aunt Viviane loves your books and will be thrilled to have the author under her roof.

That was, I supposed, good news. As for the rest, why should it matter that Léa had slept with Pierre any more than that she was currently sleeping with the physicist, Robineau, and others for the time being unknown? I didn't really care, except that after my first night with Léa I thought I had fallen in love. Had I told her? I didn't believe I had, but I wasn't completely sure. If I had, perhaps such declarations were so much a part of the routine that Léa hadn't paid attention. Perhaps they weren't. In that case she must think me a fool. Not the first fool, of course, to love a promiscuous mistress. In any case, what I meant by falling in love with Léa would have to be reexamined, I told myself. Meanwhile I could only pray that I had confused a temporary infatuation with love. I decided I wouldn't question Pierre about his "fling" with Léa. Instead, I let fall that after the interview she told me that she was a painter as well as a journalist. Did he know her work? Was it any good?

He told me he had seen her paintings; they were unusual in subject and the technique she used to achieve a smooth, almost glossy surface. Quite like the surfaces of Ingres. Yes, he thought they were good, which didn't mean anyone bought them. He had told her he couldn't help. He had never handled contemporary art; his one desire was to stay away from it.

Pierre had to leave to meet Marianne at a concert. We embraced, and I went back to my room. In the morning, Léa had told me that she would be at the hotel no later than nine-thirty. I had interpreted that to mean ten o'clock and ordered canapés from room service for that hour. I also ordered for ten-thirty a cold meal of roast chicken, Russian salad, cheese and fruit, and a bottle of red wine that was respectable and relatively inexpensive. I hoped she would find it sturdy enough.

The cost of the celebratory long weekend was beginning to get on my nerves. Then I took a bath, shaved a second time, put on a pair of flannel trousers and a sweater, and, contrary to habit, since I seldom write in the evening, turned to my text. Once again I revised what I had written and composed an additional page. And once again I found myself bone tired. Only this time I did not get into bed or masturbate. I fell asleep head down over my manuscript.

The waiter bringing the hors d'oeuvres and a bottle of champagne on ice awakened me. It was five minutes after ten. In general, I really do not dislike waiting. But unless I have a good book to read—not one of my own!—it's far better to wait in public places, where you can watch people coming and going, study their faces, and do a little eavesdropping. Unfortunately, when I am working on a novel, and particularly if my novel is not very far along, which was then the case, I have to avoid novels written by others. You don't want some other writer's voice in your ears, and there is a huge risk of that when you read good writers. Of course, instead of reading, you can let your mind wander. That is how I have gotten some of my best ideas. But it would have been useless to daydream just then. I was drained by the day's work. Instead, I washed my face with cold water and, *faute de mieux,* took a *Time* from the coffee table. As you can imagine, I am not much of a magazine reader. At ten-thirty very precisely, the same waiter wheeled in the table with our refined collation. I asked him to open the wine and pour me a glass. It was better than I had expected, another confirmation that buying costly wines is necessary only if one wants to give the sort of impression I never want to give, but it made me realize at once that what I really wanted was a big glass of potato vodka and that I was famished. The waiter set off in search of the vodka while I reviewed the situation. Clearly, I wasn't irritated enough to tell the concierge that I was going to sleep and didn't want to be disturbed by any visitor. In fact, the longer I waited the more I wanted Léa in my room and in my bed. I wouldn't eat the cold chicken without her unless she was more than an hour late—that line would be crossed in twenty-five minutes. However, there was no reason that I shouldn't eat the canapés—all of them if I liked. She had forfeited any right to champagne or to the hors d'oeuvres, the cost of which, as I calculated it rapidly, was more than half the price of the dinner. *Knock, knock.* It was not the young lady; it was my faithful waiter with the vodka, so cold the glass had thick frost on it, and a carafe with more in a little ice bucket. I blessed the man and gave him a large tip, every centime of which he had earned. Once I had finished the canapés and drunk all the vodka, my mood lightened. I didn't even notice when the magic hour of eleven came and passed. *Knock, knock* again. According to the clock on the mantelpiece it was eleven-fifteen. I opened the door. Ah, Mademoiselle Léa, in a white silk dress with black polka dots the size of grapefruits, cut wide so that I could think of nothing but the unobstructed access it offered to her person.

She had been obliged to go to the dinner that followed the opening, she explained, and she had sat through it without eating. Could we eat? Or should we make love first? Before I could get the words, Let's make love, out of my mouth, she said no, she wasn't sure that we were going to make love at all, so we had better eat. Very well, said I, let's eat and let's drink. I do believe she told the truth about not having touched the food at the restaurant because she demolished her half chicken in less time than it had taken me to eat the canapés, moved on to the cheese, and finished what was left of the wine. I rang for the waiter, who must have been standing behind the door, he arrived so fast, and I asked him to clear the table and open the champagne. Having the champagne opened was a preemptive strike worth making, although I certainly didn't want any. The thought of all those bubbles made me sick. I feared that, given a chance, she would ask for more of the red wine, which was so evidently to her taste. But bringing another bottle would have taken some time—this not being a wine the hotel was pushing—and I wanted our midnight snack over and done with so that the party could move to the bedroom, the couch, or even the floor. The tempo of Léa's ingestion, however, was slowing to an *andante ma non troppo*. She began to tell me about the sculpture show, how much I would like her friend's constructions and the artist himself, how she had in fact arranged for us to get together at the gallery before lunch, so that I could see the work in his presence, and how we could perhaps take him to lunch with us afterward. The dinner had turned out to be fabulous too. I would have liked the restaurant and the decoration—coffeepots of every sort, paintings and drawings of coffeepots, and a very nice *patron*. Thereupon she made a moue, wrinkling her nose in a manner I found irresistible, and said she knew I wouldn't like what she was going to tell me now: the real reason for her being so late was that Robineau insisted on sleeping with her—just one

fuck, is what he said; he was not asking her to spend the night–
so they had to go to his apartment, which is all the way on the
other side of the Luxembourg, and then she had to find a taxi
because she didn't want to ask him to drive her to the place
Vendôme as that would naturally have led to his asking all
kinds of questions. That is, she concluded, why she wasn't sure
she was going to sleep with me.

You can wash first, I suggested. She turned red and I fully
expected her to throw a plate at me or hit me with the wine
bottle. Instead she said, You are a *salaud* too, just as bad as he,
but I deserve what you said. I just don't know that I can sleep
with you tonight or–she brightened at the thought–I don't
know whether we can make love. We can sleep in the same
bed, like brother and sister, because you are almost my great
love. At that point, I was no longer certain of what I wanted
more: to get her into bed and treat her like the little whore she
was showing herself to be, or send her back to her studio with
an envelope full of cash. Not for personal services but for the
painting, since I was surely not going to renege on my purchase. She settled the issue for me, saying that I was right, she
would take a hot bath. Perhaps I would take it with her in that
enormous tub before we went to bed.

Time after time that night she protested that we should just
make love very simply, like an old married couple, but I was as
tough with her as I had intended to be at the height of my
annoyance and demanded every accommodation she had
offered during our first time and more, answering each Please
not tonight, with Then get dressed and get out of here. She
stayed and I suppose enjoyed herself because, before we finally

stopped, and while I was somewhere between sleep and waking, she whispered in my ear that I had made her happy, and that she was wishing again I could be her great love. We slept late. One of the great advantages of being in Europe is that neither your family nor your agent wakes you unless you are still asleep at three o'clock in the afternoon. Some little alarm clock in Léa's head must have gone off, reminding her of the appointment at the gallery, because she started nudging me to open my eyes and begin the day we were going to pass together, getting to the rue de Seine well before the sculptor had grounds to complain that we weren't punctual. We had breakfast in bed. I asked her to take off the peignoir she had put on in preparation for the waiter's arrival so I could look at and play with her breasts as she ate. I thought that my feelings for her, however I might characterize them, had not diminished. Most likely they were made up principally of an intense desire which, having been fulfilled, was turning into tenderness. Also, I thought she amused me; I found she was original. That view of her, as you will see, was destined to change. No doubt, what we had done during the night, and the promise I made to myself of what we might still do before going out or after lunch, had put me into a state of considerable exhilaration. I was returning to the thought that my time with Léa might be good for me and for my work, and that it need not harm anyone.

She had finished the contents of the basket of croissants and brioches and was working on the basket of fruit when I asked her why she had gone to bed with me the first time two nights before, why she continued to sleep with me, why she had gone off with Robineau on her way to me, what it was that drew her

to so many men at more or less the same time–I said I could
sense there were many–and what did it all have to do with
monsieur the physicist, her great love. That was quite a question, as she pointed out, but I managed to ask it well and very
nicely. In any case, she did not get angry; she answered. She
loved the physicist, she told me, because of his intelligence
and what she could only call his nobility of soul. Besides,
although he was old–fifteen years older than I, whom she
thought in that regard just right since she liked men older
than she–he was very sexy. And good at making love. As good
as Robineau? No. Robineau fucks better than anybody, she
said, before adding, out of politeness, except you when you
don't come too soon. That's why I went with him last evening;
he said if I didn't he'd never sleep with me again. The others?
She had not found anyone she wanted to marry who wanted to
marry her, and she wanted to marry and have children. So she
was still looking. How was she to find someone, unless she
went to bed with the men who appealed to her? Besides, she
added, you know that I like it and that I know what I'm doing
in bed.

I thought about her reply then, and later that day, returning
to it often while we continued on our strange road together. I
knew that many men, myself included before I married Lydia,
would go to any length to sleep with every attractive woman
they came across. That was so, I believed, because the male
desire for women is situated right here–North tapped his fly
with his index and median fingers, I guess to make sure I
didn't miss the point–and for them the great existential puzzle
comes down to this: Why does the penis sometimes become a
club, when it's neither wanted nor needed to be one, and why,

even more perversely, does it so often shrink, hide, and refuse to show itself when, happily, our desire is faced with its very object? I know there are answers to these questions, but we needn't go into them now, North said, raising his voice. He must have thought I was going to contradict him or add my own two cents' worth of theory.

But for women, I believed at the time, North said, desire is less specific. It must be accompanied by fondness for the man, a sense that the conditions for the fulfillment of desire are right; certainly desire cannot be purely carnal because why else would women seem to be quite genuinely attracted to certain repulsive men? You have never seen that happen in the other direction, a man besotted by a female of monstrous ugliness. Bear in mind that I have always avoided books on sexology, gender studies, and the like, from Simone de Beauvoir to Betty Friedan, so that this theory is based on my own field research and observation, in which I have never engaged full-time. The result is quite necessarily that its authority is limited. But I have begun to wonder whether great literature, that highest and most reliable source of learning about human nature, does not contradict the "woman above mere flesh" thesis. Take just two notorious examples: Anna Karenina and Emma Bovary. Can Rodolphe and the other creeps for whom Emma sells her soul be explained by anything other than a raw, irresistible desire to have their phalluses up her vagina? Don't answer me now. Just think about it. Please. And Vronsky? Why does Anna give up everything for him?

Meanwhile, North said, I'll get on with my tale. The day wore on pleasantly. I didn't even try to avoid inviting the

sculptor to lunch. Politeness or my luck? He had to leave
before we had coffee, to get back to the gallery. Over cognac—
we had already agreed that we were going to take a nap after
lunch—Léa returned to the subject of her painting. She would
arrange for its shipment, unless I had other ideas. I didn't.
Then she would have it shipped as expeditiously as possible,
because it was important for her to regularize the situation, so
far as Lydia was concerned, so that all three of us could be
friends. You really will be able to invite me to dinner at home
once the painting has arrived, she told me. By the way, Jacques
Robineau invited me to go with him to New York in July, so I'll
be there. I want to meet Lydia and see your apartment. But I
don't think that we'll hang the painting in the apartment, I
told her, I bought it for my office. You see, I find it magnificent, but Lydia will think it doesn't go with the other art we
have. It takes her a long time to accept new things. Or she will
say it's too large, we would have to move everything around to
place it. Another thing: we will be away from the city in July. As
you can imagine, I did not think it necessary to express my
views about her going to New York with Robineau, and perhaps planning to bring him to visit as well. She answered that
if we were in the Hamptons—I had told her that is where we
have our country house—we might be together anyway.
Jacques had friends there he wanted to visit over the weekend.
She named an investment banker. If not, she would be in New
York again in September. You will have to find a way to introduce me to Lydia, she said, very distinctly. I know you will
manage it.

And I knew the name of Robineau's friend in the Hamptons:

a Venezuelan of French extraction, a fellow in his late thirties, I thought, who worked for one of the big investment banks on Wall Street, North said. He and his wife were then in possession of a house in East Hampton, on Lily Pond Lane, and moved in pretty fancy circles. Even Lydia's parents occasionally invited them to their big cocktail parties.

Lily Pond Lane, I murmured.

Do you know it? North asked. Then you realize that, as the crow flies over Hook Pond, it isn't all that distant from the Frank family strongholds on Further Lane. The problem was that we would indeed be there on the Fourth of July weekend–Lydia's parents are comically serious about national holidays, and I couldn't see asking her, for no reason at all, to abandon East Hampton on that particular holiday when for years we have spent most of the month of July there. And though we almost never go to cocktail parties in the country–they cut into the working day so Lydia goes to them alone, if at all–there are invitations to Fourth of July shindigs given by old friends one really can't refuse. It occurred to me that the Venezuelans, with that fellow Jacques and Léa in tow as houseguests, might even turn up at the Franks' annual bash, or at the McEwens' or Sartors', people we have known forever. Of course, I would greet Léa. I would greet Robineau as well. And if Lydia was close by, I would introduce her to them. Nothing could be simpler: the journalist who interviewed me for the article in French *Vogue* that Lydia had liked–because the issue in which the piece was to appear would be out by then, and Léa would have sent a copy that I, in turn, would have shown to Lydia–and this is her friend, with whom I dined at the

Lalondes. And afterward, would Léa find a ruse—or would it be I who found it—to ease out of the crowd, so I could show her the view from the deck above the dune, or even escort her down some battered steps to the beach? It was probable, I thought. She would review the activities the Venezuelans had organized for the weekend and find that she had a free morning: because Jacques and the Venezuelan husband and wife were scheduled to be on the golf course, and she had never taken up the game. In that case, would she propose that we meet at one of the motels on Route 27? That too seemed likely. Whether there would be a vacancy at any of them during that supercharged weekend was another matter altogether. That dodging Léa and keeping her away from Lydia would involve lies and take a good deal of my time were clear enough.

North stopped speaking, as though to catch his breath. There wasn't much whiskey left in the bottle. He emptied it into our glasses, pouring carefully so that we each got an equal share, added ice cubes, stirred with his index finger, and ordered another bottle. They will keep it here for us, he said. I don't expect we will finish it. By the way, North added, it helps that you are a good listener. You make me want to continue.

Seeing the danger, North said, I decided I must lay down some rules of conduct for Léa so that she would know what I expected—and with regard to discretion, I thought that her touchiness about being seen with me in restaurants, at events like that sculpture show and so forth gave me some ground for hope. I told her she could call me at my office whenever she liked. If I was writing, I wouldn't answer. But if she left a message, I'd call her back as soon as I could. The fact is that I have a second line which I always pick up, whatever I am doing. It's for Lydia and my sister, Ellen; the gang that services the bodies that used to belong to our mother and father; and nobody else. Naturally, I did not reveal its existence to Léa. But I will write to you, she told me. I replied that she could send letters to my office address, but she wasn't to expect any from me. I told her the truth: writing letters takes time and effort I can't spare. Not even for business letters. My agent or my accountant takes care of them. I discourage people from writing personal letters to me. Of course, I don't always succeed.

She thought this over and said she understood. You want to be able to fuck me when you feel like it and have a spare moment and don't think that Lydia will catch you. The rest of the time, I am not to get in your way.

I laughed and told her that was a harsh way to describe the good time we were having. She agreed that we were having a nice time. Then let's not spoil it, was my reply. For the record, though, I reminded her that in my solar system Lydia was the sun, and everything revolved around her. I will never forgive myself, I said, if Lydia comes to be hurt by what we are doing. If it is your fault, if it is because you have talked, I believe I will kill you.

I suppose I looked quite fierce—that was certainly my intention—because after a moment of silence she said: I think you would. We should stop what we are doing right now. And she burst into tears.

Of course we didn't stop. Neither of us wanted to. We took our nap after lunch, which means that first we fucked and then we slept; she went home to change, and we had dinner together; she spent the night and most of the following day with me until it was time for her to go to a family meal with her brothers and parents—the parents turned out to live in one of those splendid buildings on the quai Anatole France overlooking the Seine, the Tuileries, and the place de la Concorde. This was consistent with the widely held theory that bourgeois families of the Seventh Arrondissement are more likely than any others to send sons to the Polytechnique and the École des Mines, the latter being the finishing school for the most brilliant of *polytechniciens.* I noticed that she did not suggest that I meet the parents and brothers and perhaps stay for dinner. This I took to be another show of reserve and discretion and a good omen. Perhaps we could keep our lives separate except when we were conjoined in bed. She called me after her dinner as she was leaving quai Anatole France. I met her halfway, at the corner of the rue de Rivoli and the rue St. Florentin. We walked back to the hotel together, and soon we were so conjoined.

The next morning we said goodbye at the hotel before I left for the airport. She cried at first and then suddenly cheered up, saying it was silly to get into such a state. We had been happy and would be together again very soon. Somehow I would make it happen. It's paradoxical, considering how I feared hurting Lydia, I too believed I would bring that about. What I have already described to you, the transformation of sexual appetite into tenderness, had continued. If I did not exactly love Léa, I am certain that I felt for her something virtually indistinguishable from love, the distinction being only the one inexorably imposed by my marriage. It was out of the question that I should ever leave Lydia; there was no one with whom I had a more perfect understanding. All of this sounds very banal, but I assure you that it was or anyway seemed very real. And Léa? Perhaps she was a nymphomaniac, if those mythical creatures really exist. But where was the evil in what she was doing? For the moment, I could not find it; on the contrary it seemed to me that love of one's own body and of the body of another—which was after all the essence of her exploits—was good; not evil. For the same reason, it seemed to me that what she and I did could not be condemned en bloc, unless I failed to protect Lydia from hurt and humiliation. I should tell you that even then, in the moment of my greatest exaltation with Léa, I was not under any illusions about Lydia's accepting the fact that I had a mistress in Paris and allowing me to have concurrently two happy and sexually exciting lives. Not only was I convinced that Lydia would tell me to pack my bags at the merest hint of such a thing, but I realized that her acceptance of any such arrangement, which was inconceivable, would be repugnant to me. It would end our marriage as we had understood it. Wouldn't you, if I ever let you get a word in edgewise, ask what was that understanding? Why, that we were united and trusted each other in all circumstances. Nothing spoken or unspoken should separate us. Now I can see you beginning to rise from your comfortable armchair, waving your arms as though to chase a wasp—careful, don't spill your whiskey on your shirtfront—because you don't see how I could possibly reconcile this high-minded notion of marriage with the position that adultery is wrong only if it is discovered. Base hypocrisy? Yes. But I thought that was the way to do the least harm.

You will recall perhaps that Lydia had offered to spend the weekend following my return from Paris at our house on Martha's Vineyard, North said. That is what we did. How she fought off the senior Franks and her siblings to disengage us from their plans for East Hampton, I will never know. She didn't say, and I didn't ask. But I felt grateful and happy like a little boy who gets his dearest wish.

The house on Further Lane in East Hampton that Bunny and Judy gave to Lydia as our wedding present is quite wonderful. By the way, why the Franks didn't have the street renamed Frank Lane or Frank Keep, since they all have houses on it, is one of those mysteries of tycoon lore—but never mind that for now. Imagine a deceptively simple, single-story wooden house with a great many rooms, built in the fifties by a sensible architect of no renown who understood that a beach house must be all light and air. Wild roses guard its approaches. But like all Frank houses, it sits well behind the dune, so that the winds do not kill the real garden on the side that faces away from the ocean, of which you have an unobstructed view from our terrace. There is no better view and no better beach in the world except one, on Martha's Vineyard, that I will tell you about later. In a way, the house I own on the Vineyard is the perfect opposite of the house in Further Lane. The Vineyard house lies hidden in the Chilmark woods, and the only view is on the garden, beautifully laid out but under my care allowed to become too lush. Overgrown. I inherited the house from a bachelor uncle, who designed it and planted the garden; he left his money—not a great sum—to Ellen and me, but bequeathed to me alone the house and his boat. When I was a boy, I spent several weeks with him each summer, sailing and swimming and cooking. He was a great chef as well as a sailor and believed that meals should be as good at sea as at home, although the menu might be different. The house has become valuable because of acreage that goes with it, but it wasn't very valuable then; the boat, which probably meant even more to me than the house, fortunately was not valuable at all. You don't get many people willing to pay anything near replacement value for an absurdly narrow forty-foot wooden sloop, even one of such exquisite beauty. Or one so well equipped: my uncle had installed every gadget ever designed to make it possible for one man to sail her quite comfortably. I didn't think it was fair to divide the money with Ellen and keep the house for myself, even if that was what my uncle intended, and owning a share in the house was of no interest to her, so I gave up in her favor the money that was to come to me under Uncle's will and threw in some more besides so that we came out exactly even based on what the property was worth at the time. That was a great extravagance, especially considering that Ellen and I have yet to inherit what little may be left by the devouring nurses when both my parents are dead, and that I already realized that Lydia and I wouldn't make much use of the house or the boat, the house in East Hampton being so much nearer the city and easier to get to. It was a still greater extravagance if you add the upkeep of the boat. Uncle named her *Cassandra,* after his favorite character in Homer. As it turned out, even after the payment to Ellen, the house is the best investment I ever made because prices on the Vineyard have gone sky-high ever since it became chic. In fact, if I took into account how much I could get for the land alone if I subdivided, I could begin to think of myself as a rich man, but the land will not be touched so long as I can prevent it. Anyway, marriage to Lydia made hash of my thoughts about money. I still count pennies, but only out of old habit. She doesn't need my money. It doesn't matter to her how much or how little I earn by writing, how much it costs to maintain the temple to Dr. Alzheimer in Washington, and what if anything will remain for Ellen and me. How much there will be in my estate doesn't interest her. She doesn't count pennies, but she is not a spendthrift either. She is quite simply as sensible about money as about everything else. But to give the devil his due, it helps in these matters to be part of the impregnable and unbeatable Frank consortium.

Are you on the lookout for the monster of envy as I talk? Yes? Then you must have seen him at the entrance of the lair, his ugly ears perking up. Mentioning the Franks will do it every time. Sometimes, to fool my conscience, I say that it's their own goddamn fault: always treating me like an outsider, while the spouses of Lydia's siblings and their children stand within the magic circle. Perhaps it would have been different if Lydia and I had had children. Their having given the house on Further Lane to her only, and not to us as a couple, that's what got me really started on the exclusionary theory in the first place. Curiously enough, that transaction or its resonance may have made me choose the wrong way at the fork in the road when Lydia and I had our first discussions about having children. Her saying to me—in complete good faith, and very nicely too—that she would bring up our child alone if I didn't think I could help, on a base and shameful level had on me the effect of a provocation. Ho, ho! I said to myself. I'm not needed. No Frank grandchild needs anyone except other Franks! Well, if that is so, who am I to complain? By all means, let Lydia do it. That was a great pity. Although my repeated lectures about the needs of a writer and his limitations as a parent were given in good faith, and expressed honestly held beliefs, they didn't need to be my last word on the subject. Children are seductive; I might have succumbed to their charm. But the monster made me dig in my heels and resist. A writer doesn't always choose what is best for him as a writer, or if he does, his actions aren't always consistent with that choice, and that may not be a bad thing. Besides, who is to say that childlessness, or indifference toward children if he has them, is good for a writer? Does it not cut him off from life itself? The issue can be debated. I have gone around for years, quoting, as an excuse for the messes I have made, Yeats's lines about the intellect of man: how it "is forced to choose / Perfection of the life, or of the work, / And if it take the second must refuse / A heavenly mansion, raging in the dark." Alas, it's true that, except in my writing, I have never taken the time or made the effort to do my best, let alone seek perfection. I don't believe that will ever change. But, in fact, I have never fooled myself; I have always known very well that it was one thing for Yeats to choose his work over his life—not that he was absolutist in his choice either; he was too smart for that—and quite another for your humble servant. As you know by now, I am by no means convinced that my work has been built to outlast bronze.

Forgive me. I have allowed myself to become distracted.

Distracted from the memory of the total serenity of that week-end and of my own happiness, but I think that I must make a confession to you, although you have probably guessed what I was going to say. The Franks are like other big families for which everything has gone well. They like fellow Franks better than other people, and expect whoever marries into the clan to adapt. If I moved in that direction, they would have treated me with affection, kids or no kids. But that is not my way; I'm no good at joining groups and rather proud of my misanthropy. Therefore, the Franks have been courteous and kindly, and really quite patient. But that was not enough to satisfy the monster. As for children, the fault is entirely mine. No wonder Lydia lost her nerve, because that's what I think happened. She became afraid I would be a resentful as well as absent father, and that her love for our children would come between us.

Enough self-flagellation. My happiness and contentment consisted in this: Lydia and I were in the house on the Vineyard and we were there alone. Had I been asked by the most fearsome of judges whether there was anything more I desired, and had I laid my heart bare, as I am doing now, the answer would have been: Nothing. I had all I wanted and all I needed. You are probably wondering about sex: Was I content with it too, did I not miss the ministrations and submissions of Léa? You will not be surprised if I don't give you an explicit account of Lydia's and my lovemaking. You might indeed be offended if I undertook to do so. I can tell you though, without hesitation, that when I was in bed with Lydia I never missed what I had done or could be doing with Léa, and that I never asked for anything like it from Lydia. Thoughts of Léa, images of Léa—they were stored somewhere, among many other memories of the same sort. I review such memories occasionally, with varying degrees of interest and pleasure, for instance on the rare occasions when I masturbate. They do not intrude on my day-to-day life, and certainly not when I am in bed with Lydia. I am convinced that I would not have regretted Léa's disappearance from my life, and would have made no move to see her again, had she not kept after me, had she not come to New York, and had I not been obliged to go to Paris for the filming of my book. A question for you: Was I really "obliged" to go to Paris, wouldn't old Joe Bain, my schoolmate, let me off the hook? It would have taken but one phone call to him. Ah, yes, you would like to ask what went wrong, because you sense that something did. You are right; just look at the facts. Léa had been consigned, without a conscious decision on my part, to a forgotten, out-of-the-way suburb of my affections. It was not a place I visited. Nevertheless, I went to Paris, although I might have arranged to stay in New York with Lydia. There is possible justification for my behavior, but an explanation can be given. Haven't I told you that I had come to love Léa? If it wasn't love according to your or my best definition, wasn't it at least an infatuation so powerful as to be almost indistinguishable from it?

We did not go out on the boat. Lydia has no real fondness for sailing. Besides, I must admit that *Cassandra* is not very comfortable even as racing boats go. You have to love her before you can enjoy her. Therefore, I took her out alone, for a short spin outside the harbor, in a good wind, and that was the one moment when I thought spontaneously of Léa. She had told me that she was a good sailor, and I could imagine the fine sight she would be at the wheel. The ocean was, of course, too cold for swimming, even on the bay side. But Lydia and I love walking on the beach, and that is what we did mornings and afternoons, because during those days I made no attempt to work. Lydia asked about Paris; she was surprised I hadn't gotten around more. My answer, that I had seen the Lalondes, once for dinner with both, once for drinks with Pierre alone, and had to spend more time than I had expected on the telephone with journalists, seemed to satisfy her. I also told her that I had been trying to write *Loss,* although my heart wasn't entirely in it because of the way I had come to feel about my work. She repeated over and over the only useful thing you can say to a writer who is in that situation: that my work wasn't boring (my worst fear as she knew), that my novels had been praised by very intelligent critics, and that, whatever one thought, the judgment of history about novels and literary reputations could not be predicted. All that really counted, she said, was whether I believed I had written honestly and had tried to write as well as I could. Since the answer to that question was yes, she said my duty was to go on writing and trying to do my best. I told her that I would have to spend a fair amount of time in Paris while *The Anthill* was in production there, and about Pierre's offer of the apartment. We agreed that we would try to be together at least once every two weeks. Either she would come to Paris for the weekend or I would go to New York.

The Vineyard people we know fall into two categories: New

Englanders I have known since childhood, and our New York friends who happen to have houses there. The former belong to the sort of dowdy good society that amuses Lydia more than it attracts her. I sometimes look them up on the visits I make alone to my house and to *Cassandra*. As for the other group, on the rare occasions when Lydia or I have said, Let's invite Jojo or Bubbles to dinner or lunch, the other has invariably asked, Why? Isn't it enough that we run into them in the city? So we remained blissfully alone.

The Fourth of July weekend found us in East Hampton, at our house on Further Lane, as full-fledged participants in the Frank circus and guest artists in the circuses of various other moguls. As you know, a surfeit of literary figures of all kinds may be found in Southampton and East Hampton, and the villages that lie along Route 27 and to the north between those poles of fashion. Writers with real reputations who still write, wrecks of such writers hollowed out by age, malady, and booze; so-called cult writers whose only readers are members of their special sect and fellow writers likewise in search of a public, editors, agents, journalists with intellectual pretensions—all reducible to a common denominator: sufficient money to own or rent a house out there, with enough left to buy food to supplement what they consume at book parties. At parties given by members of the American senatorial class, such as the Franks or the Sartors, writers (myself included) appear as entertainers or, if you prefer, the twentieth century's equivalents of Greek slaves. Years of practice have taught me to assume that the host and hostess—and the guests they want to impress by my presence—will treat me as a star among Greek slaves, although the notion that they actually take any pleasure in my company and conversation still makes me giggle. Marriage to Lydia Frank enhanced my status: I became an anomaly, the entertainer who rose to be a provisional member of the Frank clan's class. My recent prize and the news that Robert Redford would star in the film *The Anthill* had a similar effect. In short, Lydia and I were a very desirable couple during that season.

Already in June, I knew from the front page of the *New York Times* that fate had saved me from the menace of Léa's irruption in East Hampton. Jacques Robineau's Venezuelan friend was indicted for looting accounts he was managing for his firm's clients. He was out on bail, in seclusion. The *Times* did not say where. A week or so later came the report that the wife and children had returned to Venezuela. About the same time, Léa left a message on my answering machine that she and Robineau were still coming to New York, but, since they couldn't stay with the jail-bound banker, Robineau was postponing their trip until the second half of July. She would call me on arrival. I am very sensitive to people's voices. Hearing her say those words made her totally present to me; they rescued her from the oubliette and made me want her. At the same time, they put me in a state of panic. There was the danger of her insisting once again that she must meet Lydia. She would badger me if I did not make it happen. In any event, I would end up sleeping with her. Where and when, I didn't know, but clearly it could become necessary to lie to Lydia in the evening about what I had done during the day. I loathed the prospect. The only escape I could think of was to tell Léa

when I called back that she shouldn't count on seeing me.
Lydia's plans and mine for that second half of July were uncertain, I told her, and I didn't know where I would be. Her
answer, recorded the next day, was: I expect you to be in New
York, don't disappoint me.

It was, in fact, certain that we would be in New York,
because the project Lydia was directing continued to advance.
She wanted to be there to oversee it, and we agreed that she
should take no more than two weeks of vacation. In keeping
with our usual summer schedule, we drove out to East Hampton on Friday evenings and returned late Sunday night or early
Monday morning, depending on Lydia's work. As for the rest
of the week, I doubt that you can imagine the monotony of a
writer's life—obviously I am speaking about a writer like
myself who constructs novels out of materials already stocked
inside him, as I described it to Léa at the Flore. Unlike most of
my American colleagues, I don't teach creative writing and so
don't have horny students or poisonous faculty squabbles to
distract me. It must be quite different for writers who gather
material for books on travel, organized crime, lesbian priests,
affirmative action, and God knows what other exciting subjects. I am mostly alone. I start work early in the morning and
write as long as I can before lunch. Afterward, I return to my
typewriter and continue until I feel I have been squeezed dry.
You shouldn't assume that I write during all that time. That is
possible only when the work is going well. Otherwise I may be
sitting at my table unable to write a coherent sentence until a
headache, combining with the sensation of having nothing—
nothing whatsoever—in my head, drives me into hiding. In

such cases I may go to a museum or an afternoon movie, the latter though very seldom because I am afraid of being taken for one of those men who go alone to the movies mainly to rub their elbow against the woman in the next seat. In principle, I play squash three times a week, even in the summer, but that too is a bore because, having no squash friends, I play with the pro. On the squash days, because I want to get an early start, I walk with Lydia to the hospital and there catch a taxi to my office. It is an office I have had forever, since before Lydia and I were married, consisting of a large dark room in a building on Forty-eighth Street between Fifth and Madison Avenues that will surely be torn down soon to make room for a narrow tower. For the time being it houses law firms, such as the one from which I sublet my room, and a couple of medical doctors with odd specialties. We have a dermatologist and an ophthalmologist. Why they practice in that location is a mystery. In the old days you would have suspected they were secretly doing abortions. A travel agency, a couple of import-export firms, and an accountant complete the list of tenants. My office gives directly onto a corridor straight out of *The Maltese Falcon*. The door has a frosted-glass panel, though my name is not stenciled on it. Inside my office, but for the addition of a halogen desk lamp and daybed which was Lydia's birthday present to me, nothing has been changed since I moved in. The daybed replaced an old chesterfield sofa, which had been giving off an increasingly strong smell of mold. There was another change, of course, the most recent, which was Léa's painting: I hung it centered above the daybed. The law firm from which I sublet has a reception area a few doors down the corridor; I don't use it, but when I am away, my mail is delivered to the receptionist who decides whether to forward or hold it. It's a neighborly arrangement: a few times each year I bring the receptionist and secretaries chocolates and such like. My own secretary is not full-time. She comes to my office or to the apartment as often as I need her during the week, to take care of household bills, retype my corrected manuscripts, and type the letters I cannot escape writing. She does the bills and correspondence at the apartment, in a spare bedroom we converted for her use; the manuscripts she works on at her own home.

After work, I walk home. If it's not raining, I walk through Central Park. Then I read. Lydia stays late at the hospital; it's rare for her to be home before seven-thirty. Normally, we have dinner at home, unless we have accepted an invitation to a dinner party, which we do reluctantly because Lydia is tired after a day at the hospital. We have dinner late, so that she can have a chance to read something other than scientific journals. Neither of us objects to the other's reading while we have drinks. Usually, our housekeeper shops for food and washes the salad and the like. I am a good cook with a limited repertory, and most often I prepare the dinner and put it on the table. Poor Lydia has never been much use in the kitchen. I also rinse the dishes and put them in the dishwasher. The pots and pans and the silverware I leave for the housekeeper.

Since July, our housekeeper had been away, visiting her mother in Trinidad. What with the heat and my lack of enthusiasm for shopping on top of cooking and dishwashing, we went out to dinner every night, to one of the three neighborhood bistros we like, including the one I mentioned when I told you about the onset of my literary panic. Occasionally, we met friends there. Most of the time, the same couple; she is a novelist who hasn't written in a while. We are symmetrical couples: the husband is a thoracic surgeon. I like listening to his tales of sawing and breaking bones as he "goes in." She hardly ever speaks, but I know that she is the most intelligent woman in New York, Lydia only excepted. All the while I was writing *Loss,* but the work was going slowly. Each word seemed to weigh a ton.

North's eyes glittered. He smiled at me, raised his hands as though to ask for attention, and began to sing Cole Porter's "I get a kick out of you." I couldn't help wincing, he was so far off-key. He noticed, stopped right away, and raised his hands again, this time to signal capitulation, and said, yes, not being able to carry a tune has been a lifelong sorrow. It's so unfair! I know that a great tenor is imprisoned inside me—a Caruso whom malevolent fate deprived of voice at birth. Have you heard Ethel Merman do this number? You shake your head. Too bad, she set a standard not to be equaled, but even so you found my rendition deeply offensive. It doesn't matter. All I wanted to get across is the sense of amazing and blissful surprise. Merman—one of those ineffably blasé party girls Porter specialized in—is out on a quiet spree, fighting vainly the old ennui, and, Boom!—apparently no longer able to contain himself, North intoned—"suddenly I turn and see your fabulous face." Ah! How splendid. Then, returning to his normal tone, he told me I really must make it my business to hear the Ethel Merman recording.

The reason I have been carrying on like this, he continued,

is the memory, still very strong, of the jolt that got me out of the doldrums, seemed to bring me back to life. Only it wasn't a face; it was once again Léa's voice. I was in my office correcting the proof of a book review I had done for the *Washington Post*. Since I expected a call from the editor, I had set the answering machine on the mode for call screening. The telephone rang; I heard myself say: If you recognize my voice, you have reached the right number. Please leave a message if you think you must. At some point I must have found this greeting funny; I have never bothered to change it. Then Léa's voice, *Coucou, c'est moi.* Without thinking, I picked up the receiver. She and Robineau had arrived in New York the previous evening. He was in Washington for the day. She was supposed to go with him, but complained of a bad stomachache so she could stay in the city and see me. Could I come right away to the hotel? The St. Regis. Oh, I didn't want to resist.

It was a very short walk, too short to clear my head, and before I knew it I was there. I picked up the house phone and asked for Mr. Robineau's room. Léa gave me the room number and hung up. I found the door on the sixth floor. She wore a blue denim miniskirt and a black tank top. Bare legs. Red sandals with high heels that made her almost as tall as I. We staggered to the nearest piece of upholstered furniture—a loveseat, if you can believe it. Soon she was naked, except for those sandals and the skirt, which was up around her waist. It was one of those hotel rooms dominated by a huge bed. She gestured toward it. But how can we, I said, it's his bed. Her reply was, You are so silly; I will have it made up fresh. We did as she said. Later, when we had finished, and she was asleep with her head in my lap, I sat up and looked around. Léa's things, some familiar to me from nights at my hotel or her studio—I had begun to think of them as her permanent mess—were on every chair and table. I catalogued her combination calendar-and-address book, leather bound, as thick as a small city telephone directory, two hairbrushes, nail polish, nail-polish remover and cotton balls, a pink Lanvin scarf, and a cotton sweater. Intermingled with them were traces of Robineau: a black attaché case from whose presence under the vanity table I concluded he must have another one, perhaps smaller or perhaps even more capacious, that he took to Washington, file folders of different colors stacked neatly on the floor. Each stack was cinched by a canvas belt with a buckle, miniature versions of the striped or madras belts that were in fashion around the time you and I were at school. On the night table beside me I saw a traveling alarm clock in maroon leather I had not seen in Léa's studio. Probably it was his, the sort of ugly object that companies give to important clients. My God, I thought, what am I doing in this guy's bed, in his expensive hotel room, fucking the girl he has brought with him to New York so that he can fuck her? I must be insane.

It was a few minutes past one. I got up and washed, dried myself with a hand towel to preserve as much as possible the pristine order of the bathroom, and as I dressed saw myself in the mirror. I looked the way I thought I should look: dissolute, like a man who has been at an orgy. Not too gently, I shook Léa, saying, It's time for lunch. She didn't want to get up, and she didn't want to go out. Instead, she kept repeating, Let's stay here, why are you all dressed, come back to bed, it's so

nice here, let's fuck. She yielded, but only after I threatened to
leave. After her shower, when she had gotten back into her
skirt, top, and sandals—her hair still moist, face brilliantly
clear—she asked me for twenty dollars. It was for the chambermaid, to get her to make up the room a second time and put on
fresh sheets.

I led Léa to the nearby French restaurant where I sometimes have lunch with a friend or dinner with Lydia when we
don't want to go to one of those three bistros in our neighborhood that have a lock on my wallet. We've been going there for
many years. It didn't occur to me to choose another place
where I might be less likely to find people I knew and the staff
was not accustomed to seeing me with Lydia. Had I given the
matter thought, I might have gone to the French restaurant
anyway for a simple and solid practical reason: I am such an old
client that I don't really need a reservation. I propelled Léa
through the door and then to the table the owner indicated.
This was not a simple matter because he kept apologizing for
not being able to give me my usual table, and I had to shake the
hands of the maître d'hôtel and assorted waiters. Finally, we
sat down. A glance to my left told me that I had been recognized by one of the editors at my American publisher's,
though not my editor. He was having lunch with a man so
oddly dressed that I decided it must be one of his authors. A
friendly gesture with my hand in his direction was quite sufficient. A lady with a head of curly red hair sitting with a group
of four overdressed biddies in the center of the room presented a more serious problem. It was the wife of Lydia's
brother, Ralph. She had not seen me, but I would have to

speak to her on my way out, unless she noticed me sooner and we made eye contact. Even before I spotted her, it had been my intention to order for Léa so she wouldn't dawdle over the menu, to eat fast, and to leave as soon as possible. But I hadn't reckoned with the owner and the waiters whom I had already greeted. They returned, seemingly for one purpose only, to ask whether Madame—that is to say Lydia—would be joining us, and if another setting should be added to the table. No, she is at the hospital, working. One by one, they expressed the wish to see me come back with Madame soon. We might as well have gone to your wife's hospital cafeteria, observed Léa, and she was right. Midway through the meal, she said, Let's skip dessert and go back to the hotel. I replied that I couldn't. She didn't argue, and we chewed on in silence. But a few minutes later she said, All right, you have hurt my feelings. I am coming instead to see your office and my painting. Don't try to say no.

Having looked over my installation, which she said I had described well, not a surprise given my profession, she said I should consider getting a little spot to light the painting. I told her she was right; perhaps the electrician who does the work at my apartment building could do it. Then she pointed to the daybed and asked whether I took naps on it. Often, I told her. When I run out of words, you know, run out of steam. Let's take a nap together, she answered, what are you waiting for, fuck me.

There is no bathroom attached to the office. I had to guide her afterward to the toilet at the end of the corridor. When she returned she said I seemed to be a different man in New York;

she wasn't sure she liked this new personage. He was more brutal when he made love, and not as pleasant to be with as the man she had known in Paris even when we weren't making love. I said she was right. There wasn't a moment I wasn't thinking of my wife, and that changed me. The conclusion I had reached, I said, was that we shouldn't see each other in New York. It made me too nervous. She thought for a moment and said that was a problem. She had to see me, so what were we going to do about it? Robineau was coming back to the United States in early September, she told me, for the International Monetary Fund meeting in Washington, but they would be in New York before the meeting and after it. Maybe she wouldn't go to Washington at all, just stay in New York. She didn't want to be here without seeing me. Anyway, she was thinking of looking for a gallery to represent her in New York and wanted to get French *Vogue* to send her to the States on an assignment. Her editor had asked her to come up with a suitable subject. Being near me was the principal reason for all this, she concluded.

I made the sort of speech you would expect, reminding her of what I had always said: Anything we did–however much I liked it and wanted it–couldn't interfere with Lydia; seeing her in New York, as we had just discovered, radically changed the nature of our relations; anyway, soon I would be in Paris a lot, and perhaps we could meet in other places as well. But not in New York, where so many people knew me and I would be forced sooner or later to lie to Lydia. Because I didn't want to insult her, I didn't admit that I had no wish to see her in a place where I would be obliged to go from her bed–or her and

Robineau's bed—to Lydia's. I also told her a lie. I said I would be away from the city in the first part of September, with Lydia, on Martha's Vineyard. In fact, I was going up alone to sail, but I feared that if she knew that she would arrange to find herself there too.

That evening I said to Lydia that the *Vogue* journalist who had written the article about me in Paris had called out of the blue to say she was in New York and I had lunch with her. Lydia told me she knew that; at any rate she knew that I had lunch with a beautiful European-looking girl. Corinne—my sister-in-law—called and told her she had seen me. Then Lydia said that perhaps I should have invited the journalist to dinner. I replied that if she thought so, I would invite her next time, when we had someone to serve at table, particularly since the painting that I bought in Paris and hung in my office had been painted by that girl—Léa Morini. It had become clear to me that excluding Léa's existence entirely from our conversations would be difficult. At the same time I was discovering characteristics of persistence, immodesty, and, I am obliged to say, off-putting insensitivity in Léa. Did the realization come to me during our lovemaking in Robineau's hotel room, over lunch, when she suggested going back there, or at my office, when she laid out her program for being near me? I am not certain. I also made another discovery: Léa's chatter, so often incomprehensible, which had charmed me in Paris, did not have that effect in New York. To the contrary, I was on the verge of finding it irritating and, even worse from my point of view, boring. Like certain other fine products of France, her charm didn't travel well. You may have already guessed as much, but just to give you a balanced view of the matter, I will admit that I am bored by most people with whom I am obliged to converse. On the other hand, I tolerate very nicely those with whom I need exchange no more than a few words on a given occasion. Sometimes I even look forward to seeing them. The only exception to the rule of Don't Talk to Me is Lydia. I hang on her every word. Therefore, as you might infer, my finding that Léa bored me was in no small part the result of the dissipation of the absolute need to have her in my bed, as well as of the persistence of my feelings of guilt and fear about Lydia and our marriage. It all made me wish to avoid Léa.

I was able to duck Léa and Robineau's visit in September. But long before then, her telephone calls to my office had turned into a flood of messages. I returned them as promptly as I could, which was not always easy when Lydia and I began to spend long weekends in East Hampton, but I made a big effort because of my growing sense that I must meet at least in part her demands for attention—and even for my presence—lest she begin to think I was dropping her. Why did that possibility trouble me? I wasn't sure. My provisional answer was that I didn't want her to go off the deep end. What that might signify remained unformulated. So it happened that when she returned to New York almost immediately to visit a male friend, a former great love, and suggested that, since this great love was away from his apartment all day, we could meet there, I said I would prefer to spend a day and a night with her in Boston. That was what we did. I told Lydia that I needed to visit one of my former college professors in Cambridge, David Leach, to ask what he thought about certain recurring themes in George Eliot that seemed to intersect with my new novel. This was, by the way, perfectly true, and so in fact I saw David and wasn't obliged to tell Lydia a direct lie. She is so discreet, of course, that she didn't ask why the visit required me to spend the night. The sex with Léa in Boston was as good as ever. The conversation wasn't. I wondered how it would go in Paris. My work there was to begin in October, on a date that was not yet set.

North paused at this point and asked, Are you awake? I assured him I was, and on tenterhooks. That's most flattering, he replied, a moment's pause then and I will continue.

You will recall, North said, that I had lied to Léa. I told her that I was going to Martha's Vineyard at the beginning of September with Lydia. In fact, my plan was to go there alone and sail. What do you think really happened? Listen carefully. To my considerable bewilderment—and yes, satisfaction, because for once I was genuinely glad to give up time alone on my boat and the absolute silence in the house when I worked—my brother-in-law Ralph's two children asked to come with me. It was just possible to fit this in before the start of the school year at Andover, because I was going up to the Vineyard on Friday of Labor Day weekend. There were, of course, no seats to be had on any of the direct flights from New York, so we took the shuttle to Boston, and from there a twin-engine Cessna I was able to charter. A skeptic like you would probably assume that it all ended unpleasantly, as such well-meant enterprises usually do. But no: they are good kids, and quite possibly I had changed a little, because I had been obliged to look at myself so closely in the course of writing *Loss*. Perhaps there were other reasons as well. I did not do my Captain Queeg act onboard *Cassandra*, or my *Diary of a Mad Housewife* act onshore. All three of us read good books: Rob, *The Brothers Karamazov*, I suppose to gain a better understanding of his old man; Jenny, *Notes from Underground*, for reasons unknown, perhaps to gain a better understanding of me; and I selected passages from Saint Augustine's *Confessions* to see more clearly where I stood in relation to Manichaeanism. After these terrific ten days, we flew to Boston and from there I drove the kids to Andover believing that we had done well and might have an even better time repeating the adventure in the future.

Nice, don't you think? Unfortunately, I have just told you a little fairy tale. Here is the truth. Thinking that I ought to end the stalemate in my relations with the Frank family, and believing that my reputation as a child-hating ogre was unjustified, I invited the two kids to join me on my little sailing vacation. The initiative, as you can imagine, required courage and determination on my part. They turned me down. Can you guess why? Well, I assure you it wasn't because they wished to spend the little time remaining before the start of school at work for the Anti-Defamation League, or a birth-control clinic, or on any other high-minded endeavor deemed worthy of support by their near forebear, Bunny Frank. The invitation having been extended as soon as they returned to East Hampton from their white-water rafting and bird-watching camps, respectively, they told me they would think about it. Then they said no. How could I blame them? They saw me, I said to myself, as the rather strange man who is married to their aunt

Lydia. I was willing to bet any amount that neither they nor
any of their cousins had ever referred to me, or thought of me,
as their uncle. There was more to it though. When I told my
little niece Jenny how sorry I was, she blurted out that she was
sorry too. Grandma had told them not to go with me. She said
she didn't trust me. And did I blow my top or deliver myself of
coolly acidic remarks to Lydia in the privacy of our *ménage*?
No, I did not. Indeed, I kept Jenny's confidence, without having been asked to. So I went off to the Vineyard by myself, and I
am happy to report that I had a pretty good time in my wonderful house, not shaving, pissing only outdoors except the one
day when it poured, once or twice going to see my fuddy-duddy
friends over a drink, and sailing alone on my wonderful boat.

I have mentioned my escapade with Léa in Boston. We
returned from Boston to New York on the same plane. I saw
her once more during her stay in the city. She knocked at the
door of my office one afternoon, waking me from a nap I was
taking, having finished a difficult page of *Loss*. She said she
had been to Brooks Bros. to buy for *monsieur* the physicist his
preferred blue oxford-cloth button-down shirts and boxer
shorts of the same material. Strange sort of purchase, you
might think, with which to charge a young mistress, but I have
known other perfectly rational Frenchmen with a passion for
the very same items of apparel. Being in the neighborhood,
she had thought of me and realized that it was teatime. Therefore, she bought an English fruitcake. Could I make tea? she
asked. It so happened that I could. We drank it peacefully, and
each ate one slice of the cake. She wrapped the rest to take
home to her old great love. Just when I thought she was going

to leave, she said that she would like to stay quietly on the daybed while I worked. I told her the truth: it was impossible, the only person in whose presence I could write being Lydia. In that case I will go, she told me, but you should know that you have hurt my feelings. I thought you would like to have me here, after such a pleasant time together. It occurred to me later that I had made a mistake; it would have been better to humor her, even if that meant that I had to pretend I was revising some text. But at the moment I thought that if she stayed we would make love, which I didn't want, and that I would be encouraging her to undertake further initiatives of the same sort. You might say that I didn't want to spoil her.

Except for the regular postcards she decorated with grotesque and often obscene little figures and snatches of doggerel, I didn't hear from her again for a week or perhaps longer, until one morning she telephoned, leaving a message. She had something urgent to tell me. My heart sank. She didn't use a diaphragm, in fact claimed not to own one, and insisted I didn't need to use rubbers because she was on the pill. I was glad to comply, though I didn't completely believe her. The news had to be that she was pregnant. It wasn't. She told me an involved story about a dinner at which most of the guests were journalists or worked in publishing. She mentioned some of the names, none of which I recognized. Over coffee, the conversation turned to American writers, and a journalist working for *L'Express,* who had been researching an article about creative-writing courses at American universities, said it was common knowledge in New York's literary circles that I was suffering from acute leukemia. Léa claimed she had not slept all night, she was so upset, and yet she couldn't believe that I wouldn't have told her that I was gravely sick. Besides, I looked so well the last time she saw me, as she told the others right away, to prove that the report had to be false. But the journalist replied that people with cancer often didn't want it known, and indeed went to great lengths to conceal their illness. I assured her that I was, in fact, perfectly well. A few days later, she left another urgent message. When I reached her, she said that she had been at a small dinner at Robineau's apartment—just as a guest, because his great love, Françoise, was back from an assignment in Moscow. Again there was a discussion of American writers. She mentioned how she had enjoyed interviewing me. Thereupon, one of Robineau's friends, an editor who once worked for my French publisher, which is why I knew his name, said it was common knowledge in New York that I told people that I had leukemia so as to explain my frequent disappearances. The awful fact was that my spells of manic depression had become so severe that Lydia, with increasing frequency, had to oblige me to sign myself into an asylum. For weeks at a time! She couldn't remember the name of the hospital but thought it was something like the famous department store. Bloomingdale, I suggested, in Westchester. Yes, that was it, the name the editor had mentioned. She contradicted him, of course, saying that she was in touch with me and I was perfectly normal. Thereupon, another guest chimed in. He maintained that when North doesn't need to be locked up it is because the medication is working. His case is exactly like Robert Lowell's, he concluded. In addition to the psychosis, North is drinking himself to death and has advanced cirrhosis of the liver. He tries to be tanned all the time to hide the jaundice. Is any of this true? she asked me. I told her to relax, I was feeling fine and had no known history of mental illness. As for my alcoholism, surely she had observed that I drank less than most of her Parisian friends. I must have been convincing, because she laughed and said I was *un amour.*

I don't ordinarily pay attention to gossip about me. You might say I expect it, as does every writer who has had one or two successful books. As for "New York literary circles," I am ready to lead an anthropological expedition to search for them—anywhere outside the minds of society columnists and correspondents of foreign media doing pieces on the state of American culture. But Léa's chatter did trouble me, because it revealed that she was going around Paris talking about me. On one level, it didn't matter. She had done an interview with me that had received a good bit of attention. Why shouldn't she, therefore, use whatever she knew about me to shine at table? On another level, it did, because she had by now a good deal of information that couldn't have been acquired talking over coffee at the Flore. Sooner or later, people in that gossipy Paris world, which likes to visit New York, would put two and two together and begin to speak of *la petite* Morini who is so intimate with John North. My mood was turning black with self-reproach. And at the time I was once again assailed—no, the word isn't too strong—by anxiety about *The Anthill,* which prompted further misgivings about *Loss,* and of course, one thing always leading to another, about all my earlier work as well. The proposition was brutally simple and dreadful to consider: if the books are no good, if they are unnecessary books, then my life, of which I had given up so much in order to write them, had been wasted.

What set me off was nothing directly concerning *Loss;* its progress had been slow, but I was moving along and, from time to time, when I reread and corrected the text I was even amused and surprised. I couldn't imagine where I had gotten some of the stuff I had written down, but I was glad to see it was there. The screen adaptation of *The Anthill* was the immediate cause. I received from the producer a text he described as the almost final version of the screenplay. According to the contract, I had the right to review it and send in my suggestions, revisions, and so on for his and his colleagues' consideration. Nothing more than that. As drama, the screenplay struck me as pretty good. Certainly, it wouldn't put audiences to sleep. I was distressed, though, by the sentimentality of the story and the main characters. That was certainly not what I had intended, what I remembered writing, and that is not, I made quite sure of it, a defect of the novel, which I very conscientiously reread. But was it not possible that the screenwriter—I knew him and knew he was no fool—had seen through some flaw at the core of my book? Something I had not been conscious of that he had brought to the surface? And there was a touch of vulgarity to the screenplay. Had my book invited it? Or, equally sad, was there such a huge and unsuspected gulf that separated me from most of my readers? I asked Lydia her opinion. She reassured me: there was no such flaw and no such gulf. In that case, was she the only reader who understood me? Assuming that she was answering honestly, I pushed these questions away as best I could, and labored on the screenplay to bring it back to where I thought it belonged, but with little speed and little satisfaction. A freak accident relieved the pressure: an example, I suppose, of how Providence looks after writers on a tough deadline. The female lead of *Anthill* the movie, having completed a film shot in western Australia, had decided to treat herself to a weekend of water-skiing. Somehow or other, she got banged up seriously enough to postpone our shooting schedule by a couple of weeks. But I went to Paris as planned. So much of the book's action is set there, either directly or in flashbacks, that the director thought he should start in Paris and said that was where I could be most helpful.

Pierre had already called to confirm the loan of his aunt's apartment on avenue Gabriel. There is no more theatrical street in Paris, with its row of starchy white buildings that seem to preen in the autumn sunlight as they look on the back part of the garden where, as a child, Proust's Narrator, with his heart in his mouth, would wait for little Gilberte Swann to appear, in a gray winter coat with a little fur collar, accompanied by her formidable governess. Pierre met me at the apartment and introduced me to Madame Marie, the housekeeper. After they had shown me around the place and had gotten my bags to my room—I was to use what had been Pierre's late uncle's bedroom, not his aunt's—we sat down to lunch served and cooked by Madame Marie. Pierre looked well, still suntanned from his summer vacation and more fit than he had seemed a few months ago, when I thought he could no longer conceal a nascent middle-age paunch. I complimented him on his appearance. He had been making an effort, he told me, to swim seriously every day during his vacation with Marianne and the girls in Corsica and to play tennis in spite of the heat. The mention of the family vacation was reassuring. I felt easier about asking where he stood. He said he wasn't sure. There was no doubt that Marianne had gone to London with a man. In fact, soon after the trip, he figured out who it was. He knew him: the financial director of one of the big fashion houses, divorced, also with two children, wife remarried. But Marianne said nothing about him or the affair, and, except for the trips she took in theory alone, there had been no change in her behavior. Pierre and Marianne slept together less often, but otherwise all was very pleasant and coolly polite. He thought the girls understood what was going on too, but they said nothing. So he was unsure what to do. Speak to Marianne? Wait for it to pass? Perhaps in some way this was an experience she needed after having been so reasonable and so hardworking all her life. Pierre knew that Marianne used to confide in me, as a fellow writer, and it had occurred to him that he might ask me to invite her to lunch, just to see whether she would talk about the situation, but in the end he believed he should be just as cool as she and wait. I saw tears forming in his eyes, so I concentrated for a moment on the bones in the fish on my plate and told him that I thought he was right. Quite obviously, he didn't want her to leave. And since neither Marianne nor that man seemed inclined to regard whatever was going on between them as needing to be acknowledged or discussed, what better course to follow was there than to give that relationship a chance to end naturally? I said I imagined that someday he and Marianne would have to talk about it, but there was no rush. Pierre nodded. I had only said what he wanted to hear, but overall I think I gave him good advice. Marianne has remained with Pierre, the girls seemed no more disoriented than anybody else their age, and I think that they and Marianne were grateful to Pierre for his patience and discretion. The man faded out of the picture.

Pierre asked whether Lydia would be visiting me soon. I told him we had to improvise. She had devised a very promising experimental treatment for sclerosis of the glomeruli, which are small but crucial capillaries in the kidney, a nasty disease that can attack very small children and leads to kidney failure unless it is stopped. A breakthrough might come soon. She was needed at the hospital and felt nervous about even short absences. Probably I would go to see her in New York more often than she would come to Paris. Perhaps to lighten the mood, Pierre assured me that, so far as my bachelor activities went, the coast was clear. Madame Marie and the woman who cleaned had rooms on the top floor of the building and had very liberal views about the sort of lives men were entitled to lead—so long as Madame Marie didn't immediately fall in love with Lydia, like everyone else who came in contact with her. In that case, Madame Marie might begin to think she had a duty of loyalty to Lydia: at the very least, she would sulk and give bloodcurdling looks to you and whatever young person might be having breakfast with you in bed. This was unwelcome news. If Lydia managed to get away, I would have hoped to have her in this sun-filled apartment that was more beautiful than any hotel accommodation I could imagine. I had assumed that some sort of omnipresent classical Portuguese cleaning lady came with this magnificent apartment that Pierre's aunt kept at the ready for her rare visits from Buenos Aires, but stupidly I had not thought that there might be someone like Madame Marie, a retainer who had started in the family when the aunt was still a young girl and took seriously her position of moral authority in the household. The cleaning lady was, indeed, Portuguese, but she too had been in the aunt's service for many years. How to reconcile Lydia's visits with Léa's would require some thought. Meanwhile, Pierre had followed his own train of thought. He told me he had run into the little Morini at dinner here and there. Also, she was doing an article on Right Bank art dealers, and had come to the gallery to talk to him and people on his staff, and he had taken her to lunch afterward, across the street. She talks about you, he said. About your work—she seems to have become a specialist on it—the filming of *The Anthill* and how she is lining up an assignment to do a story on that, the painting you bought from her and how good it looks in your office in New York, Lydia's breakthrough project and her hopes of meeting Lydia. She's a nice girl and very gifted, but she can be as hard to get rid of as a bad case of the crabs when she thinks she has glommed on to something. Pierre's long nose with which he liked to make little sniffing noises, looking curiously about him, had always served him well. I interpreted the silence that followed as a question. I like her, I said, and I too think she's gifted. I had to hang her painting in the office because I didn't think Lydia could stand it. That came as a disappointment to Léa. I think she expected to find it over the fireplace in the living room.

Pierre nodded. Experience proves, he told me, that it's useful to bring the little Morini down to earth sooner rather than
later. She has told half of Paris about her great love—he named
the Nobel Prize winner. It doesn't matter, because his wife
doesn't care. Or maybe she thinks that one vigorous session
with Léa per week is good for the old boy's heart, not to speak
of the other organ. The old boy certainly doesn't mind letting
it be known that he can still perform. But suppose the wife did
care? The prize money is all very well, but in today's world it
doesn't amount to much, being a member of the Académie
Française is very nice, the lectures at the Collège de France,
they are very nice too, but they don't bring any money, and it's
the wife who owns the apartment in the Palais Royal, the
château in Normandy, and the villa on Cap Ferrat. Not to
speak of the income that keeps the show on the road.

It was my turn to nod. So Léa had told Pierre. Why wouldn't
she? Whom else she had told outright, where she had dropped
hints that were not too difficult to interpret, I would soon find
out. I wasn't convinced about the wisdom of my trying to bring
her down to earth. That maneuver might work for a Frenchman, in Paris, because it conformed to a locally accepted doc-
trine of relations between sexes. The way Léa talked about
people showed her to be a shrewd judge. I was afraid that if I
told her that we should be grateful for the good time we had
had, and from now on were going to continue as good friends,
she would know right away I was acting out of character and
wouldn't believe me. She might even think that Pierre was
coaching me. In any event, she would have no doubt about my
vulnerability and cowardice when it came to Lydia. Léa would

be unpredictable, I concluded, if she felt scorned. Perhaps vengeful.

I had dinner with her that first evening at the Balzar, having told Madame Marie in answer to her question that I was going out and it was unnecessary to prepare anything for me. It was a pleasant surprise, by the way, to see that she intended to treat me not as a species of paying guest—Pierre's aunt had categorically rejected my offer of rent, agreeing only that I could pay the salaries of the staff and the utilities, and, of course, pay for what I ate and drank—but as one who really lived there, over whose needs she would watch, so that every morning she inquired whether I would be having lunch and dinner and how many guests I expected, and proposed a menu for each meal I would be taking. The surprise at the Balzar was less welcome. Léa had invited a young woman who also worked for French *Vogue*, editing the feature that tells readers who has been seen where and with whom; the young woman's American friend, a lawyer working for a New York firm with an office in the place de la Concorde; and a baby-faced Frenchman whom I took to be another lawyer until I figured out that he was involved in some form of international finance and was the American lawyer's client. I was there as a special treat, a sort of human baked Alaska, except that they didn't wait until it was time for dessert. Instead, I was passed around and served as soon as we sat down. In principle, you know, I don't mind that sort of imposition: I take it for granted that, like all writers with a well-known book or two behind them, I will be used to entertain friends of friends. Recent experience in East Hampton and New York, moreover, had shown that my value as a conversation piece had gone up because of *Anthill* the movie, it being easier for guests to grill the writer about the producer, the director, and the stars than to talk about his novels, which they haven't read—or have forgotten or haven't liked. Nor did I mind forgoing a romantic tête-à-tête with Léa—as I have told you, I had decided that she was a bore, and I had felt mildly apprehensive about the conversation I would have to keep up alone with her at table before the payoff in bed. I didn't even mind too much the prospect of footing the bill for this surprise literary symposium, which I supposed was my obligation since I had invited Léa and she had felt free to invite her friends, although, hearing the consensus that we would stick to champagne throughout the meal, I realized that it would not be negligible. I was feeling flush with the film money. I did mind very much the other manifest consensus, that I was the trophy boyfriend of the young woman who had arranged the dinner. There was no escaping the conclusion. That was how they saw me. I hadn't a doubt that Léa had clued in her very pretty colleague, who would not have hidden that detail from her American friend, and, as for the French financier, my sixth sense and his self-satisfied demeanor had warned me at once that he might be one of my predecessors. In that case, he would have been informed by Léa herself. Was there anyone at French *Vogue,* I wondered, who didn't know, save perhaps the charwomen, the bookkeepers, and the cyclists who deliver advance copies of the magazine to charter members of *le tout Paris*? Who were the Paris partners in that American law firm, which I recognized as one that the Franks frequently used? I decided I wouldn't ask. Three of the New York partners were men with whom I had been at college or school. Was my baby-faced financier predecessor a supplier of financing to my brother-in-law, Ralph? The range of possibilities was dismayingly wide. And this was only the first evening of what might well be a stay in Paris of two months or more. It occurred to me that perhaps, after all, I had better follow Pierre's counsel and let the explosion, if there was going to be one, come quickly.

But you didn't, I interjected.

Of course not, replied North. I was afraid of its consequences and, worse yet, besotted.

I took her home with me that night, North continued, and kept her until the morning, although she hadn't brought clothes to wear to the office. I said it didn't matter, she could go in her black suit, or she could make a stop at her studio and change if she really cared so much what she wore. I would order a radio-taxi to take her to the rue de l'Abbaye and wait there, and then continue to the place du Palais Bourbon, where *Vogue* and other Condé Nast operations are located. All that mattered was that she be there with me through the night in case I woke up and wanted her, whether at that moment or first thing in the morning. She did as I said, and from then on, unless I met her for dinner and brought her home, she let herself into the apartment with the spare key I gave her. Usually I was still up, working or reading; otherwise she would come straight to my bed. I took her to restaurants less and less frequently, and soon refused to go with her to the theater or openings of exhibitions. When we did go out to dinner, I would choose some banal bistro, or better yet one of those old, faintly musty bourgeois restaurants that still exist in certain neighborhoods that have good food but are completely unfashionable, and would pray that no one who knew her or me would happen to be there that evening. Everywhere else we risked being observed and commented on, and possibly photographed for a media gossip page. I didn't need to explain this to Léa. She continued to insist that discretion was necessary to protect her as well—in addition to *monsieur* the physicist, and she now mentioned her parents and brothers too as needing to be kept in the dark—but that did not prevent her from pouting about it or saying I was treating her like a cheap little slut I didn't want to be seen with. Of course, that was really how it was, and I was not the man to deny it. There was no hiding our activities from Madame Marie. The sheets told her and her colleague all they needed to know, Léa not being inclined to take the trouble to avoid leaving traces. Perhaps no one had taught her how. Still, Léa was perfectly dignified when she came face-to-face with Madame Marie in the morning, which happened from time to time, although I had made it known that it was not necessary for her to come down from her sixth floor so early, and had asked for breakfast to be left instead, before she retired, on a tray that I could carry to the bedroom. At the same time, she managed to make herself somehow so insignificant and small that I allowed myself to hope that she was not making much of an impression on Madame Marie. The breakfast that Madame Marie prepared was, of course, for two. To ask for breakfast for one would have signaled to Madame Marie that I was not only a cheat, unfaithful to his wife, but also a coward too timid to make sure his *poule* got her morning orange juice, croissant, and coffee.

To make up for the shabby treatment during the week, on a couple of weekends when I didn't plan to see Lydia, I took Léa on trips to places where I thought I was least likely to run into Lydia's friends or mine. Those turned out to be Vienna, where Léa had never been, and Bourges, the site of a glorious cathedral that I had never yet gotten to see, despite my love for the high Gothic. Bourges also happens to boast a hotel suitable for clandestine weekend getaways. I will tell you more about Bourges in a moment to illustrate how my sexual obsession with Léa, which I thought was waning, had in fact reached its apogee. And weekends with Lydia? We should have spent them in Paris, in the marvelous apartment on the avenue Gabriel. But we didn't. I felt squeamish about welcoming Lydia to the bed that was the arena of my nightly exertions with Léa. I met Lydia once in London and, during one visit when I couldn't avoid Paris, we stayed at the Ritz. I said I was making good on the promise I made when I moved there from the Pont Royal on that fateful Memorial Day weekend. My desire for Lydia when I saw her was not diminished either, and quite possibly we made love more often than we would have otherwise in the same adverse conditions—her fatigue after an overnight flight, my fatigue after a week's struggle with the director, the producer, and that benighted screenwriter. But sometimes I observed in myself something that disturbed me far more than any signs of slackening of libido or performance, of which there wasn't any: it seemed to me that there were moments when I resented Lydia's not being Léa, and that was most probably the reason I made love to Lydia less tenderly. Lydia sensed this, I am certain, and was perplexed, but, as usual when it comes to our sex life, she said nothing.

Now back to Bourges, circuitously: I had a girlfriend in college whose sexual behavior was if anything looser than Léa's or that of any girl I have known since. She was always ready for anything forbidden or dangerous. I have no idea whether this girl is now alive or dead, so, out of respect, I will call her Daphne. Wild—in the parlance of that time. I recall screwing her during a game of chess we were playing in her parents' den, both of us fully dressed, I sitting on a straight chair and she astride, going up and down faster and faster, her face pressed against my shoulder, the father's bowling trophies displayed on a bookshelf directly in my field of vision, the parents in the dining room glued to the television screen, then a time in a cozy nook under the bleachers of Baker's Field while the sons of Harvard and Yale filed out past us after the game. There were also the sessions atop a pile of overcoats in a tutor's spare bedroom during a cocktail party, and in a little clearing in the woods, observed by one of her deplorable cousins who was imperfectly hidden behind some ferns. This was the boy who had initiated her at the age of twelve, and set a standard for performance I could never match. By the way, I could never match the standard set by Léa's first great love either, a loony genius who apparently never needed to come. After about a year of bliss with Daphne, she fell sick. Forehead, hands, body—all hot as a stove. It was at first taken for flu, so she did nothing about it and continued to hang around my room with her brilliant eyes, burning mouth, and burning you know what. That is when I discovered the extraordinary, unequaled thrill of dicking a body racked by fever. I cannot recommend it highly enough. Later, she turned out to have a bad case of hepatitis and was moved to the hospital where,

falsely claiming to be her fiancé, I gained entry to her room
outside of visiting hours so that I could anoint her body with
creams and taste other refined but undisclosed delights. That
certain maladies act as a powerful erotic stimulant is well
known from life and fiction. But I have strayed far from
Bourges.

The glories of the cathedral, including the stained-glass
windows that were spared in the First and the Second World
Wars, surpassed all my expectations. There reigned in it, however, completely unexpected, the cold of the lowest circle of
hell. I had not brought warm clothes with me to Paris and felt
each and every one of my bones, down to the very smallest,
turn into ice. I don't fall sick often. But already at lunch after
the cathedral I knew it was coming, the chill, the fever, and the
heat of Nebuchadnezzar's oven. Léa at the wheel, we made it
back to Paris, to the lovely and warm apartment, and the suddenly maternal Madame Marie, who set to preparing various
restorative soups, none of which I wanted to touch for some
days. I knew what I wanted: it was Léa, for immediately after
that delirious and bibulous lunch I had discovered that to
mount her cool and lithe body while mine burned was the fabulous converse of what I had experienced with Daphne and
almost forgotten. Pierre arrived, summoned by Madame
Marie, took one look at me, and wanted to pack me off to the
hospital in Paris where rich Americans go to die. Not feeling
quite ready for heaven, I refused, and we settled for supposito-
ries supplied by his doctor. The fever continued unabated for
almost a week, winning me respite from the film and *Loss*
while I puttered around the apartment, the surrender to my

passion for Léa quite complete. Also respite from calls to Lydia and lies I had been forced to tell her. I sent her a fax announcing that I had lost my voice and would telephone as soon I recovered it. Madame Marie's disapproval no longer mattered. Léa dropped in to check on me during the day—sometimes more than once. Right away, we would bury ourselves under the covers of my sweaty, disordered couch.

North downed a fresh whiskey and soda, as though he were still in a fever. You think my behavior was crazy, he said to me.

I nodded.

You are right, I was half crazy, he said, from the fever and from the sex. All the same, in spite of everything that happened, I don't think that I would give up that week with Léa even if I had the power to change the past.

A long pause ensued, after which he said: Among the innumerable book prizes that each fall occupy the minds of French novelists, publishers, book reviewers, cultural journalists, and literary hangers-on, to the exclusion of most other subjects, there exist two that are available for novels published that year in French translation. One is considered quite good. In truth, neither counts for much among the French who are in the book business, because they take little interest in writers who don't write in French. It's a case of perfectly reasonable endogamy that doesn't necessarily interfere with the love of all concerned for foreign literature. I began to receive hints that *The Anthill* might receive one of those prizes—though not the better one, because the fix was in to give it to an exiled Iranian novelist writing in Farsi. Since members of French literary juries usually work for publishing houses as editors or members of committees that select manuscripts for publication, rumors of fixes circulate wildly in Paris. Some claim that a jury must give a prize to the novel published by this or that house for no better reason than to even the score. In that setting, I was not surprised that the first hint should come to me from my own publisher: he would have been speaking to his member on the second-best jury. In fact, I imagined them devising together the winning strategy. The second hint came from Léa. It made me uneasy. To have this information about a second-rate prize, not exactly something on everyone's mind at *Vogue,* I said to myself, she must be snooping, which means she is asking about my chances and so forth, which in turn means that she is showing her special interest in me. The frequency of hints accelerated. Also, now they were all about the better prize, not the second best. They became more specific: For instance, jurors X, Y, and Z were clearly for me; the only question was whether juror B could be brought over; what could be done to give him confidence that next time around he could count on X if not Y? Were we sure that juror D had an acquaintance with my oeuvre extending beyond *The Anthill,* which he had read in English as befitted a specialist in the Victorian novel and a biographer of Dickens? There were days when both my publisher and Léa had news to report, and it wasn't unusual for Léa to be the first with juicy anecdotes that my publisher either had not heard or else had not bothered to repeat.

Finally, my publisher felt confident enough to suggest that, all things considered, I might want Lydia to be present when the prize was announced on Tuesday of the following week, because I would be receiving it. The way he put it suggested some possibility that he thought Lydia and I had broken up— and why would he think such a thing if it wasn't on account of Léa?—or of some reluctance on my part to have her at the place of honor for the festivities. I told him I would telephone Lydia that very evening; unless her work made it impossible to be away, I was sure that she would be there. By that evening I meant midnight Paris time, which was the best moment to reach her at the hospital, in her own office. Having been to dinner at her parents', Léa had just arrived at avenue Gabriel, and we had not yet made love. I found it difficult not to take her right away, especially since I could sense that she too wanted it, but I thought I had better talk to Lydia first. You probably think it was shameful to call my wife with my mistress at my side, and I suppose you are right, but compromises of that sort are forced on one by the difference in time zones. Besides, when I told Léa that I was about to telephone Lydia, she had a way of leaving the room without a word from me, so discreetly that I would not always be immediately conscious of her absence.

I believed that she had left the study that time as well. I was explaining to Lydia that my publisher's celebration dinner would be a large affair but that it wouldn't be particularly dressy, because tradition obliged us all to be astonished when the prize was announced. Thus, the dinner must seem impro- vised. Suddenly, I sensed Léa was in the study after all, but completely naked. Her hair fell loose over her shoulders in what she called her gypsy princess style. She was doing a sort of belly dance as she moved toward me, writhing and touching herself languorously on the breasts and between the legs. I gestured for her to leave the room; as you have had occasion to notice, my gestures are quite expressive. But she shook her head, knelt down in front of me—I had in the meantime stood up—and shifted her caresses to my dick. Keeping my voice under control, I said to Lydia that I had left the water running for my bath, that by now the bathtub must have overflowed, and that I would call as soon as I got the mess under control. I hung up. Léa had already opened my fly and was working on me, intent and concentrated. She finished and with hardly a pause asked whether I had really told Lydia I wanted her to be in Paris on the day of the prize. I asked how she could think it would be otherwise. She replied that she had thought that day was to be for her; for me and her together. I made no comment, and nothing more was said between us on that subject.

Once again, my friend fell silent. I sensed the imminence of another confrontation he was perhaps reluctant to describe. But who were the actors? Himself and Léa or Lydia? Or was it between the two women?

Receiving the prize, North told me, turned out to be a not-so-funny comedy in four acts. Act I was a lunch with my publisher at a Right Bank restaurant to which he also invited Lydia. His wife, my editor, and Alix, the head of public relations, were there as well. To my horror, said North, I saw that Léa, arriving late, was the remaining guest. I will return to Léa's role in these festivities. We waited for the official news from the jury, which was having a more leisurely lunch while deliberating at Fouquet's. Except that they weren't deliberating; that too was just a part of the pantomime, good for the prize, though, because it builds suspense. Before coffee, a telephone call is made to the publisher of the book they have chosen, and the publisher together with the lucky author, who just happens to be at his publisher's side, rush over to Fouquet's in a waiting cab that just happens to have been ordered in advance. Act 2 was played in a private dining room of Fouquet's, North told me, and asked whether I knew that institution on the Champs-Elysées.

I shook my head.

A wonderful relic of Parisian life between the two world wars, he said. Downstairs, it's a café where gentlemen of a certain age, *embonpoint,* and income may sit on the terrace and eye younger ladies having their coffee or drink alone at a table. These ladies tend to be so well groomed and so dressed up that one is able to guess at a glance that this one is a manicurist, that one does facials, and the one near the potted palm sells ladies' hats. One may turn out to be wrong, of course, any one of them may be a *bonne bourgeoise,* married to exactly the sort of gentleman who is ogling her. Upstairs there is a restaurant that serves standard good food in the brightly lit main room and in private rooms, like the one we were ushered into. At a table that had been cleared of everything but flowers and glasses of brandy sat the five jurors, obviously in the best of humors. Effect of the meal, the wine, and the cognac, or of the satisfaction of having agreed on the right novel? I was introduced by Xavier, kissed the hand of the sole female juror and was kissed by her on both cheeks, and then kissed the cheeks of all the others. Very sweet people, I must say, and authors of decent books. I had more or less expected the president to clear his throat and harangue me for a couple of minutes about the merit of my book before handing over some sort of diploma and an envelope with a small check, but nothing of the sort happened. Congratulations and kisses were all I got. Act 3 consisted of interviews in an adjoining but larger private dining room. All sorts of journalists, television cameras, and photographers. Alix, who arrived after Xavier and me, was the ringmaster. I don't think I need to describe the circus to you. It was like all the circuses that you have seen. A longish intermezzo separated Act 3 from Act 4. It was played out at my publisher's office. There I gave interviews that Alix had decided were important. I bared my soul to the elect, over coffee and scotch and sodas. Rather like here, don't you think?

I nodded, and for some reason that made North laugh.

Intermission is over, said North. Act 4 is the impromptu dinner for two hundred guests or more at a not-quite-first-class hotel. I had never been there before for any purpose, public or private. As I have told you, Lydia was at the lunch. Both at lunch and at the dinner, she was seated on my publisher's right. Since the intermezzo was a solo performance by me, she told me she would return to avenue Gabriel and rest, and then work until dinner on a paper she was giving at the New York Academy of Medicine. A perfect plan, I said, I'll pick you up there. Of course, I didn't think this was a good plan at all; I didn't want her to spend two hours or more alone with Madame Marie, but I didn't see what I could do about it. My shock at finding Léa at the lunch, on my left, Xavier's wife being on my right, was redoubled when she reappeared at my table for dinner, once more seated on my left. I found this bizarre and thought that the weight of *Vogue* must be far greater than I had supposed, unless there was a current or former great love, so far unknown to me, lurking within Xavier's publishing house who arranged these things for her. Worse yet, I found Léa's behavior appalling. When I introduced her to Lydia, Léa spoke to her in English though Lydia had addressed her in French, and Lydia's French is flawless and elegant, which could not be said of Léa's English. But in the same conversation Léa persisted in speaking to me in French, although in my exasperation I spoke to her only in English. After a moment of this, I realized why she was so insistent about speaking French to me: it was to be able to demonstrate our intimacy by using the familiar *tu* in every sentence, although I pointedly used the neutral *vous*. That was willful and unnecessary and unexpected in a girl as well brought up as Léa. She reached the summit of obnoxiousness, I thought, at the end of dinner, when Lydia and I were on our feet, receiving congratulations from quite a crowd, including many who were complete strangers. I found Léa at my other side, her arm under mine, leaning against me–to get the full effect you have to be able to visualize her cleavage–and saying to Lydia that she envied her, because she was married to the most desirable man in Paris. Then she corrected herself: in Paris, New York, and East Hampton.

What a marvelous evening, said Lydia when we left. I am very proud of you.

It had been pouring during dinner. The rain had stopped, but when we got to avenue Gabriel the sidewalk was still glistening. The air smelled of autumn and rotting horse chestnuts. Lydia wanted to walk a little. Afterward, she took a long bath. By the time I had taken my own bath, she had turned off her reading lamp. It was clear that she wanted to make love. I was surprised. She had come to Paris on the night plane, and it had been a long day. But I was relieved too, because she did not seem to hold against me whatever it was that Madame Marie might have told her or what she had inferred from the events at lunch or dinner. We slept late. I woke up first and waited very quietly until she opened her eyes. What a lovely room, she said when I drew aside the curtains. I asked whether she would like to have breakfast in bed—that was our habit when we traveled. Naturally she said she would, whereupon, in accordance with my arrangement with Madame Marie, I went to get it in the pantry where it was waiting with the newspapers. I set the tray in the middle of the bed so that it would be between us, and offered Lydia the *Herald Tribune*. The *Figaro* was bound to have an article about the prize and I was eager to see it. There was nothing wrong with it and I showed it to Lydia. She read it at once, squeezed my hand, and kissed me. A little later she asked why Madame Marie hadn't herself brought up the lovely tray. Was it because I had told her to respect my privacy while I was still in bed? I laughed, and said she had seen right through me.

We were in a taxi on our way to the airport when she asked who Léa was. I reminded her about the interview and the painting I had put in my office. It was curious that she had forgotten. Of course, said Lydia, how silly. Such an energetic young person! She seems very fond of you. But then why shouldn't she be? I replied that Léa must be taking her first steps as a literary groupie. There could be no other explanation for the fuss she made about a minor figure like me. That was a foolish thing to say, and Lydia made no comment.

The Paris shooting of *The Anthill* was soon completed. I found myself more satisfied with the result than I had expected. I gave up the apartment on avenue Gabriel, said goodbye to Madame Marie, who accepted my large cash gift with stiff politeness, and returned to New York on Christmas Eve, glad to have left Paris and Léa. My relationship with her had changed. I was angry and made no attempt to disguise it. She was defiant. In our sexual encounters, we competed to inflict pleasure on each other. When she announced that one week before my scheduled departure she would leave for Megève to ski with her older brother and his family, I didn't pretend to be disappointed. The truth is that I was glad.

North was silent while the waiter emptied the ashtray, took away glasses in which the ice had melted, brought fresh ice and clean glasses, and set out canapés. Then he spoke again.

I think you realize, he said, that I have brought you to a watershed in my story. The affair between Léa and me had been carefree in the main and on the surface harmless. It is about to take on another coloring. If I tell you truthfully what followed, which is what I would like to do, there may be moments when I will feel overwhelmed. We both need to gather strength. The food is mediocre here. But it's harmless, if one sticks to the simplest offerings. Will you risk dining with me?

Of course, I answered.

Good. Then take a look at the menu. I know it by heart. Meanwhile, I will collect my thoughts.

I followed North's lead and chose the sort of fare that any establishment with a name like L'Entre Deux Mondes should be able to prepare competently even with the chef asleep at the stove. Normally, I would have felt obliged to keep up some sort of conversation during dinner. But North had the distant look of someone deep in thought and I was reluctant to disturb him. We finished our meal in silence broken only by the orders he gave to the waiter with a peremptory precision that seemed habitual. Both of us took coffee. After the table was cleared he asked for a cognac. I declined to have one. I had decided to continue with the red wine until the bottle was empty, and only then to switch to whiskey. I expected North to disapprove.

I wasn't wrong. Shaking his head, he told me that too much red wine leaves one sluggish, not to speak of what it does to one's girth. But suit yourself, he said. We have other things to talk about.

Thereupon, he pushed his chair away from the table and stretched out his legs. I suffer more and more often from cramps, he said, carefully massaging first one calf and then the other. That task accomplished, he made sure that the cigar on which he was puffing drew correctly and went on with his story.

From the beginning of the new year, time seemed to pass with such unaccustomed haste that I needed to consult my pocket calendar several times a day just to find my bearings in the week or the month. Lydia had been invited to speak at a nephrology congress in Kyoto about those sclerotic capillaries in babies and research into new forms of treatment which, if successful, would make dialysis unnecessary. This area of pediatrics was receiving increased international attention. She asked me to come with her. I knew that I should, and mostly I wanted to: she had been especially tender toward me ever since I returned from Paris. Often, her tact and gentleness brought tears to my eyes. Nevertheless, I couldn't bring myself to say yes. For one thing, I really found it difficult to imagine giving up my work for ten or twelve days as the trip would require, even if we skipped all sight-seeing in Japan outside of Kyoto and Nara. That in itself was a problem, because I knew that she had her heart set on seeing the Inland Sea of Japan and the Japanese Alps. But she also wanted to go afterward to Taiwan to visit the museum in Taipei and to see the treasures that Chiang Kai-shek stole when he fled from the mainland. She was particularly curious about the Kang Xi emperor's collections on account of her maternal grandfather, the husband of the lady she had loved so much and who taught her German. He had been a connoisseur of objects from that period and left many very good pieces to the museum in Boston. But the pressure of the tasks that lay ahead was bringing me close to panic. I was rewriting *Loss* almost from scratch, moved by a reconsideration of the concessions and mutual accommodation that may be necessary in a marriage. On top of that, there was my new project. I had gotten along well with the director of *The Anthill,* and he asked me to try my hand on an adaptation of George Eliot's *Daniel Deronda.* That is a work I admire enormously, as much as her *Middlemarch* and Dickens's *Our Mutual Friend.* For me, these are the three peaks of the Victorian novel; I would gladly enter them in a contest with the best of what was written at the time in French and in Russian and would expect any one of them to place, if not to win. Besides, I have always thought that *Daniel Deronda* should be filmed. It seems made for the camera, one scene after another. Take the bad couple–Gwendolen Harleth and Grandcourt. They have real Hollywood glamour. Of course it's a frightful oversimplification to call Gwendolen bad; she is like one of those magnificent young women who inhabit the novels of Henry James–for instance Kate Croy– who would have been good if only they had inherited a little money. Grandcourt is my special favorite. I looked forward to the screen treatment of the breakfast scene with the dog. Just think of it: The innocent and quite beautiful animal is slobbering over Grandcourt with affection. Grandcourt considers the problem and addresses his loathsome toady Lush. "'Turn out that brute, will you?" is what he says quietly, without raising his voice or looking at Lush. Lush complies at once. He lifts the dog, although she is heavy and he doesn't much like stooping, and disposes of her somewhere. A beautiful example of economy in malevolence: the spaniel and the toady are humbled in one instant. Why would anyone, however decadent, want to humiliate a dog? You tell me. I didn't want to miss the chance to do this film, even if the completion of *Loss* had to be postponed for some months, and I was obliged to work on it with less than my usual intensity, perhaps only a couple of hours a day. The thing was to keep at it. It is an incalculable risk to lose contact with a book you are writing. With each day of absence, you think about it less. Your grasp of the characters weakens. It may happen that when you finally return to them, you find yourself face-to-face with strangers.

That's when inconsistencies in psychology develop. Sometimes these off-the-wall new insights are really very good–valuable–and on rereading you don't want to delete them. But in that case you become involved in tricky fiddling to make the inconsistencies fit.

The scene in *Deronda* I have just described, for all the light it casts on Grandcourt, is minor. But there is something else that has haunted me since I first read *Deronda*–I guess when I was still in college. It's the sailing accident. You see, Gwendolen marries Grandcourt–let's say for his money, although it's more complicated than that. He carries her off on an interminable and, for her, appalling cruise aboard his yacht in the Mediterranean. Grandcourt is fond of sailing and the absolutism with which you can order life aboard ship. It drives Gwendolen nuts. In the course of a squall, the yacht is damaged, and they are forced to put in at Genoa for repairs. A week will be needed. The prospect of a week ashore seems bright to Gwendolen. Grandcourt cannot bear it. It will be too boring. You see, when he is not active, not exercising minute-by-minute mastery over his entourage, he is bored. That he is a colossal bore is another matter. It's altogether astonishing how boring English gentlemen were allowed to be. Therefore, he hires a sailboat. He can handle it alone, but insists on Gwendolen's going out with him, ostensibly to hold the tiller while he looks after the sails. The real reason is that he will not leave her ashore alone. He is too jealous to endure it. On one of their outings, all of a sudden they jibe; the boom, swinging violently, smashes Grandcourt on the head. He falls overboard. Guess what: apparently, this is a rat who doesn't know how to swim. He calls out to Gwendolen: "The rope!" It's at her hand, but she doesn't throw it to him, and Grand-court drowns. I cannot tell you the resonance of this scene within me.

North fell again into one of his reveries, during which I think he sometimes forgot my presence. After a while, he shook his head, as though to rid himself of a persistent and annoying image before his eyes, and began to speak again.

I've resolved to tell you, North said, even the shabby sub-texts of my story. Therefore, I will confess that my eagerness to do the adaptation was not unrelated to the taste I had devel-oped for the money you can earn from working on a movie. This is the kind of sordid reason for my actions that ordinarily wild horses couldn't drag out of me, and you may be sure that I didn't reveal it to Lydia. Whether she guessed it, when I explained the demands work was making on me just at that time, is another matter. If she did, she must have taken my decision as an insult. You see, she truly believed that we—she and I—were bound together completely, so that to make such a choice for such a reason I must be either stupid or indifferent to her happiness. She knows that I am not dumb, so why at the cost of time we might have together would I seize the opportu-nity to earn a sum of money that she would say I absolutely didn't need? I fear, though I am not certain, that Lydia had measured the extent of my egotism and envy and knew how resentment of her and her family's wealth made me incapable of generosity and equal partnership with her. I do not think that she despised me for these feelings. You see, she loved me too much. Instead, she pitied me, and tried with all her strength to forgive. But on this occasion the result of my obstinacy and sour pettiness may have been too much even for her.

To make matters worse, I advanced another reason for not accompanying her—an outrageous reason, though not without some bits of truth in it, that I had cooked up on an impulse. I claimed specific aversion to the idea of going to Japan. I stuck to this position, although I knew it upset her, because she is too utterly honest and rational to tolerate that sort of stuff, and because it put me in a bad light. I carried on and on about how I feel lost in countries where I can't even make out the newspaper headlines, street signs, and so forth, much less the spoken language. I also talked about having observed the entire spectrum of Japanese tourists, on the one end in their bizarre versions of Western casual attire swarming over every tourist attraction in the United States and Europe, and, at the other luxury and power-play end, tight little groups of Japanese businessmen in lobbies of the best hotels, bowing interminably to one another or sleeping on armchairs, heads thrown back and mouths open. These field observations, I asserted, had led me to the unshakable conclusion that the Japanese were a people I could never understand or want to understand even if that were possible. Why should I, in that case, expend a great deal of effort and cash to find myself in their midst? I asked. The photographs of the gardens and temples of Kyoto, many of which I had seen and admired, were quite sufficient. That was the windup of my peroration. Ordinarily, disagreements between Lydia and me were set straight right away; they did not survive to cast a shadow. This time it was different; Lydia stopped speaking about Kyoto, but I could sense her disappointment. She may have thought there was a touch of racism in my bombast. She is extremely sensitive about that, and rightly so. Perhaps it was just as well, therefore, that I was able to advance my starting date in Hollywood. She left for Kyoto, joylessly, I fear, some weeks after my own departure.

To close this long parenthesis before I return to the main thread of my story, said North, I should add that I was not sorry to slow the writing of *Loss*—a novel I continued to like even as its hold over me caused me great discomfort. I have told you that my views on marriage had been in flux. That condition continued. I kept asking myself why things on both sides of the line—the line by which I divide the good from the bad—that seemed easy to others were so difficult for me. For instance, adultery, the wrong I was doing to Lydia. Why was being unfaithful to a wife or husband a matter of so little concern for the many ostensibly decent men and women I knew, and such a torment for me? I am leaving God out of this, because I have no use for God or religious faith, but one is aware of apparently serious believers on whom the sin of adultery, the scandal of betrayal, does not seem to weigh heavily. Or how difficult, if not impossible, it was for me to accept what Lydia had to give and wanted to give me in such abundance: her love, bestowed unconditionally although her personal qualities are so far superior to mine; her infinite patience with my eccentricities and selfishness; her wealth and the carefree material comfort it purchased for both of us. Any other man, I kept saying to myself, would fall on his knees and give thanks, while I, immobilized by my contradictions, squirmed like a moth pinned to a preparation board by some bastard who won't use ether.

Writing a screenplay based on a great novel is foremost a labor of simplification. I don't mean only the plot, although particularly in the case of a Victorian novel teeming with secondary characters and subplots, severe pruning is required, but also the intellectual content. A film has to convey its message by images and relatively few words; it has little tolerance for complexity or irony or tergiversations. I found the work exceedingly difficult, beyond anything I had anticipated. And, I should add, depressing: I care about words more than images, and yet I was constantly sacrificing words and their connotations. You might tell me that through images film conveys a vast amount of information that words can only attempt to approximate, and you would be right, but approximation is precious in itself, because it bears the author's stamp. All in all, it seemed to me that my screenplay was worth much less than the book, and that the same would be true of the film. The best I could say, to comfort myself, was that I had avoided pushing Eliot's work toward melodrama. Somehow, my camaraderie with the director survived this operation–miraculously, in my opinion. I worked as rapidly as I could, and left for New York after six weeks, exhausted and sick. The studio doctor told me I had nothing more than a bad cold. Rest and sleep, he said, rest and sleep. I got off the plane with a cough worthy of *La Traviata,* uncontrollable and loud. I was grateful that Lydia was still in Japan and would not return for another week or ten days. I decided to move into the guest room when she arrived unless I was really better, even though we have always slept in the same room and in the same bed. In fact, I doubted that she would allow me to move, but what with the noise of my coughing and wheezing I thought she would never get any sleep. A day or so after I returned, I was reminded of a meeting of my old school's twenty-fifth reunion committee. It would be indecent, I decided, to miss it on account of a cold. I dressed warmly and drove up there.

A classmate, with whom I was later at college, a Manhattan internist, was also in attendance. We had been friends. He had been on the wrestling team and I was glad to see how compact and quick he showed himself at forty-three. Since we were staying at the same inn, I had a nightcap with him and his wife after the committee dinner. As we were leaving the bar, he asked whether I was taking antibiotics for whatever it was that had made me spit my lungs out at the headmaster's table. I told him about the Hollywood doctor's prescription. That's odd, he told me, I will come to your room and listen to your lungs. I didn't believe that in this age of telephone medicine there were doctors left who still traveled with their little black bags, but he certainly did, and from it he produced a stethoscope that he applied to my back. Which hurts you more, the right lung or the left? he asked when he had finished. Neither, I told him, whereupon he said I had pneumonia. Then thirty miles away he found a pharmacy that was open on Saturday night, and drove there himself to get the pills. I should make clear that in keeping with what my city physician has called my nihilistic attitude toward medicine, I had not consulted him when I returned from the West Coast. After church the next day I went to the meeting and to the lunch and was very pleasant with everybody, mostly, I think, because I knew that I was quite sick. Having seen that I could rise above it somehow put me in a good mood. I didn't bare my claws for one second. The good mood continued in New York. I sent a case of wine to my doctor classmate, put aside the screenplay of *Deronda* I had agreed to revise one more time, as well as *Loss,* and hung around the apartment, allowing myself unlimited naps. There was no question of taking to my bed. The last time I did that I was ten with a bad case of measles. I don't count the business with my flu in Paris. This last observation provoked a fit of laughter in North.

Seeing that I did not share his amusement, North raised his eyebrows and continued. Finally I felt good enough to make a short visit to my office. There were messages on the answering machine, all from Léa. The only other person who regularly leaves messages at the office is my literary agent, and he knew that I was in Hollywood and had my number at the hotel. You may wonder why I didn't listen to messages from home, like everybody else. It is more a matter of my modus operandi than of some Luddite conviction. Quite simply, I do not want messages that I have consciously channeled to my office to follow me around when I am not there. They and the people who left them can wait. Lydia and Ellen, the only people alive who mustn't be kept waiting, don't need to leave messages. And my parents' keepers always know how to reach me if they can't find Ellen. Didn't I love Léa once, you want to ask. Whatever the answer to that question might be, by this time I probably didn't. But even earlier, I had instinctively decided that she could always wait. Léa's recorded voice was even more breathless than usual, and some of what she said I couldn't understand: there were words she had swallowed, moments when she was incoherent or quite inaudible. Normally, I erase her messages as soon as I have heard them. I did not do so this time. In fact, I listened several times to the entire series, trying to put the events she talked about in some order. By the way, I realize now that I did not tell you that following the shoot of *The Anthill* I had returned to Paris three times, though never for more than a couple of nights. I would call Léa a day or two in advance, half hoping that she wouldn't be there, or that she would have appointments, work, anything at all that might oblige her to say she couldn't see me. That never happened. She came to my hotel room only after dinner, like a call girl, as she put it, and we went through our repertory which, I have to hand it to her, we somehow managed each time to enrich. Her unfailing availability, the body so unquestioningly offered, the pleasure she manifestly took–all of it unnerved me. As for my pleasure in our lovemaking, on the most primitive level it had never been greater because it was sex in its undiluted state. No courtship, no preliminaries, no hesitations; rather like one's body functions when all is going well. I stopped giving her presents. There seemed to be no point. There was nothing she seemed to want that she didn't have, and there was nothing I particularly wanted to offer. Besides–harden yourself against another sordid confession–I preferred not to spend the money.

The story that emerged from the messages remained confusing. It seemed that there was a new great love in her life, one whom she could marry in the sense that there were no obstacles such as a wife he was unwilling to leave. It was possible that she might even want to marry him, but she wasn't sure. It was also possible that she and this man, whom she didn't identify, were formally engaged. As to the meaning of that, in her case, she gave no clue, but she asked herself whether she should go on sleeping with me and her physicist *monsieur* once she was engaged. Was this a hypothetical question or a problem that was actually presenting itself? I cannot tell you. And what to do after she got married? Would she still want to sleep with me, or her *monsieur?* Or men that she would meet in the future? Would marriage make her more attractive or less? She was also making plans for her wedding, at the Crillon in Paris, and wanted me to promise to come. All her loves would be there, so she could dance with them. Midway through the series of messages, I learned that the marriage was postponed. It also seemed possible that she had broken with her intended. Her career took center stage. She had decided to leave *Vogue* and either devote herself exclusively to painting or to go on with journalism, but as a freelancer, so as to be able to spend more time in the studio. Obviously, there was a good deal of turmoil in her life. I wondered whether she had all of a sudden inherited a round sum of money. I didn't think that her father or her mother had died—she wouldn't in that case be so cheerfully scatterbrained—but aren't there always, in French bourgeois families, childless aunts, uncles, and cousins whose fortunes are parceled out, in strict obedience to the civil code and the guiding spirit of family loyalty, to nephews, nieces, and other cousins, however distant? I had told her I would not check my messages while on the West Coast and had refused to give her my number there. But she knew I would be back around this time. I dialed her number in part because I was curious about these developments and, more important, because of the policy I had adopted of avoiding anything that might drive her over the edge. Shutting down communication between us could become such a provocation, I told myself. This time it was she who didn't come to the telephone. I hung up without leaving a message, because I didn't want her to own recordings of my voice any more than I wanted her to have letters from me, but called her every other day or so, without success.

Meanwhile, Lydia returned. My attention was wholly engaged. I watched for a sign. Had the breach between us healed? Where did I stand? I wasn't sure. She was serene and chatted cheerfully about the dreadful journey, almost twenty hours door to door, that took her from Taipei to Narita and from Narita to New York. She brought me as a present a jade netsuke of great beauty. But was she so loving because this was simply her way, or was it because she had forgiven me? I felt a great unease. When I compared this reunion with so many others when I had returned from abroad, and she greeted me at home, I could not identify any difference in her behavior. But we had never before, during our long and harmonious marriage, parted other than in good cheer, clinging to each other. There had never been need of a reconciliation. If one was needed now, I didn't know how to go about it. A question to her—on the order of You aren't angry at me anymore?—I feared might reveal to her more about my offense than she already realized. In fact, at the moment I was no longer sure what my offense had been. That I didn't want to go to Japan? But that was surely because I was nervous, needlessly, perhaps, but quite genuinely, about my work. What kind of crime was that? That I had made asinine remarks about the Japanese? I am so self-centered, you see, my work being included in the "self," that it is not unusual for me to forget what I have said quite recently to this or that person—even to Lydia. I don't consider my outbursts important. Others tend to remember them, alas all too well. Unless the trouble was not connected at all with the Kyoto Congress, and came because Lydia had sensed that I was having an affair with Léa. I turned away from the thought; it had made my hands turn ice cold. You must find truly remarkable the faculty I was displaying for the disregard of inconvenient truths about myself and my situation, no matter how well they were known to me. I would have to agree with you about that. Time passed slowly, but it was past lunchtime, Lydia's plane having landed at about ten-thirty. I was watching her unpack. In a moment, she would disappear to take a bath. I put my arms around her and said we could have scrambled eggs at home or go out for a bite. I had thought she would prefer to go out. She nodded and told me she wouldn't be long. Her good manners were impenetrable. There was nothing I was going to learn over our hamburgers. If I was to understand whether anything important had come between us, it would be when we made love.

After lunch I waited in bed for her while she spoke to her parents, brothers, and sister. I noticed that she called them in the order of seniority. They were lovely conversations, not only about monks sweeping the gravel smooth in a Zen temple, or the painted faces of Kabuki actors. She had stories that were interesting and droll, whereas I, a professional story- teller, as a rule have nothing to relate. When I call my sister, which I do more or less every week, I am unable to say much more than that my work is going well before I switch to our only real subject, the parents and their keepers. But Lydia's conversation was full of giggles and shared confidences, those I could hear, because I was at her side, and those that I could read on her lovely and expressive face. Did I envy her? Cer- tainly, the monster was at my side, even as I was at hers, but for the moment it was overcome, neutralized by happiness, by the wonder of saying to myself that this is my wife, the woman whose mouth I will kiss, who will wrap me in her arms, whose body will yield to mine.

Do you remember Wyatt's lines: "They fle from me, that sometyme did me seke / With naked fote stalking in my cham- bre"? Rest assured, Lydia did not flee. She came to bed, naked and trusting. And having been chaste during the weeks of our separation, I was a battering ram while I waited—oh, on a reduced scale, I'll agree, this being no time to boast—but as soon as I drew her to me, so that, lying on our sides we faced each other, well, I became nothing, and no amount of her ten- derness could change it. We talked for a while—about the museum in Taipei, of all things! Then we fell asleep: she because she was so tired, I because there is no safer place to hide. She was first to awake and, in her usual way, very careful not to disturb me, reached for her book and began to read. Our bedroom faces south and west over the roofs of adjoining buildings; she did not need the light of the lamp. But she moved, and that was enough to break my sleep. I struggled back into consciousness and for a while lay very still. Her nearness soothed me; it calmed my fears. I dared to begin to touch her. She smiled, a familiar sign that told me she knew and liked what I was doing. Soon she put down the book. Relieved beyond measure, joyous, I was all right. And what did I learn? That she gave herself without reserve, and that the act, as almost always, brought us great pleasure. It did not, I realized, prove anything except that she loved me, which I knew, and that it didn't matter how much she had guessed—if at that time she had guessed anything at all. Jehovah did not need to call out to me to ask about my sin: I knew I was the author of my own expulsion from the garden where I had been so blessed.

Lydia is a conscientious physician. She was appalled by my cough, which I seemed unable to shake, my loss of weight, and my insistence on keeping to my regular work schedule, in fact, to my usual schedule in all aspects. Perhaps because I had been yielding so recently to my body's maleficent demands, I now refused it any concessions. I had finished the second round of revisions to the screenplay and it didn't seem likely that I would need to do more until the project advanced to a further stage. You must take a vacation, Lydia had been telling me, someplace where it's warm and you are separated from your novel and George Eliot. At the same time, it was clear that she would not come with me. In retrospect, she considered that she had already taken too much time off going to Japan. I had no desire to go away alone—I felt weak and unadventurous—and I didn't want to go south to a resort, whether it was Florida, Mexico, or the Caribbean. I will rest here, I said, I like our apartment. I will make a point of getting to bed early. In reality, I was tired. When I sat down to write, my eyes would begin to close after a mere hour, sometimes less. I tried my system of quick naps on the couch in my study, removing only my shoes and lying on my back, my hands crossed behind my head. Ordinarily, half an hour of sleep in that position, without other preparations—like pulling down the shades or disconnecting the telephone—is enough to let me go on with work until I produce two or three pages and prepare a jump-off platform for the next day: a sentence pointing in the direction I want to take. But not this time. I slept much longer and awakened feeling broken. Or I awakened in a half hour as I had planned, but the moment I was back at my table the same lassitude as before would overcome me.

Of course, I asked myself whether these were not symptoms of a failure of imagination, signals that I was writing the wrong book, punishment for my sins, the definitive proof that I was a writer without talent whose shame was being revealed—all the maladies typically lumped together under the label of writer's block that feed a writer's hypochondria. I knew, though, that something unconnected with my writing was acting upon me, perhaps in addition to all the foregoing ills, because I tired unnaturally when I attempted to walk to my office, the forty blocks I have always covered at my habitual trot being so clearly too much that, after a perfectly serious attempt, I would hail a taxi. I found myself forced to stop midway through the first match of squash that I scheduled with the pro to get back in shape. I was too weak and couldn't stop coughing. Did I consult my doctor? Yes, because Lydia insisted on it and, although I protested in my usual fashion, I quite saw that it was not unreasonable to speak to him. I have little faith in medicine, except when it comes to extreme maladies, such as the ones that Lydia tries to combat or that manifestly call for surgery. The rest of it, the care of normally sturdy men like me, I consider high-priced tinkering, at best less harmful to the patient than the bleedings and purges administered by the leading lights of the medical faculty in the seventeenth and eighteenth centuries. That sort of medicine killed the Sun King, and he and any other man capable of thinking straight would have rejected it indignantly had he not been weakened already, as much by such treatments as by the disease, and browbeaten by the physicians. My doctor, who is actually a perfectly fine fellow, appropriately skeptical about his own science, confirmed that my travails as a writer were not alone to blame. I was suffering from a variety of deficiencies and insufficiencies that had their source in the pneumonia or trailed behind it. He said, Give yourself two months off—or, if that seems impossible to you, one month. And get away from here to a place where you do not wake up each morning thinking that you should work. You can't work productively just now; the botched attempts leave you frustrated and add to your fatigue and depression. Could I have come to the same conclusion myself, without the office visit, the blood tests, and the bill that followed? Certainly, but I suppose that since this sort of rest meant not working, I needed the validation of a medical authority to relieve my guilt.

Two places tempted me as possible retreats. One was, naturally, my house on the Vineyard. The other was Spetsai, an island off the Peloponnesus, to which I was drawn by number-less memories, not all of which I had used in my first novel and, therefore, not all of them dead. For me—I don't know to what extent this is true for other novelists—memories strong enough to power a novel are themselves displaced once the book drawing on them has been written. Only pale ghosts remain in the nether land outside the book, so feeble and distant that they can no longer command the offering of the smallest dish of blood. But of my Spetsai past I had put into the book only the violence and danger of a first love and, in a laboriously transformed form, a political intrigue in which my father had involved himself, and the treachery—so it seemed then, but perhaps it was only a mixture of necessity and foolishness—of his best friend, a French diplomat who, like my father, had behind him *une belle guerre,* but had developed unfortunate connections with the extreme right. So I had left to me a good deal to revisit: the gentle landscape of that rarity which is a green Greek island; its friendly coastline, with stretches of deserted rocky shore interrupted here and there by unexpected sandy beaches and sheltering coves; the perfection of its size. Spetsai is large enough to afford a sense of physical freedom, and yet so compact that one can traverse it from one end to the other in a four-hour purposeful walk across dry, aromatic brush, and a strong swimmer has no difficulty swimming around it in a day.

People my parents saw every day during the season for lunch, drinks, or dinner, or at picnics organized aboard a caïque, lived in the area bounded on one side by the old harbor, where yachts stood anchored amid the boat building and

repair activities centered there, and on the other by a spur of
the island that looks on Hydra. Just behind the old harbor a
row of tall white houses built two centuries ago by Venetian
shipowners looks grimly over the seawall. A handful of other
old houses climbs the hillside, less strict in appearance and
surrounded by stands of lemon and fig trees and laurel and
bougainvillea. At the extremity you will find modern villas
built at the very edge of the sea. Smooth rocks at a distance of
not more than a hundred steps from their terraces constitute
the owner's private beach. Among my parents' friends were
the sort of Greeks who populate the Pierre in New York and
the Plaza Athénée in Paris, French people neither very rich
nor very aristocratic nor very glamorous, but more than suffi-
ciently pleased with themselves in these regards, and other
foreigners who just happened to live there. Father and Mother
were unofficial permanent local representatives of the United
States and hosts to a line of American and British friends long
enough, Ellen and I thought, to circle the globe—all loosely
bound by government service or the war. There were also the
special cases, certain luminaries defined by no fixed criteria.
Among these were two Swiss men from Zurich, painters who
had lived together since art school, both enjoying a fair degree
of success, especially in the German-speaking part of Switzer-
land, and both remarkable cooks. Apart from domestic
chores, which somehow Max had made Johann understand
from the start were Johann's responsibility exclusively, they
did everything together, inseparable to the point that everyone in their circle referred to them simply as the Painters. It
was easier than using their names. They adopted me when we

first went to Spetsai and didn't become less affectionate after the appalling mess my father went through, which caused my parents to sell the house in disgust and abandon the island. I never lost contact with them; indeed, I stopped off to see them in Zurich at every opportunity. Their first trip to America was to attend Lydia's and my wedding. The Painters had been writing to me—actually it was Max who wrote, that activity being his alone—and occasionally telephoning, with rare persistence, to urge me to visit them in Spetsai. They wanted me to come before the island changed under the waves of tourists, and while they were still living as they had in the old days. That they were at most five or six years younger than my parents was very much in my mind, as was the state to which my parents had been reduced. They would not last forever. Springtime is enchanting on Spetsai. I was seized by an urgent desire to take them up on their invitation, and telephoned to accept it.

I told Lydia that evening over dinner that, since I had agreed—reluctantly, I made that clear—to my prescribed rest, I very much hoped she might find a way to be with me, at least for ten days, especially since the place was to be the island that meant so much to me, which she had never seen. I had decided I would stay for three weeks, perhaps four, according to the compromise I had reached with my doctor. To my surprise, she did not even seem to consider the question seriously; otherwise, wouldn't she have said, Let me think about it and speak to my staff, we'll talk about it tomorrow when I come home? Instead, she laughed and said she would feel lucky if she managed to get away on weekends, to East Hampton. Then she added, gratuitously, it seemed to me, that Spetsai—for better and for worse—was "North country," perhaps it was just as well if she didn't go there and introduce an alien element into my family myth. That closed the subject: I was too proud to mention it again. I remembered, of course, how when we first met she had talked with special intensity about my Spetsai novel, although it was the only one of my books that she never mentioned after we became lovers. That silence had struck me as strange and made me wonder whether in relation to that special period in my family's life and mine there might be a chink in her otherwise imperial, almost triumphant self-assurance, which seemed to exclude feelings even remotely like jealousy. Was it the love story that I described? I doubted that; other liaisons of longer and shorter duration and varying levels of intensity—most of them I am constrained to confess imaginary!—live in my other books. It may have been her thinking that in that novel I had written about a magic circle of my own, from which she and, who knows, perhaps the Frank tribe as a unit would have been excluded. That would be perfect nonsense, of course, but people—even of the highest intelligence—sometimes apply what goes on in a novel to themselves. The consequence is that you can probably find some poor fellow in New York, with a literary culture and a taste for Tolstoy, perfectly accustomed to dining with Royal Highnesses, employed by this or that auction house, asking himself: Suppose I had run into Oblonsky and Levin dining on oysters, halibut, and rib roast at Stiva's favorite hotel, could I have greeted them? Would they have asked me to join them at their table? And so forth.

No hypothesis could be excluded. The fear that our relationship was indeed damaged tormented me, as did questions for which I had no answer that brought peace. What explanation was there for dismissing out of hand, without apparent regret, the chance to be together in this unusual circumstance? Since she had insisted as strongly as my doctor that I get away for a rest, could she not find a way for her colleagues and assistants to carry on while she was absent for such a short while? Suppose it was she who had fallen sick: Wouldn't an arrangement be worked out to cover? I know about the maxim that what is sauce for the goose is sauce for the gander, and I didn't for a moment forget that I had refused to accompany Lydia to her congress in Kyoto because of my work, but there was, it seemed to me then, a difference between our situations, and I think so even today. No one could write my book or screenplay for me, or even, if I may say so, keep it warm and prevent a rupture from developing between me and the text. As though to forestall any doubt that I had been genuinely sick, I took pleasure in recalling that I have never babied myself—on the contrary, as Lydia knew well, I had always put a high value on my considerable indifference to fatigue and aches and pains. All this hodgepodge served as the basis for a dubious and unfortunate conclusion: that Lydia's refusal to come to Spetsai for my convalescence was unjustified. Moreover, I felt myself authorized to regard it as an action more significant than my refusal to attend her congress. In my thoughts I took to referring to that event as a tax dodge, designed to let one hundred and fifty nephrologists and their consorts whoop it up in a place that had no more connection with childhood diseases of the kidney than—why not!—Ulan Bator.

We parted, therefore, a week or so later, rather the way we

had said goodbye when she left for Japan. We had dinner the night before at the French restaurant to which I had taken Léa. I ordered a very good wine without a murmur inside me about its preposterous price, my serenity reinforced by the two payments I had just received from Hollywood. We made love nicely when we got home. But I knew that in my heart all was not well and was almost sure that that was also true of Lydia. So there, said North, as though he were abruptly snapping shut a book. It's late and I am tired. If you wish to hear more, meet me here tomorrow. I bid him goodnight.

The next morning, North was waiting for me at the door of L'Entre Deux Mondes. His eyes were red, showing ugly enlarged blood vessels. The eyelids twitched. He cried, Welcome, most welcome! And led me to the table. Our half-empty bottle of scotch and a bottle of soda were already there. He made me a drink, refreshed his own, and said the place looked dingy. Never worse. I followed his gaze and nodded, although honestly I could not discern any change from the day before or any other day I remembered. His own appearance was another matter. The middle button of his tweed jacket was missing–I was certain it had been there when we parted–and his necktie had congealed egg yolk on it. Remains of his breakfast? He hadn't shaved. Perhaps, having slept late, he had decided to skip his morning toilette.

Have you guessed what happened next? he asked me. I am willing to make a large bet you haven't, although it should be quite obvious.

I shook my head. I had not even tried to guess. In any case, I dislike bets.

It should have been easy, North said. Since Lydia refused to accompany me to Spetsai, I invited Léa. Need I say that she accepted? Here is how it came about. Two days before I was to take the direct plane to Athens, Johann telephoned to tell me that Max had suffered a minor stroke, a sort of warning of things to come. His whole right side was affected, including his hand and face. I asked whether that meant he was paralyzed, and Johann told me he wasn't, not quite; it was a partial loss of mobility and feeling that could quite probably be reversed. Max could speak, but it was hard to understand him. They had gone to Zurich almost immediately, and Max was at the hospital for tests, therapy, fine-tuning of his medication, and so forth. Johann said in these circumstances it was especially important for them that I make no change in my plans, and go to stay in their house as though nothing had happened; Max had insisted on it from the start, making a great effort to speak. It would be a blow to them both if I refused. He, Johann, had already worked out all the arrangements. He described them in detail, down to how he had hired one of those double-ended fisherman's boats with a primitive but powerful motor that I could use for picnics and swimming, as in the old days. That was a wonderful thing to have done, because some of the best places to swim in Spetsai take too long to reach on foot. He had also drawn up lists of things to do and all sorts of instructions and then realized that they were unnecessary, since I knew the house and the island so well, but there they were anyway, waiting for me. Max knew about everything Johann had done, and it made him happy. Out of the blue, he added that there was great significance in my having announced that I was going to visit them on Spetsai: long ago, they decided to leave the house to me in their testaments, but having done so, from time to time they wondered whether I still loved the island. Perhaps it had been spoiled for me. I was, of course, immensely moved, because it had never, absolutely never, occurred to me that those two old birds liked me quite so much. I expressed my feelings as best I could. As you can imagine, I was upset as well as moved. I told Johann that I would certainly go to Spetsai, if that was what they wanted, although the idea behind my plan had really been to spend that time with them, but I wanted at least to stop in Zurich on my way, to embrace them. Johann said that was out of the question: Max didn't want anyone to see how his mouth was twisted or how he drooled when he tried to speak; as for himself, he had no time for anyone except Max. He spent all day every day at his bedside and slept on a cot right there. The time to see them would be when Max had recovered. That left no room for argument. I decided I would keep to my original schedule.

And Léa? After what had seemed a long calm, she had taken to telephoning again, to complain that we hadn't seen each other, that she had drifted out of my life, although I was a permanent part of hers. She wanted to go on a short vacation with me—anyplace I wanted, provided it was soon. There were all sorts of *emmerdes* she needed to tell me about, and it couldn't be done over the telephone. I wondered what these real or invented troubles might be. I would never have thought of taking her to Spetsai if Johann and Max were going to be there; the danger of the news getting back to Lydia would have been too great. I don't mean that they would have told Lydia. Nothing that simple, because that is not their way; they could not bring themselves to harm me directly, and they weren't at all close to Lydia, or even in contact with her. In fact, she had felt uncomfortable on the only two occasions they met, at our wedding and at the dinner after the first show of Max's paintings in New York. But the Painters entertained every night. We would have seen all their pals on the island, most of whom had been pals of my parents. There would have been a lot of gossip, because of my parents, and because of my having become so well known, and word might have gotten back to Lydia. I would not have risked that, not even if four weeks of sex with Léa were the other side of the bet. There was also the Painters' uncontrollable urge to meddle. One couldn't predict what intrigue, possibly well meant, but nefarious in its effects, it might spawn. But with them absent, there was no reason that I should see anyone at all on the island, except the couple who worked for them. I knew them both well. The husband also looked after the Painters' garden and the gardens of others, including, for a while, my parents'. He would laugh his head off beating Ellen and me and sometimes even my father at backgammon. It seemed that anytime the board was out he would appear from behind the laurel bushes he was watering, sooner or later join the game, and outwit us until we gave up. The wife cooked; not as well as my parents' old cook, but well enough. After everything these two had seen working for the Painters for so many years, my sexual activities would be of no interest. And whom could they talk to about them? Maybe Max and Johann, on their return to the island, but by then the news that I had brought a young woman with me would be stale, and perhaps the Painters would simply think that Léa was Lydia. So the danger seemed small. The truth is that a rage of sexual longing mixed with a dose of resentment and spite had possessed me. If I wasn't to work on my book, if there were going to be no dinners and lunches to distract me—parties the like of which no one but the Painters knew how to organize—if Lydia refused to come with me, I would make sure there was another woman's body at my side that I could plow. I wasn't about to start picking up German tourists. If not Lydia, then Léa. I told Léa to meet me at the airport in Athens; we would take the hydrofoil to Spetsai together. Her answer was *Youpi!* We will swim and swim. She said she was jumping up and down, she was so pleased. *Siga, siga,* I said, which is Greek for "easy does it," I am taking you with me to fuck, not to swim. But bring a wet suit, just in case. The water will be cold.

It seems that one can change physically beyond recognition and not be aware of it. In the long years since I had last been on Spetsai, I had not gained more than five or six pounds; my hair was somewhat thinner but hadn't turned gray; my bearing and the way I dressed had remained the same. I had merely aged. But the context had fallen away: I appeared no longer as my father and mother's son, the boy from the yellow house on the bluff above the old harbor looked after by Roxane, the best cook on the island. My exploits in the small centerboard sailboat my father gave me for my fourteenth birthday—the wrong craft for the passage, swept by fierce winds, between Spetsai and the Peloponnesus—if not forgotten by the locals had been reattributed by them to someone else, remembered as performed by another kid who, no doubt, had continued to frequent the island and these days sailed over on Saturdays from Athens in one of the chubby ketches that anchored below the terrace of Vasily's. Close enough so that when Léa and I were at table, drinking retsina and eating little squares of feta cheese, I could think that I saw him, portly and content, cigar in his mouth, disporting himself on the deck of his ship, while an overdressed woman too young to be his mother shouted at him tirade after tirade. Or to a fellow just like him. In a word, I had become invisible. With one exception—a *Paris Match* photographer who dined a couple of tables away from Léa and me at Yiannis', the taverna we used to call back then the Maxim's of Spetsai—no one recognized me. Not the old guy who sold newspapers from the kiosk at the new harbor, not the crazy dwarf with a mongoloid idiot's head and features who used to make faces at Ellen and scare her, not the owners of Vasily's or Yiannis', and certainly not the elegant elderly Greeks, snapping their fingers at the waiters because their grilled fish was slow arriving, who used to drink gin and tonics at my parents' cocktail parties and chatter in thickly accented French with other guests and even among themselves. The one person who would have recognized me and would have been wonderfully happy to see me was my parents' cook, Roxane, whose *keft-edes*—lamb meatballs delicately flavored with mint and deep fried—will be my madeleine if ever I am lucky enough to taste their equal. She has been dead for years.

The Painters' house is one of those that sit right on the water, with steps of poured concrete leading from the lower terrace down to a big flat rock from which you can dive into the sea. Climbing out is tricky when the sea is up, but you get the hang of it pretty quickly or you wait until the wind dies down. The view from the bathing rock, the terrace, and the window of the guest room I took for Léa and me is superb. On your left, you see the shoreline of the Peloponnesus. Directly before you, at much greater distance, lies Hydra, like a green mountain rising from the sea with flecks of white foam on its flank that are in fact houses. Once I had shown Léa the Dapia, which is where the hydrofoil and other tourist boats dock, the old harbor, and some of the tiny churches that dot the island, and we had taken a morning walk through the wilderness of laurel bushes and olive trees that begins almost immediately at the end of the road to my parents' house, which I pointed out after some hesitation, it hurt me so deeply to pass by it, there was really little reason to go out. She asked to visit my parents' house. I refused, not wanting to make contact with the new owners, a Swiss banker I vaguely knew and his English wife, or if they were away, which was probable, with the servants, to whom I would have had to explain who I was. We stayed at home, which in the end seemed prudent, except to walk over to the old harbor to board the boat the Painters had chartered and return from it to the house in the afternoon, when the torpor of the siesta had already descended on the island and the only living creatures to be seen were donkeys, in one dusty plot or another, picking at the burned grass. We did go to the two good tavernas when we wanted to eat fish. You see, on islands like Spetsai, fishermen sell their catch first to restaurants, then to the locals, then to the cooks of the rich Greeks from Athens, and then they divide what's left over, which may not be much, among the most prestigious of the cooks working for foreigners. And only those foreigners who are longtime house-holders. Roxane was such a cook. I would have thought that the Painters' Marina also enjoyed those privileges. But the few times when, tired of her lamb and chicken, I ventured to ask for fish, she sighed tragically, and, in one of those phrases that begin with the word *tipota* and that Greeks seem to reserve for discourse with barbarians, made it clear that fate would not permit it. Most likely, she didn't want to waste her credit with the fishermen on the likes of Léa and me. She would keep it intact until the Painters returned. I couldn't blame her. But she prepared with gusto the lunch basket of hard-boiled eggs, canned tuna, cheese, wine, and fruit I took with us to the boat. We would leave the old harbor around eleven and chug out noisily to an anchorage at a beach or cove where we were sure to be alone. There were many such places. By noon, the deck was broiling hot. I would cover it with beach towels. We lay on them, making love, then resting from our exertions. Around one-thirty, we ate lunch. I seemed to sleep a lot, especially after the heavy Greek wine. Sometimes a mountainside gave us afternoon shade. Otherwise, I would stretch the awning over the open cockpit, and Léa read there while I slept. I hardly read at all, although I had stuck a couple of books into my duffel bag, and the Painters' library was full of treasures. My fatigue was far greater than I had thought. I was getting over it very slowly. When I did read, it took me minutes to get through a page and very soon my eyes would begin to close. A strange thing happened. All my life, I have been plagued by nightmares. During that period, on the contrary, my dreams, especially those I had on the boat, were so interesting and unthreatening that I found myself looking forward to them and the intricate high adventures they brought. I tried to prolong certain dreams, even as I felt my grasp of the plot and its meaning was weakening, or the dream itself had faded without resolution. But perhaps the effort wasn't wasted: after the border between sleep and waking had been crossed, a residue of what I had experienced and perhaps understood left me momentarily encouraged and naively hopeful.

The truth is that dreams and swimming had become my means of escape. Escape from what? I see the question taking form on your face with such insistence that I begin to wonder whether for once you will find the force to break out of your mutism. Will you ask the question, man? Will you ask, What is it that ailed you, John North, on this paradisial isle? What was there to flee from? I see that you won't. You would rather remain silent, true to form. Perhaps you think of it as a way of letting me tell my story without interference. I have begun to think it's a form of disdain.

It seemed to me that North had become peculiarly agitated. Coming on top of his strange appearance, his nervousness worried me. To calm him, I held up my hands, palms open toward him, outstretched fingers spread wide. I believe that is a gesture universally understood as a plea for conciliation. If necessary, I might even have spoken. But I had succeeded in pacifying North without that. He smiled and said, Don't worry about my outburst. Just to show you that the tantrum is over, he continued, I will give you the answer to the question you couldn't bring yourself to put. What I was fleeing, what I was absolutely driven to escape, was the shame of what I had done, the colossal stupidity of having gone on a whoremaster's holiday with Léa. The most time I had spent with her previously was two consecutive days in Bourges and Vienna while *The Anthill* was being filmed in Paris. On those occasions, I was providentially distracted by sex and tourism. Yes, tourism, even though I know Vienna too well to be a tourist. There is always, when you travel, the tourist's business of actually getting there and arranging to leave, getting accustomed to the hotel room, dealing with the concierge about dinner reservations and the like, and visiting at least one museum. It was a marvel that those occupations left any time for screwing and, conversely, perhaps an even greater marvel that, with the amount of screwing we managed, there was also time for lunch, dinner, and the opera. Certainly, I have no memories of talking to her then at length. But our routine on Spetsai left plenty of time for that, or more precisely for Léa to talk to me. You will perhaps laugh, North said, and then, correcting himself, continued, no you won't, it's not your style, when I tell you that I am fundamentally taciturn and tire easily of chatterboxes. But it's absolutely true. When I am not on parade, by that I mean at literary dinners or on panels where my job is to shine, I am perfectly capable of saying not a word for hours, and being happy about it too. Is that your case as well, is that why you never speak? North asked me. Then he said, Never mind, I don't want to force you. But here is the truth: the nymph silence is my ally. Without her, I wouldn't have written my books. She gives me time to listen and to think. Silence has been one of the cornerstones of my happiness with Lydia. Of course, Lydia is not so averse to speech as I, since my aversion borders on boorishness, while she, as part of the beautiful manners she was taught by that German-speaking grandmother, is able to converse with anyone–with a wall–without falling into despicable small talk. Lydia too needs to think–about her work. Her best discoveries are not accidental. They are the product of long, concentrated reflection.

We had finished our drinks. North refreshed them and drank his at once almost to the bottom of the glass. That's much better, he told me.

A moment of silence followed, and then he said, You see, that is what I was forced to think of while I listened to Léa's unending chatter, parts of which, by the way, I couldn't understand, either because I wasn't paying close enough attention or because of the way she swallowed entire groups of words and radically changed pitch in the middle of a phrase. These oddities seemed to have become increasingly accentuated, as though to keep pace with her growing happiness. Ah, she was happy in Spetsai, and tried to assure me of it by exclaiming, at weirdly inopportune moments, Alone at last! I am convinced that certain odious forms of intimacy she tried to impose were linked to that vision of new bliss. For instance, she took to sitting down on the toilet with the bathroom door open. I discouraged that particular initiative by shutting the door myself, perhaps more ostentatiously than was necessary. More than once, when I was in the bathroom taking a leak, she entered unheard–when she wanted to she could move as noiselessly as a Sioux warrior–and, reaching from behind me, without a word took hold of my member and played with it as with a garden hose. I didn't doubt her good intentions, or that her other great loves were aroused by shared defecation and so forth. The sad or not-sad truth is that I am not; other generally unmentionable activities are more to my taste. In the end she repeated the stories of the various *emmerdes* she had been hinting at on the telephone for me to pierce the mystery of her worries. In fact, it had all to do with my least favorite man, Jacques Robineau, who had gotten married with a reception at the Racing; Léa had been planning no such a wedding for herself at the Crillon. You see how completely I sometimes misunderstood her. Indeed, the principal *emmerde* was the lack of a serious candidate for her hand. There had been two she took on approval, as she put it, only to return them to the store. A married professor of medicine with a talent for cunnilingus but unwilling to divorce, perhaps because of his children. Another was an Algerian documentary filmmaker. Here the wife was no problem: the Algerian was ready to leave her in a heartbeat. The problem was money. The Algerian hadn't any, and Léa had decided her husband would have to be rich or at least, like Robineau and me, live as though he were. The woman Robineau had married in the splendor that so impressed Léa was none other than the journalist with whom he was living, according to Marianne. The journalist turned out to be Léa's best friend. Manifestly, that circumstance had not stood in the way of Léa and Robineau's relations before the marriage. The question now preoccupying them, or perhaps only Léa, was whether there was any reason that those relations should not resume. Logically, she thought, there was none. She was waiting, though, for him to make the first move, perhaps the next time the journalist was sent off on assignment. But for the time being, the field was pretty thin, just her great love, the physicist, and me. She announced that to me, said North, with the usual *Youpi!*

Gone were the days, North told me, when telephone communications between Spetsai and the outside world were truly awful and calling the United States took considerable time and perseverance. Still, receiving calls at the Painters' house was complicated, because the phone rang also in the quarters occupied by Marina and her husband, who naturally answered, because almost all calls were in fact for them, and I made it a rule not to answer so as not to have to convince some voluble Greek to stay on the line while I ran to fetch Kosta or Marina to the telephone. I arranged, therefore, to call Lydia every third day, at the same hour, just before she left the hospital. Efficiency and predictability were my goals, but the system also made it easier to make sure Léa was out of the room. The risk that if she saw me telephone Lydia she would immediately want to perform once again the services inspired by my call to Lydia from Paris about the French prize would have been intolerable. I spoke to Lydia, therefore, unconstrained either in my lies—necessary to brush Léa out of the picture I gave Lydia of my daily activities—or in my tenderness. I listened carefully, weighing each of her words, as she gave me news of her work and the family, told me which friends she had seen, and so forth. It all rang true; there was nothing feigned I could detect. Lydia's intelligence and good nature, and innate rectitude, shone through every word. She showed no trace of guilt or embarrassment about not having come to Spetsai. That meant, I concluded, that she didn't feel any. So far as she was concerned, she had acted sensibly, having considered, in perfect good faith, the competing claims: my health and need to get away; my reluctance to be alone; and the demands of her work. Perhaps she had not even bothered to articulate for herself the reasons for her decision. It was enough that it had been made. She didn't feel the need to review it. And I didn't hear anything that suggested trouble still brewing between us. If there had been such a thing when she left for Kyoto, or when she returned and refused to come to Spetsai, it had disappeared. It followed, said North, that I had spitefully and recklessly brought Léa to this island, and every moment of the day chipped away at the foundations of my marriage, when there was nothing to be spiteful about. I found my own stupidity intolerable. The sex I had imagined with Léa, and the fervor with which I had wanted it, now seemed of secondary importance in the decision. After all, I wasn't utterly unable to exercise any sort of self-control. I would hang up after speaking to Lydia from the Painters' studio, pour myself a scotch, and drink it on the terrace to delay the moment when I would have to enter the bedroom for the replay of the nightly scene: Léa's leap out of the bed, her attack on my clothes until I too was naked, maneuvers to encourage tumescence, penetration this way and that. Afterward, I lay awake, ashamed and afraid.

Don't feel sorry for me, said North. Even now, I am not sorry for myself. The gods are just. I got what I deserved. All the while, I also felt blessed. Blessed by the incomparable shining sea which, wrinkled by the breeze and playful, waited for me as I rose from my adulterous couch. At first I would swim alone, the water being really too cold for someone not used to the North Atlantic. It wasn't long though before Léa went in as well. She turned out to be a remarkable swimmer: powerful and elegant in her strokes and very fast. Obviously I was stronger, and I suppose that when I was in normal health I had greater stamina for long distances, but really she was better. Someone had taught her very well and she had talent. We swam off our rock immediately after breakfast, then off the boat, and then off the rock again, at the end of the afternoon, before having drinks on the terrace. I picked the anchorages that were good for swimming and had a great view, and, one after another, I took her to all the places I had liked best. My favorite spot I saved for last, when the water had warmed up, a deep bay with not a house nearby, facing Spetsopoulos, Stavros Niarchos's private island. There were rumors and scandal in the seventies tied to his adventures, conjugal and otherwise. I was out of touch with this sort of gossip. Still, examining his installation through binoculars added spice to being there. The second time we went, I proposed to Léa that we swim out to one end of the mouth of the bay and race from there to the other and back. She said we had better double the length of the race if I was to have any chance of winning.

Until the last leg, I kept maybe a length ahead of her, falling back a little from time to time to see what she was up to. It wasn't all that easy to stay ahead. She had one of those freestyle strokes that make you think of what a virtuoso does with his bow. Back and forth it goes, all by itself, so natural and simple, except that only a Heifetz or Milstein can do it. But I was all right. In fact, I knew I was keeping my strength undi-

minished, in reserve. The rest cure had worked. We started on
the fourth leg, and I really let go with everything I had. The
only discomfort I feel when I swim in salt water is the smarting
of my eyes. They have always been very sensitive to strong
light and to salt. The concentration of salt in the Aegean is
greater than in the Atlantic, and swimming as a boy in Spetsai
I had sometimes really suffered. On this swim, though, I was
wearing goggles. For this reason, and because I had timed
myself well, my happiness was complete. I pulled ahead of Léa
easily and then just kept going at the same pace, which was
much faster than what I had done before. I knew I could sus-
tain it. There seemed to be no reason that I should ever have to
stop. The high of *mobile perpetuum*, an unveiling of the secret
of perpetual motion. If she liked, we could triple the race, I
would not rest until the moon rose. At some moment of my
euphoria, for no reason I know, I turned my head to look for
her. She was not anywhere near. I stopped, stripped off my
goggles, and shading my eyes against the sun looked again,
carefully. There she was, perhaps thirty-five yards away, waving her right arm and calling out. I called out in turn to say I
was coming and rushed toward her. She was crying by the time
I reached her. I could not understand what had happened, and
at first thought she might have been stung by jellyfish. Big
ones are rare in those waters, but they do exist, and they can
hurt a swimmer. No, she sobbed, I lost you, I didn't know
where you were or which way I should go, and I am freezing. I
felt a sudden chill myself, which was, I think, the cold of panic.
Of course, she was blind as a bat, but it was easy to forget it
because so much of the time she wore contact lenses which, of

course, you have to take out to swim. The rest of the time, if she didn't have her glasses on, she faked it. Her technique made me think of Marilyn Monroe in *How to Marry a Millionaire*. She had never had to worry before when we swam, because I was always near her. I hugged and caressed her until she was calm and we swam to the boat slowly, very close to each other. Once we had climbed onboard and she had warmed up—I wrapped her in towels that had been baking in the sun—and I had gotten her to drink some of the terrible Greek brandy I kept on the boat for old times' sake, I got on top of her without asking for the usual services and we made love very sweetly. This was a change that I think she noticed. I had been brutal with her since our first day on the island, and, as a matter of fact, was surprised that she didn't complain.

When the *meltemi* blows hard in Spetsai the sky can remain perfectly clear but the quality of the light becomes very different. It acquires a cold sort of luminosity, as though the island were all of a sudden under a different sun. Light suitable for natural disasters and mourners. That's what happened the next day, not to the island or the general population on it or to Léa. Only to me. My sister, Ellen, telephoned and said that this time my father was really dying. I had better get to Washington as fast as it could be arranged if I wanted to see him alive. He had been demented for so long, all real contact between us rendered impossible, that for a moment I hesitated. Couldn't I tell Ellen that I would be there as soon as possible, and then take my time? The man occupying the bed in the best guest room of my parents' beautiful house—the master bedroom was where my mother reigned alone in her own Stygian gloom—

resembled my father, but that was all. Nothing good could pass between him and me before I closed his eyes. But I didn't have the courage to stay away. Instead, I called the lawyer in Athens who had been willing for years to look after my parents' real estate and tax problems, not because these paltry issues were worthy of his attention, but because of who they were, a point he never failed to make in any of his conversations with me. I did not seem to impress him nearly as much. It was the perfect moment in the morning to try to catch him: not so early that it was unthinkable for him to have arrived at the office, and not late enough for him to have left for his lunch and the nap at the house of his mistress. I was in luck. He agreed to charter a helicopter to pick me up at the tiny landing strip across the water and take me to the airport in Athens. That is where I said goodbye to Léa and managed to catch a direct flight to New York. Lydia was already in Washington, and met me at the house in Georgetown.

Have I told you that I had made it a rule to go down there every three or four weeks to look in on father and mother? Sometimes it seemed to Ellen and me that they recognized us, but the flicker was brief and of uncertain significance. Certainly, they were unconscious of the lapse of time between our visits. That was the doctor's opinion, and also Ellen's, who went to see them more often, living relatively nearby, in Virginia. The lawyer who was the executor of their estates and paid the staff didn't disagree. Nonetheless, I went there, sat by their bedside, patted their hands, which had become white as flour, and usually kissed them. It wasn't really unpleasant. They were always clean and sweet smelling despite the unimaginable indignities of diapers, uncontrolled breaking of wind, and so forth, and their clothes were spotless and suited to the time of day and season. My father was shaved as carefully as when he was still alive–yes, this is how I thought of it, how I distinguished between his former and current states. In fact, he was shaved daily by the same man who came to do my mother's hair. I thought they looked as they had always looked, but in reality they were specimens stuffed by an expert taxidermist. Not unnaturally, I came to believe that this part of my visit–the kisses and caresses–was really for my benefit, not theirs. Ellen's and my more important task, I thought, was to check on the nurses: Were they alert? Were my mother and father so admirably cared for every day, or was this treatment reserved for days when an appearance by Ellen or me was to be apprehended? Was the linen really changed twice a day, rooms aired, food freshly prepared, massages carefully and punctually administered, clothes for them chosen according to our instructions? In other words, were we getting our money's worth? It was difficult not to think of money as one added in one's head the weekly salaries of the day and night nurses, the cleaning ladies, the cook, and the orderly whose presence had become superfluous when my father's strength ebbed to the point where, even in his greatest agitation, his nurse, perhaps with the assistance of my mother's nurse, could subdue him. But the orderly stayed on, just in case. What kind of case? I wouldn't have been able to say until father bit the nurse and drew blood. Ellen and I clung to the vision of the house as it had been. Except for the hospital beds that had replaced the Queen Anne four-posters, nothing in the house on O Street was changed. We liked that. But in moments of exasperation, speaking to Ellen, I called the house a fake Egyptian tomb, a waiting room between life and death, from which, in breach of promise, we the heirs would eject the imperial couple, one after the other, as soon as the hour struck for embalmment and other serious business. In the meantime, I must confess on behalf of this particular heir that he devoted almost equal attention to the way his parents' keepers treated the furniture. There were many glorious pieces in the house, and they deserved respect. I never left O Street without having made sure that the curtains were drawn where necessary to keep out the destructive rays of the sun, and that those glistening surfaces, polished by so many years, had been dusted and waxed. Probably you think that I am too hard on myself. It can't be helped, because you end up with a load of guilt on your back no matter how conscientious you dare to believe you have been as a son. The dreary truth is that doing your duty is no substitute for love, and I can't claim that I loved those troublesome bodies and their unremitting functions. At best, I felt sorry for the bodies and loved certain memories. So giving a harsh account of yourself is a form of defense, mounted before an attack has been launched.

Because I had been sick, and then had gone to Spetsai, I had not seen my father for a long time. Eight or ten weeks, I suppose. During my last visit, I found him in his normal Madame Tussaud form, sitting by the window in a wing chair. He was dressed as he would have been if he had kept all his marbles: in a dark red cashmere turtleneck sweater, gray flannel trousers, red socks that matched his sweater, and loafers that had been shined within an inch of their lives. I remember my satisfaction: to keep the keepers on their toes, I had not telephoned before reaching the airport, just before the fifteen-minute taxi ride to the house, and so could tell myself that this was really how he was turned out every day, this wasn't staged for my arrival. We thought, Ellen and I, that it was beneficial to have them dressed as they had used to be, to see familiar objects when they looked about them, to have fresh flowers. The doctors didn't contradict us, though what they really thought was another matter, and who is to say what percolated in those damaged brains. I disliked the geriatric specialist, an unctuously slimy fellow, and never believed a word he said of comfort or otherwise. Or his silences. Of course, that last nice viewing of my father had its obligatory moment when the balloon of my self-satisfaction was punctured. The poor guy was fiddling with a ring of plastic sausages of various colors that could be detached and reattached—a toy for kids between the ages of one and two. For a dreadful, sentimental moment I thought that the nurses had found it in our old playroom. Then I realized that it couldn't be; we had cleaned out that room when it was going to be used by the orderly. Besides, I didn't remember our having this particular toy. So the nurses had bought it. I didn't think that my father recognized me. If he did, he wasn't glad because right away he began to swat me with the ring, going for my face, whereupon the nurse took that toy away, and gave him in its place a sponge shaped liked a football that he could squeeze.

This time I found my father on the hospital bed, twitching and twitching. Since that last visit, he must have lost thirty pounds, perhaps more. He was mostly on his back, in skimpy pajamas that looked like a hospital garment. From time to time, he gave a big jerk, and for a moment turned on his side. Perhaps because he had become so very skinny, it was obvious that he was wearing a huge diaper. The room was very warm. He was uncovered, and his feet were bare. Was it possible that I had forgotten what they looked like? I had no idea how long it had been since I last saw him barefoot. Those feet were appalling. Big bunions had grown on them, the kind that deform the foot even when the sufferer is wearing shoes. I had always winced at that sight and here they were, disfiguring my father. Whoever had clipped his fingernails had forgotten about the toenails. They were horny, long, and cracked. If they had not been so very clean, I would have said they were the toenails of a homeless bum. He tried to cross his legs, but couldn't manage it so I took hold of his ankle and tried to help. He pulled away with a violence and strength that surprised me and continued his own efforts. Then I looked carefully at his face. When I had first come into the room, I found I had to avert my eyes. Now I could look, and saw that something strange had happened. His face–indeed, his entire skull–had become longer, as well as narrower, as though it had been squeezed in a vise. Naturally, the jaw was narrower too. I did not want to think how the teeth had adjusted to it. I could not bring myself to kiss him on the cheek, so close to that mouth; it seemed to me that the gesture would be a histrionic one, in bad taste. Perhaps I was wrong. Lydia kissed him and that seemed, in fact, very right, but by then it was too late for me to follow suit. I resolved to kiss him on the forehead–that unfamiliar, pointed forehead—but only as I left. Ellen pushed me toward a chair. I sat down, and put my head on the pillow, as far away from his as I could. A sort of monotonous mumble was to be heard, occasionally words I recognized: my name, Ellen's, the geriatric doctor's, but not my mother's, disconnected expressions like "with such desire" that came back again and again, the names of days of the week as though he were rehearsing them to make sure they were all still there. Some sort of newsreel of hell was passing before those seeing and unseeing eyes, and then I suppose repeating and recombining itself. He attended to it with the greatest care. Ellen came over to my side of the bed, tapped me on the shoulder, and led Lydia and me out of the room. I had not noticed the nurse, but she was there, sitting in the corner. I deposited that kiss before leaving.

The two doctors and the lawyer were in the library, drinking coffee. It was really quite simple, explained the neurologist. The reflex that makes us swallow food had been lost; if we were to feed him it would have to be through a tube that reached through his mouth and esophagus to the stomach. The lawyer began to mumble, much like father, about how we had nothing to say in the matter because that procedure wasn't covered in father's instructions and for once I interrupted him. I told the doctors we wouldn't allow the feeding. Lydia held my hand as we went to my mother's room, across the wide white hall from father's. Silent blue and green parrots were swarming in the wallpaper. She too was in bed. The nurse stood up and put her finger to her lips. Mother was sleeping. Her face seemed fuller. Perhaps she had gained weight. There was nothing to criticize

about the way her hair had been set, or about the pink angora
bed jacket, or the gleaming white of her bed linen. I whispered, Does she know? The nurse smiled and shook her head.

The funeral service in the cathedral was the best I have ever
seen, except for Jack Kennedy's, of course, which I had
watched rebroadcast on a television set in a hotel room in
Athens. Father received full military honors, so a brass band
played on and on while the coffin covered by the flag was
brought in by six marines in dress uniforms so stiff they
creaked like a new harness on a horse, and it was a wonder that
they could move at all. His best friend and classmate at school,
who had been secretary of the navy a number of administra-
tions back, delivered the eulogy. This old boy still had his wits
about him. He managed, Lord knows how, to get hold of all the
reports on father at school that the masters and the head had
written, some of which had been sent to my grandparents and
some of which I suppose had remained in the school's files.
That he had been a model student was no secret. Mother had
drummed it into Ellen and me with the sort of unintended perverse effects on our own academic performance you would
expect. But the stuff the secretary read painted father as a
young god. When we talked about it later, Ellen and I agreed
that we weren't really surprised. Some of it may have come
through to us, like an exotic scent, through the overlay of the
war and government service and father and mother's social
life and many other things better forgotten. There was also the
adulation that surrounded him whenever his school friends
gathered at the house. It was a pity that mother could not have
seen and heard it all—I mean seen, heard, and understood. We

debated with Lydia and the neurologist whether she should come to the service, and in the end we brought her, sedated as the neurologist advised so that there was no risk of an outburst, and she sat through it all in the front pew between Ellen and me. We put two of the nurses right behind her. Although she didn't utter a word, which made me ask myself whether the goddamn doctor hadn't gone overboard with his Valium, she cried from the moment the marine band began until taps, which they played while the detail bore the coffin to the hearse. She cried noiselessly, without sobbing. Just tears and more tears. Perhaps one may conclude that she understood. But perhaps she cried because she had been to so many funeral services and so many burials that she was conditioned to cry as soon as she received the sensory stimuli associated with them. The neurologist did not express an opinion. We did not take her to the cemetery, because that was going to be another drawn-out affair, and the nurses, whose judgment we did trust, and who, I am certain, would have enjoyed seeing more of the military show, thought she was really too exhausted.

Funerals affect people in ways that those who are most immediately concerned—such as I, the grieving son—do not think about in advance. Too busy or inward turned for it? I am not sure. An example that I was made aware of immediately, and that came across to me as bittersweet, but also slightly comical, was the way the Frank contingent suddenly realized that my parents were really important people, in spite of what Bunny and Judy Frank used to regard as their lack of seriousness and, in secret, perhaps even foolishness. Bunny took Lydia and me aside when we all came back from the cemetery to the reception at O Street and confessed that he was shaken. With all his achievements, past and ongoing, he did not think he would rate a send-off like my father's. Or such obituaries in the *Times* and the *Washington Post.* I couldn't tell him he was wrong, or that such things didn't matter, because he wasn't going to believe me. Instead, for the first time in my life, I clasped Bunny in my arms and said, Don't talk like that, you will be with us for a very long time still. Besides, I said, it's not your fault you were too young to be in the war and to do all the follow-up stuff the Establishment then reserved for its own. Those were the rites of a dying world; you have been building for the future.

I did that for Lydia. It didn't matter that I was telling him the truth; I wouldn't have been kind or said those words except as an offering to Lydia. And I didn't do it only because I knew that without her help I would have broken during that week of death, or because I felt guilty about Spetsai, although these things surely had their effect. Do you believe in redemption? North asked.

I didn't answer.

Of course, said North, either you have no view or you won't express it. One is at a loss trying to decide whether you are a case of low affect or caution. I don't believe in redemption, North continued, in a religious or even a Tolstoyan sense, because I don't believe in God and the associated claptrap. But with my whole being I believe in the possibility of change. Two powerful demonstrations, like masques staged to instruct more than to entertain. Could they have done it? The Masque of Lust in Spetsai, wherein the hapless wanderer disports himself in a waste of fevered pleasure, and the Masque of Love that heals. I abjured adultery. You might say that was the easy part, though I realized that a lifetime of penitence and effort might not suffice to expiate. For once, you are laughing. Is it the liturgical aroma of the word "penitence" or my buffoonery? Please, don't mind me, keep laughing. Depending on your point of view, you may come to think that further events have proved you right.

By the way, North asked, have I told you that after I was born my mother entered into an adulterous relationship that lasted until she began to lose her mind? She did. When Ellen and I were little, we began to understand that something was wrong, and that it was mother's fault. Yet we loved her without reserve because she was good to us, and beautiful, and perfect in every other way. We also loved our father. He had to leave on missions, and when he wasn't away he and mother were usually busy in the evening, entertaining at home or going out to dinner with important people, and he was aloof—naturally aloof and reserved, not at all indifferent to others—but he was also very fair and even tempered. He always talked to us as though we were grown-ups, listened carefully to what we had to say, and remembered it. He knew about a great many things—and his information was accurate and detailed. We admired him.

At some point, I suppose I must have been seven or eight, and Ellen is two years older, we realized what was wrong: mother had a lover. We didn't need to talk about it; we knew quite naturally who he was. To my knowledge, there was never anyone else. We didn't find out about it through an indiscretion or through any specific thing either mother or father said or did. One day, the knowledge materialized; it sat there like a very large piece of furniture. I think we were too little to speculate about what mother and her lover did and how it was arranged. Those matters became the subject of endless and sometimes heated discussions between us only after our understanding of the mechanics of sex expanded. Can you guess who he was? I don't expect you to, you don't know the milieu or the cast of characters. Surprisingly, but, in fact, I think also quite inevitably, it was none other than father's closest friend at school, the best man when he married mother, his comrade-in-arms—yes, that's right—the once-upon-a-time secretary of the navy. No wonder he eulogized father with such authority, intimate knowledge, and penetration. As long-running affairs go, I suppose this one was uncomplicated. The secretary had never married, so there was no betrayed wife or confused and embittered children as our opposite numbers. Does this bit of family history help you peer into my soul? I loathed the connivance among that trio— to this day I cannot understand why any one of them accepted it. How could father go on being such good friends with that man? But were they really good friends? I can't tell. I used to think that perhaps father enjoyed tormenting him; the fact that the secretary couldn't so much as yelp. Because, I should add, insofar as Ellen and I could tell, father and mother never stopped living like a real husband and wife. They gave each other elaborate birthday and anniversary presents, organized parties, and so forth. So you might say that mother was moonlighting. Why didn't they divorce? Money couldn't have been the reason or, for that matter, fear of society's disapproval. Their friends were divorcing left and right. As I have said, the secretary was unmarried and, therefore, theoretically available as a husband if my mother felt she needed one. But they stayed together, this improbable threesome, drawing on inexhaustible reserves of voyeurism, masochism, and sadism. I wish one of them had explained to me what they thought they were doing, but they didn't, and I never had the courage to ask. It may not be too late to put the question to the secretary, even if it brings on a massive heart attack. I can just see him in his corner office at the law firm, where he is still a partner, rising to his full height—he is six foot four and weighs a good two hundred pounds, all of which if you happen to touch him feels like muscle—frothing at the mouth a little, and hitting the floor, spilling in the process his tea, overturning the chinoiserie gueridon, perhaps gashing his forehead on a corner of the desk. Believe it or not, until we were teenagers, Ellen and I thought we were the only ones to know. My Vineyard uncle disabused us of that notion one summer. We were staying with him alone, and after a day's hard sail and his fourth whiskey sour, he began a rambling lecture on character traits prevalent in our family and step-by-step got to the case of mother and father and the spectacle their form of *ménage à trois* offered to their friends, and to society at large in Washington and Paris. A lot of this was hearsay, because my uncle was an eccentric architect and did not move in any society, but Ellen and I didn't disbelieve him. In fact, it wasn't a *ménage à trois* in the classical vaudeville sense, because the secretary never spent a night under our roof that I can remember, not even when the house was full of weekend guests, for instance on Spetsai. I read some time ago a memoir by Nigel Nicolson about his celebrated and very interesting parents. They were both bisexual, the mother's orientation toward women being probably more pronounced than the father's toward men. The father, a diplomat like my own, had to be more careful, I imagine, than the Bloomsbury mother. He seemed to me more the typical product of English public school education than an out-and-out queer. The son used a pretty phrase to sum up the moral aspect of the parents' way of life. "Honor was rooted in dishonor," he wrote, or something just like it. Balls, is what I say. At best, it was honor among thieves, if you think that being polite in the midst of depravity is a badge of honor.

I need to stretch, North said suddenly. It's the stirrings of my sciatica. Arm in arm we walked to the door. The light outside was still quite harsh. He took out his dark glasses and, whether because his handkerchief wasn't clean or he had forgotten to put one into the pocket of his trousers, wiped them carefully with his necktie. I had seen him perform this act with a silk square taken from the breast pocket of his blazer, but for once his breast pocket was unadorned. In the process, he noticed the egg-yolk stain. He worked on it for a moment with the nail of his right index finger, but the result didn't satisfy him. Shaking his head with an air of despondency, which might have been intended to be humorous, he took my arm and led me back to our table. It's the great retreat from daylight, he said, and ordered more whiskey.

To finish the story of my mother's adultery, you can imagine how Ellen and I felt when we learned that in his testament father specified that, if he died first, the secretary was to be asked to deliver the eulogy. Fiendish, don't you think? And absolutely no other speakers; the instructions couldn't be clearer. The task of conveying father's wish fell on me, and it cost me dearly to carry it out. Since adolescence, I had been careful to avoid contact with that man. So had Ellen. By the way, I don't think I would have had the strength to telephone him and get those words out if it hadn't been for Lydia. Until a few minutes ago, when I began to tell you about this page of my family history, there had been only two people on earth with whom I had spoken about it: Ellen, naturally, and Lydia. It was Lydia's tenderness and good sense—I don't know how to separate one from the other—that calmed me and gave me the necessary courage. She made me understand that I didn't have to see in father's wish a diabolical scheme designed to visit public humiliation on mother and her lover. You see, said North, at the time father had his testament drawn up, there was no hint that mother was sinking into dementia, so that one could imagine father constructing and refining his pillories for the disloyal friend and the adulterous widow. For the man the pulpit from which he would address the assembled congregation, for her the front pew where she would sit enthroned between Ellen and me. Such was my firm conviction. But Lydia showed me that one could quite as well imagine father's having in mind a definitive reconciliation: the recognition of the permanent value of a friendship, admittedly imperfect, that until the last moment bound him to his wife and schoolmate. A public reconciliation, of course, for the benefit of those who knew the facts, of whom there must have been more than a few in attendance. I will never know whether Lydia's interpretation was the right one–unless I speak to the secretary and he doesn't have that heart attack or refuse to speak. Father did not leave any clues. But her view was in keeping with father's character and the influences that had formed it. Team spirit, you know. Come to think of it, the old man, unlike me, would have loved the concept of honor rooted in dishonor: it can give cover to more than one kind of shame, including activities associated with certain aspects of government service. But I don't want to drift away from my purpose, which is to give you a true if miniature likeness of Lydia. She had poured balm on Ellen's wounds and mine. She had formed an absolutely just opinion of a complex and fundamentally secretive man whom she had seen only at family gatherings–and that over only the relatively short interval between our marriage and father's decline.

I am tired, said North abruptly. I will leave you here–I don't mean to say that, of course, why should you stay here?–and take a walk or sit down on a bench and put my face in the sun. I had a bad night. You have probably deduced as much.

Within some thirty minutes he was back. Soon after the funeral, North told me, Lydia and I resumed our yearly summer routine: weekdays in the city and weekends in East Hampton, three-day weekends whenever Lydia's work at the hospital allowed. The manuscript of *Loss* was waiting for me; finishing it, I decided, was a challenge I had to meet. I reread the one hundred eighty or so pages anxiously, and was relieved to find I didn't completely distrust or dislike the story I had written. It would be a rather short novel in an age when it seemed that the proof of serious purpose and rich imagination was to write a work of eight hundred pages without a plot and without a single memorable character. But my method of composition has always been to write down all that I have to say on a given subject and stop. To strain for more is like adding Hamburger Helper. Usually, after so long a separation from a text, I would start by reviewing it from the first to the last page, making big and small changes as I went along. This time I was astonished to discover that I did not need to do that. Nor did I feel that I had to do over the chapter I had finished just before I left for Spetsai in order to jump-start the book or get back in the mood. Those are tricks I have used successfully when I have felt stuck. Quite miraculously, there seemed to be no obstacle to resuming work right away, at a steady pace. I welcomed the arduous task and the heavy fatigue I felt at the end of each day: these were, I thought, the only possible means of reestablishing my physical and mental health. By the beginning of August, I was able to hand to Lydia, always my first reader, a completed first draft. I decided that I would revise it only if her judgment was favorable. You must understand that revisions are a task to which I invariably look forward, however long I estimate they may take, because at least the book is palpably there. It's a blessing to be relieved of every writer's recurring nightmare: that he will find himself, perhaps without warning, unable to complete what he has begun.

North paused for a moment. Then he said: I want to correct myself, because I am in danger of misleading you. I should have said my own recurring nightmare just now, my own dread of the failure of imagination or will. How other writers func-

tion is the ultimate mystery, no matter what sort of absurd or
mendacious revelations they have volunteered on that subject
in memoirs or interviews. Also, you are not to think that I had
overcome the doubts about the quality of my work that had
been tormenting me since *The Anthill*. They were still there,
horribly alive and present, but I was able, at least for the time
being, to suffer them as one of the apparently infinite number
of aches that afflict us. The failure of a project because of a lack
of means—imagination, to be precise—to bring it to a close, I
think, cannot be borne because it announces paralysis and
utter annihilation. Clearly, a return to the serenity of my life
with Lydia had become the indispensable condition to going
ahead with productive work on my novel. That condition had
been met: the unease I had felt, and had suspected in Lydia,
was gone. As though there had never been such a thing.
Whether in bed, or in our banal daytime activities of a working, childless couple accustomed to living face-to-face with
little room for anyone else, everything functioned happily. I
knew that I could once again turn to Lydia with perfect confidence—she had earned it so richly in the days that preceded
and followed my father's death—and receive her advice and
myriad kindnesses without constraint or suspicions of occult
meanings behind her words and gestures. I was also able to
observe an unexpected development in my attitude toward
Lydia's family. It could be traced, I believed, to the moment
when I found myself able to give a tactful response to what I
had come to call—in my thoughts only, never in conversation
with Lydia—the beautiful manifestation of Bunny Frank's obituary envy. When I answered him then, I spoke out sponta-

neously. I was too consumed by past and present grief to think, and for once I forgot I owed it to myself to be unpleasant! That was ground for hope that I could purge myself of my greatest shame: ignoble envy of the Franks, their opulence and their simpleminded happiness. Perhaps there was enough goodness in me for that. I longed to suppress once and for all the resentments that had been thriving on it like anaerobic bacteria. If I succeeded, Lydia would know it at once—I was convinced of that—and I would have added to her happiness.

Meanwhile, my manuscript had remained on her desk exactly where I had put it. She didn't seem to have begun to read it. That was, I have to admit, an unexpected annoyance, but I understood the reason. She was herself writing a long paper that was overdue at the medical journal, and she had not solved problems of argumentation and structure that worried her. I hesitated at first, and then began revising *Loss* without further delay. If I had waited, doing nothing, she would have noticed. And that might have put unfair pressure on her; she might have imagined I gave greater weight to her opinion than was ultimately the case. There was a well-known side benefit from moving forward that I took into account as well: the process of revising a book has always absorbed me totally, steadying my nerves. If it turned out later that Lydia did not like what I had done, being at work, I thought, should make me able to deal with my disappointment more calmly. Besides, my thinking about *Loss* had changed somewhat. Without articulating it, I had reached the decision that the test of whether this novel should ever be shown to my agent would be the success of the revisions, not Lydia's response to the first draft. In some ways, my state of mind was not dissimilar from what I have experienced upon the publication of any one of my novels: a moment of panic, followed by the realization that the best remedy is not to leave town or refuse to read newspapers but to be busy writing.

For some time now, listening to North had been making me feel apprehensive. He had reached a point in his story at which it seemed some new development was to be anticipated. It would not be pleasant, or easy to shrug off, even here, at L'Entre Deux Mondes, even in my unsettled state of mind oscillating between extreme sympathy for North and a numbness for which I blamed the effort I had been making to follow the meandering course of his story, the lateness of the hour, and, to tell the truth, the alcohol. I thought that I detected in his bloodshot eyes something like sadness in place of the habitual mockery and defiance. Perhaps a similar anxiety had taken hold of him and accounted for his silence. I did not dare to interrupt it.

Look, said North, things are rarely as simple as one tells them. For instance, it's quite true that I had finished my novel, had reread it, and, after due allowance for its uncorrected condition, found it no worse than its predecessors at that stage of their existence. Or let me put it differently: What I read didn't bore me. No, don't protest, there is nothing abnormal about being bored by what you've written. Far from it: I have found myself falling asleep over my own typewriter while I slogged through some description of a girls' school in Salonika or the New York subway or other foolishness of the sort that for some reason I found valid at the time and I thought I absolutely needed to stick into my story. And my eyes have closed when I was rereading the stuff. Can you imagine the horror of finding that an entire work you have labored over is like that? You shake your head. Let me tell you that I can, although thus far I have been spared that particular humiliation. So I revised and revised, less curious or anyway less concerned about what Lydia might say, and in the meantime my own position evolved again. I realized that the last scene in the book, which I had mapped out in considerable detail before beginning to write—in fact, I had a pretty good draft of it before I started the first chapter, and it would not be an overstatement to say that I wrote *Loss* so that I could get to that scene—needed a significant fix. Not one that required many deletions or a lot of new text. It was a matter of a few sentences to correct the version I had given of the cuckolded and abandoned husband's feelings, without which the end of the novel, such as I had written it, was inconsistent with what had become my real intention and, besides, too cruel for me to bear. I performed the operation and found it successful. It was a Wednesday morning in August. Both my club and my favorite restaurant—yes, the same one to which I had so stupidly taken Léa—were closed. I knew that Lydia was at an all-day staff meeting. Nevertheless, I shaved, bathed, got dressed to the nines, and treated myself to a celebratory lunch at another restaurant that I like but usually avoid because, unless you eat there every week, which I don't, or reserve ten days in advance, which I never would, they tell you, with a little smirk in their voice, that they're fully booked. In August, it's a different story. They were actually glad to see me, and the quality of the service, the meal, and the half bottle of wine for once justified their outrageous price.

Do you know why I have just told you this? North asked.

I shook my head.

The reason is not apparent, but it is this: while by a little bit of writing, by changing a few words, I could affect profoundly the climax of my novel, I cannot change the course of the story I am telling you. You see, no price, not even my own life, would be too high, he continued without pretending to give me an opportunity to answer, if I could make that story end now, or if I could rewrite its outcome. There are no such miracles. Words once said cannot be unsaid, and I tremble at what I must tell you.

You see, North continued, I have described to you a moment of triumph. Don't think that I exaggerate: writing is a solitary business and its great joys—the rare moments of elation—come when you are convinced, even for a short while, that you have solved a big problem and your book is going well. If you remember that, you won't be surprised if I tell you that during this period when I was finishing my novel, and then launched into revisions that seemed to me successful, Léa vanished from my mind. It was as simple as that. I wrote every day and was totally absorbed in my work; I was happy when I was with Lydia; there was no room or need for Léa or anyone else. There had been times in the past year, in fact quite a few, when I missed, almost physically, the intensity of the sex with Léa, something that, as you now realize, I had never attained with Lydia. Nothing of the sort intruded during that August. Léa shattered my tranquillity by her own acts.

I was again receiving messages from her at my office. They seemed to grow in length. I did not always listen to them in their entirety, in part because she was repeating herself and in part because it would have taken so much time. Because of the heat wave, I went to my office irregularly, mostly to check my mail, both the walk and the ride downtown in an overheated taxi being so disagreeable that they hindered getting down to work. In fact, if I hadn't from time to time erased messages on my machine when I was there, it would have filled up. I don't know exactly what she would have done if she had realized that her messages were not being recorded, but given her subsequent behavior, I don't think that she would have given up trying to reach me. What I did hear in these messages was a hodgepodge of her usual exclamations, assurances that she loved and missed me in certain specific ways that she sometimes described, imprecations that I join her in Ramatuelle, where she was for some of this time, and complaints of being badly treated by a new love—a man whose name I thought I recognized from previous accounts of the comings and goings in the circle of her journalist and art dealer friends. When I called her back and she wasn't there I didn't leave a message myself, true to the principle of not leaving incriminating evidence in her possession. Once, she was at home. I told her I would be traveling in the West with Lydia and couldn't talk. Nonetheless, messages accumulated almost daily. None of this, I should tell you, interested me greatly. Unofficially—in the sense that I hadn't consciously formulated the decision, and as you can see was far from having communicated it to Léa—I felt that my relationship with her, our love affair, call it what you will, was over. For me it ended when we left Spetsai, for no reason other than that I hated being unfaithful to my wife and found that Léa's company no longer gave me pleasure. Except during sex, which I thought I could do without. These were the excellent reasons I was willing to give to myself when I directed my conscious thoughts to Léa, which I did rarely and very reluctantly. Léa had become a hugely unpleasant problem, one I didn't want to deal with. In the meantime, I was planning a stay in Martha's Vineyard for the Labor Day weekend, and perhaps two weeks more. I hoped Lydia would come with me, that I could pry her away from the hospital and holiday weekend festivities in East Hampton. I thought I would go to the Vineyard even if she didn't, but in that case only after the weekend, which I would spend with her. A year had passed since I last visited my house and, more important to me, my boat.

During the week before Labor Day–, North said, and then he paused, looked puzzled, and corrected himself, no, it must have been over a longer period, perhaps ten days, perhaps two weeks–the content of Léa's phone messages changed. They were alarming, and I had to admit that I didn't believe it was all pure fabulation. A series of them were from Ile de Ré, where a new love and she were staying with his married friends. Like all her great loves, the new one was supremely brilliant. She gave me the highlights of his career at the two *grandes écoles* he had attended–but she was discovering in him a streak of mean brutality. There were unreasonable demands and anger when she didn't comply. She didn't describe the nature of these demands, but I couldn't help supposing that they must be quite unusual, perhaps extreme, since she was not a novice in such matters. When he invited her to Ile de Ré, she had agreed to stay until the end of the month, but now she thought she had better leave. But how? Tell him and her hosts she had to get back to Paris? But what would she do if he said that he was leaving with her? Or if he turned on her violently? The married friends were so very polite that she wasn't sure they would protect her. They might think it was indiscreet to get involved. She was also afraid that if she left he would follow her to Paris, where she would be completely alone. All her friends were away on vacation. Then came a message from a pay phone on a railroad platform, on the mainland. She had taken advantage of being alone–while her love and the host were out sailing and the host's wife had gone to shop for groceries–and run. The ferry was on the point of leaving, but she made it, and she was about to board a train to Paris, where she would take another, from the Gare St. Lazare to her parents' house in Normandy. Once she was there, she would call again; she had to speak with me; she needed my advice.

I didn't want to counsel Léa; in fact, I didn't want to talk to her. Although nothing had been said between us, she was far too sensitive and intelligent not to have understood where we stood, and I told myself that was sufficient. Almost all the women with whom I had love affairs before I married Lydia are still my friends. We may not meet for lunch as often as we should or exchange letters, or do any of the things that in theory friends are always doing, but I do not discern any bad feelings or hostility. I saw that this case was different: there would be no continuing friendship. To the contrary, I would want, quite passionately, to have nothing more to do with her. It may or may not be clear to you but, as I looked coldly on our relationship, all I could see was its sordidness. I was ashamed of what I had been doing. This was a fact, not a judgment subject to appeal. I don't think that Léa ever came to any general judgment about our activities. She attached no moral significance to them. You wonder whether being ashamed justified heartless behavior toward a young woman I had been delighted to screw whenever the occasion presented itself and I felt like it. The answer is no, it didn't, but I had become angry as well as ashamed. In any event, for the time being I was let off the hook, and glad of it because it seemed to me there was nothing I could do for her, and no words of wisdom to impart that she wouldn't find insulting. If I were to give her my honest advice, I would have had to say that she should stop being a little slut and give up sleeping with men who didn't meet some modest threshold level of kindness and decency. I had no doubt that this would make her laugh, and I could imagine her riposte: You mean I should let myself be laid only by true gentlemen like you! The answer to that question was: Of course, you should have stayed away from me, and very little effort was required to stop my advances. But that is not what she would want to hear.

North paused as though to give me an opportunity to speak. I said nothing, and after a moment he continued.

I am giving you here, said North, an example of my sour propensity to renounce and reject parts of my past. My growing determination to shun further contact with Léa is really of a piece with how I often behave in much more trivial matters, when I have been disappointed or when I think I have been in the wrong. Take restaurants where I have been a regular guest. If I am served a surprisingly bad meal, or if I think I have been treated disloyally–for instance, I am kept waiting, despite having made a very precise reservation–two outcomes are possible. The first, which is happy, and consistent with my general predilection for untroubled dealings and loyalty when it comes to places where I eat and drink, get my teeth cleaned, fill the car with gas, and so forth, is that the restaurant owner or headwaiter will apologize at once in a manner that I find sincere. In that case, all is forgiven, and I never give the offense another thought. But if no rescue operation is performed, and I allow myself to get worked up–as I got worked up after that comical epiphany about the true nature of my affair with Léa–all hell breaks loose and there is literally no going back. To the restaurant, or to the person. My annoyance or worse at whatever it was that set me off–it sometimes happens that I forget the precise nature of the wrong I have suffered–is from then on compounded by feelings of guilt about my own role in the breach of faith. It's all childish and absurd, I know it is. Nevertheless, there are streets in more than one city that I avoid because they happen to be where this or that establishment I have broken with is located, so that walking along them might expose me, for example, to the risk of an encounter with the barber who cut my hair for years and surely felt hurt when I abandoned him. It would be kinder, I say to myself, to let him think I had moved away from the city, or never returned to it, or, best of all, had died. There are addresses that I have had to expunge from my address book and would, if I knew how, expunge from my memory, so that if a friend asks me, Do you still go to Igor? referring to the barber who offended me, I could lift my eyebrows in bewilderment and reply that I have never known any-

one by that name. The truth is, of course, that no rescue operation was possible in Leá's case, but that fact, including my
not-so-dim awareness of it, had no influence on the outcome.

Thereupon, North rose and told me he was going to the
men's room. Did I need to make a visit? he asked. I accepted
the offer gratefully. When we were back at table, North said
that it was possible that the oddities of his character he had
been discussing did not interest me. If that is so, he told me, I
was underestimating their significance. After I had assured
him that there was no danger of it, he refilled my glass and continued.

I must get back to the events that were unfolding, he told
me. You see, up to that point Léa had made avoiding contact
with her wonderfully easy for me. She had never mentioned in
any of those messages where or how I could reach her, which
isn't surprising because naturally she wouldn't have wanted
me to dial the number of that house in Ile de Ré. On the other
hand, I could have broken my rule and left some words of comfort on her Paris answering machine. I knew that she checked
it compulsively. But with the unity and coherence of my feelings toward Lydia, and my conviction that I had finished with
Léa, these appeals of hers were particularly unwelcome and ill
timed.

She called again, from her parents' place, just as she had
said she would. The town in Normandy turned out to be Trouville, a dreary resort a short distance from Deauville. The
mention of Trouville made me recall a cold and clammy weekend I once spent there with a wilted American couple who
had rented a villa for the summer. The memory intensified my

disgust. They had quarreled incessantly during my stay, which for them was probably the equivalent of treating me like a member of the family. I must have felt obliged to accept their invitation because the husband had been a protégé of father's. Why else would I have gone there? I don't think that I had any illusions about Trouville or my hosts. Had someone asked me to describe them, I believe I would have given a prophetic answer: The sort of people who ask, when they see you, if you are going to the beach, whether you have brought your own beach towel, and, if you haven't, which was my case, produce a worn-out white washcloth and say you can't have one of the landlady's good towels because you'll ruin it. So much for my novelist's foresight. It can provide you with accurate information, but you don't always act upon it. Superimposed on the memory was an incongruous and humoristic vision of Léa, an almost blind Aphrodite, her tan perfect and her breasts insouciant, who is discovered, having lost her way, walking up and down that gravelly strand among a population of pale petit bourgeois covered with goose pimples and shivering in the cold. The most recent message included a telephone number. I was to be sure to call that same day, after eleven in the evening, when her parents would be asleep. The telephone rang in her room and we would be able to speak privately. To this she added, in English: You had better call me. I didn't like the words or the tone. Still, shortly after five in the afternoon, which corresponded in France to the hour she had named, I telephoned from my office. I too wanted privacy. She answered at once, but it wasn't to talk about Ile de Ré or her disquieting new love, or to seek my advice. It was to announce that *Vogue* had offered her a reporter's position in New York and she thought she might accept it. Therefore, she was coming to the city the following week to see the woman who would be her new boss, and also us, both me and Lydia. If she was going to live in New York, she wanted to make our situation transparent. That was the way she put it, and she added, again in English, a variant of the unlovely locution she had used in her last phone call: You had better be there. Perhaps she was practicing how to cope with her tough environment-to-be. My astonishment was so great that then and there I made a fatal, unforgivable mistake. I should have said, Terribly sorry, *ma petite chatte,* Lydia and I are leaving for Australia and Tasmania and won't be back until the new year. I told her the truth. I said I would be on Martha's Vineyard. Really, she asked, alone? Again I told the truth, that I wasn't sure. And then, because I could no longer contain my rage, I shouted, I will kill you if you come near Lydia. I regretted instantly what I had said, but it induced in her a fit of laughter. When she was once again able to speak, she said this: You have no sense of humor. I remember our pact. But, even so, I am going to see Lydia. If not this month, then the next. It doesn't have to be on your island. I want to get her to move my painting to your apartment. It doesn't look right in your office and, anyway, I want it to be where it can be seen by the important people who come to your house. I hung up without saying goodbye.

There is a bottle of whiskey in the bottom drawer of my desk that I keep there for emergencies—usually a bad headache brought on by getting stuck in my work. After a stiff drink, I began to think about the situation more calmly. It seemed very unlikely that she would show up on the Vineyard. She didn't even know where it was! The last time I had mentioned my house there she seemed to think that it was off the coast of Maine. But even if she found it on the map and made a serious effort to get there next week, the logistics would defeat her. Commercial flights to the island from New York, Washington, and Boston over the Labor Day weekend would have been fully booked since early May, even those going only as far as Hyannis. I couldn't imagine her chartering a small plane, even if she found one available, or flying to Boston and renting a car she could drive to the ferry in New Bedford. Anyway, the ferry too would be fully booked, so she wouldn't be able to get her car on it. As fully booked as all the hotels, inns, and bed-and-breakfasts on the island. The real threat was the news that she had a job she liked waiting for her in New York. But that prospect also attenuated the more immediate threat. If she was going to live in the city, perhaps merely a few blocks away from us, where was the need to make heroic efforts to get to an inaccessible island during the worst moment for travel in the whole year, especially if she had no place to stay once she managed to get there?

It was late by the time North and I took leave of each other. Neither said that we would meet the next day. Had the question whether I would see North the next day occurred to me—I was so tired that I am sure it didn't—I would have dismissed it. I knew that, if God gave me life, I would be inside L'Entre Deux Mondes waiting for my strange friend.

As it turned out, he was waiting for me when I arrived, looking again as though he had spent a sleepless night. But this time he was carefully shaved, and his clothes were fresh. I thought he looked oddly festive. Perhaps that was the effect on me of the nicely faded red shirt and the knit tie of a darker red.

All happy weekends are alike, North announced as soon as we sat down at what had become our usual table, and in consequence there isn't much that's interesting to be said about any one of them. Therefore, he continued, if I inform you as I now do that my long-awaited Labor Day weekend with Lydia on Martha's Vineyard was exceptionally happy, you won't be surprised to find that my account of it is brief. Perhaps even banal.

Here is how it went. Lydia did manage to take part of Thursday off. The traffic to La Guardia was light; there were no accidents on the bridge and no delays on takeoff or on landing. To arrive on the island during the most beautiful afternoon of the year with Lydia, in our state of shared happiness, was a blessing that filled me with exhilaration and gratitude. Out of superstitious fear of inviting an immediate reversal of fortune, I tried to avoid making my beatitude obvious. One by one, my charms worked. Robbie, the caretaker, who had worked for my uncle and stayed with me, met us at the airport with my station wagon. We dropped him off in West Tisbury and drove on home. There we found that he had opened all the doors and windows, so that we could smell in the house every herb and every flower in the old overgrown garden. I kept hugging Lydia while she unpacked and kissed her on the neck, because she is so ticklish there. She put up little resistance. We went on with our childish pursuits during the four days that followed. The night we arrived we had steak, which we had brought from the city. During the rest of our stay, dinner was either lobster steamed in the big lobster pot on the stove or broiled, freshly caught bluefish. For lunch, we ate scrambled eggs or pasta with pesto that I made with basil from the patch outside the kitchen. These are things I cook quite expertly. Lydia had left word at the hospital that it would be impossible to reach her. Just in case some resident or intern decided to try anyway, I disconnected the telephones throughout the house and the answering machine with them. We saw absolutely nobody—not a single one of my fuddy-duddy friends. Toward the end of the afternoon, we swam from West Beach, which is a long stretch of dune and sand, open only to the families of members of the association that owns it. As my uncle's heir, I am a member. It's only a few miles' drive from the house. You have on your right two ponds, first Menemsha and then Squibnocket. The ocean is always on your left. Then you come to a place at Nashaquitsa where only a narrow finger of land separates the pond from the ocean. You drive over it with extreme care. Once you have made your way across, you are at the parking lot of the Squibnocket public beach, which is itself quite fine. At the end of the lot begins a road like a track in the sand, the entrance to which is barred by a gate. If you are a member of the Squibnocket Association, you have the key to the padlock. You unlock it, drive through the gate and just beyond, lock up, and continue down the little road until you reach sanctum sanctorum. By that I mean a beach of the purest soft white sand with nothing behind you but dunes and dune grass, nothing before you except the ocean and Ireland beyond it, and nothing on either side of you as far as the eye can see but more beach. Families with young children come earlier in the day for the extraordinary beauty of the setting and for the swimming, which is perfect for kids and for strong swimmers who want to cover a long distance, because in normal circumstances the surf is very manageable without any threat of an undertow or treacherous currents. People bring lunch, and groups mingle with the sort of constrained politeness and gaiety that have always set me on edge. To be frank, I can't bear it. But in the late afternoon, West Beach is absolutely deserted. My fellow association members are all on their own or their neighbor's screened porch, decked out in faded L.L. Bean togs and cackling over Dubonnet and gin. And what did we do during the day? Lydia read my manuscript. To keep out of her way, I ran errands and pruned the garden, which is the part of gardening I like best.

On Monday, I took my boat out for a run toward Naushon. She had been in the boatyard for her annual visit, and since I wasn't using her, they had delivered her to the Vineyard Haven berth only the week before. I had never seen her in better shape, and it made me feel guilty when I thought of how little time I spend on her, but that's a whole other matter and another example of my childishness. As I have told you, Lydia is not a keen sailor, so when she said that she would stay at home and finish my manuscript, I was not surprised. In fact, I was glad to have her finish, although I must say that when I was out on Vineyard Sound running before the wind, I regretted that she wasn't there because I thought this was the best I could offer her, better than all my literary pretensions. I got home in good time for drinks, and over drinks and dinner we finally talked about *Loss.* Then it was early Tuesday morning, time for me to take Lydia to the airport. To be on the safe side, and catch the first flight to New York, we left the house before seven. A heavy fog had come in before dawn and was billowing over the road, which is not unusual, but though I had to drive very slowly there was little risk of being late. The pilot wouldn't take off until the fog had lifted. Shortly after we arrived it did lift, majestically, like a curtain rising on yet another gorgeous day. I kissed Lydia goodbye and waited in the hall while the passengers boarded. There seemed to be no end to my childishness. I found it so difficult to let Lydia go that I left the building and went to the edge of the tarmac and waited there some more, waving as the plane rose toward the sun, banked sharply to the left, and disappeared. Only then did I go back to the car, trying to cheer myself with the thought that the rest of the stay promised to be pleasant. Lydia had agreed to return on Saturday, and if possible remain through the end of the following week, in which case we would leave for the city together. That gave me time with my boat—I might sail over to Nantucket and have dinner with an old friend and his rather new third wife. I would accept the offer of a shower, but certainly I would sleep on the boat, and then take them out for a spin and lunch onboard before heading back to Vineyard Haven. I would also have enough time to finish my revisions before Lydia and I left the island. The background music for these cheerful thoughts was our dinner conversation the night before. She had told me with great conviction that she really liked *Loss,* to the point of believing that it might be my best book, more moving than *The Anthill* and stronger. The wayward wife had impressed her especially, because she was drawn with a sympathy and an understanding that she thought were new in my work. Since it was Lydia's standard complaint that I treated my female characters unfairly, this was the comment that counted. I did not abrogate the principle that a wife is not an objective judge of her husband's work. But Lydia was telling me that I had overcome a defect that she had always criticized before. That bestowed on her praise, I thought, greater authority. Anyway, I might as well confess it: I wanted terribly much to believe what she said. Her liking *Loss* and saying it so convincingly had reinforced my trust in her and my consciousness of our union; it had put me in a state of exaltation. There is no other word for how I felt. Thus, said North, I couldn't understand what had happened when I got into my car and realized, with total clarity, that all the contentment I have just described to you had suddenly vanished, and that its place had been taken by a terrible grinding nervousness and anxiety. My panic seemed utterly irrational. You need to get home at once, I said to myself, drink a cup of strong hot tea, and get to work. That was good advice except that, as I realized very soon, my jitters were the result of a remarkably timely premonition. Something inside me was keeping watch.

North was silent for a moment and then said, Forgive me, I must now interrupt my story to tell you something that concerns the present. I saw that you noticed immediately yesterday, when I arrived here, my considerable disarray. My disarray and distress—yes, that would be an even more accurate description—were so visible because I had hardly slept during the night and had mishandled my insomnia. I knew I would have trouble falling asleep, so before going to bed I took the pill that usually knocks me out at once. This time it didn't work at all, and in despair I followed up by drinking a good deal of whiskey. But even that, coming on top of what we had drunk together, didn't quite do it. It gave me perhaps an hour of unconsciousness in the morning. Mixing liquor with barbiturates is not the recipe for looking respectable. That's why, quite shamelessly, I came before you with stubble on my face, stains on my clothes, and so forth. I apologize for it. It's unpleasant to look at a man in that state.

I began to mumble something about there being no need for apologies, but North stopped me.

Thank you, he said. It was quite apparent that I shocked you, and if you have forgiven me I am grateful. The reason for my sleeplessness must be obvious. I am deeply upset by the revived memory of the events I have been describing for you. To say that it unstrings me wouldn't be overly dramatic. Constantly, as I speak to you, I am at the same time asking myself why I did the things I am telling you about, why I didn't foresee more clearly their consequences, why I allowed myself to be so weak. There is never a good answer, and it seems that there is to be no rest. And then, the night before last, I began to worry obsessively about a different problem that is important to me, although it will almost surely strike you as trivial. I have hinted at it before. You see, I am a writer, not a talker, and yet here I am, talking and talking. The question I have had to put to myself is whether it isn't a colossal mistake to tell you my story, when I should be faithful to my craft and set it down on paper. That is how I could give it a proper conclusion, so that you and every other reader would know, when you reached the last line on the last page of my book, exactly how the story ended. Now you may never know. Who is to say that the story is finished if I am still alive? If you are curious about the ending, you may have to arrange somehow to be there to bear witness when I draw my last breath. An even more important failure is that while I may never in real life resolve the conflicts that have torn apart the real John North, I think I could resolve them in a novel. You ask how? By inventing: erasing what's inconvenient and bringing in whatever is useful and getting rid of what is improbable. Against the rules of logic. There is no other way. But real life is improbable and refuses to be governed by logic. That is why I have been right to insist always, whenever the question has come up—as I did to that wretched, stupid girl—that I didn't want to write memoirs. That is the resolution I should have perhaps stuck to instead of allowing myself to play Jean-Jacques to you here in L'Entre Deux Mondes. At least Rousseau had the good sense to write it all out: that gave him the chance to reconsider and rectify his indiscretions. That's already a lot more prudent—and more artistic—than spilling it all to you over bottle after bottle of booze on the threadbare hope that you will understand and won't betray. By the way, it isn't as though I spent much time worrying whether you would betray me. The risk of my betraying you, by not telling my story as it should be told, is far graver.

My surprise was so great that I blurted out a question. Is there something to prevent you, I asked North, from making a novel out of your story later?

I don't know, he replied. For some time now I have thought that we never get closer to the truth than in a novel. Gide thought so too. It may be that, as I speak, my story acquires a shape that will resist change, that there are things I have said to you that I will not be able to take back. Perhaps someday I will make the attempt. If I do try and succeed, and you bring yourself to read what I have written, you will find out whether I was right. For the time being, I am inclined to go on with my tale, such as I remember it, and such as I can tell it now. Will you stay with me, even after my warning?

I nodded vigorously.

Thank you, said North. You are probably right. Here is what happened. I drove home faster than is my habit, because I was sure that Lydia would call from La Guardia when she landed— unless there were lines to get to the pay phones, in which case she would call from the hospital—and I didn't want to miss her. In reality, there was absolutely no chance of that even if I dawdled. The pretty drive from the airport to my house in Chilmark couldn't take more than twenty-five minutes, and Lydia wouldn't be getting off the plane for another half hour to three-quarters of an hour. But this made no difference whatso- ever, because my nervousness and anxiety had spread, like a summer storm cloud, to cover everything. I restrained myself from running to the house from the driveway. Instead, I walked ponderously, stopping to uproot grass and weeds peek- ing from between flagstone steps, made tea, had a first cup in the kitchen, and sat down behind my desk with another. My papers were laid out neatly—I had done that the evening before—and I started to work immediately. Some time had passed, I don't know how much, when, as expected, the telephone rang. I picked up the receiver and said, Hi, you've been gone for a little more than two hours, and already I miss you. Was it a smooth trip? I heard a woman giggle happily at the other end of the line and at once I knew. It was Léa calling, not Lydia. She said, Then you haven't been expecting me? I am very disappointed, and giggled some more.

She had found *Vogue*'s offer so good that she accepted the job on the spot. There was a sublet on the Upper East Side waiting for her. We would at last be neighbors. Best of all, when she told her editor that she wanted more than anything else to be on Martha's Vineyard for the Labor Day weekend, the editor had her secretary make some calls and it worked like a charm. She had a funny room with a big bathroom at a rather odd little hotel in Vineyard Haven, right across from the harbor. She'd been there since Saturday morning. The hotel didn't matter, she said, Martha's Vineyard didn't matter, she had come to see me. But when she called on Saturday morning upon arrival there was no answer and since then she had been calling nonstop. Where had I been? I said I had been out on my boat. Then my voice cracked, because I had exhausted my self-control, and I told her in a strange artificial tone that I can still hear today that she was mad, completely lunatic, if she thought she could get away with pursuing me to Martha's Vineyard, against my wishes, when I had expressly told her that Lydia might be here with me. She could stay on the island or go away, I said, there was nothing I could do about it, but she had no right to call me at home, I wouldn't have it. What I meant by that last statement I didn't know and I didn't care, because I had lost my head entirely, but somehow I felt it had some effect. She must have sensed besides that I was going to hang up because she said, Don't, don't hang up, let's talk for a moment, there are things I have to tell you. I said all right, but she had better make it quick, and she said, All right, listen to me, I was teasing you because you are such an idiot. I know you don't want me in New York and I have accepted that, and I am not taking the job, although it is every bit as good as I described, and I am not moving into the studio on Seventy-eighth Street, although it is full of sun and looks out on a garden and I liked it immediately, because I love you too much to cause you worry or hurt you. But stop being a bastard. I've come here to see you because I can't stop thinking about you, so let's see each other and tomorrow I'll go away and the next time you will see me will be wherever you want. In Paris or Moscow, it doesn't matter, I'll go to the ends of the earth to be with you. I could hear her begin to sob. I have never been able to bear a woman's tears. I guess it began with my mother, who used to cry at great length from frustration whenever Ellen or I disobeyed, which was a relatively frequent occurrence. Tears would make me want to hide—disappear—it didn't matter where, under the table, behind the sofa, in the coat closet. Or, when I got older, made me flee altogether.

Stop, I told her, stop at once, and then we will talk, said North. In a moment she did, indeed, relent. Whereupon, North continued, I told her she was wrong to treat as a joke something she knew was essential to me—keeping what she and I did away from my life with Lydia. And I told her again that she was wrong to have come to the island. However, since she was there, and since Lydia had gone back to New York, I told her we would break the rule I had made and see each other here. I have to confess to you that I was buckling under the force of sudden desire for Léa. There was a particular image—of her nipples, very small and upright even before she had been caressed, and the way that her breathing would accelerate and she would turn red in the face as soon as I squeezed them—that was before my eyes the entire time that we talked. And with it, the knowledge of her immediate and complete availability and submission to every wish, to every need. At the same time, I didn't want to spend the entire day with her. Boredom would outweigh the satisfaction of the senses. I cannot imagine greater ignominy. Therefore, I thought for a minute and said that yes, we could indeed be together until she left the next day but we had to do it right. There was no place on the island I could show myself with her without feeding immediate scandal. Not in a restaurant, not at the inn where she was staying because the owners knew me, not at the boat basin in Vineyard Haven where *Cassandra* is moored, and not on any of the beaches where there are other people—I was simply too much of a public figure in the community, my face was too well known to too many people I couldn't even begin to know. And she couldn't come to the house immediately because my handyman had just begun to fix a leaking pipe and it was impossible to send him away. Find something to occupy you through lunchtime, check out of the hotel, and wait for me on the sidewalk outside the movie theater at two. I will pick you up, in a red station wagon. Then I asked about her flight back to New York. She said it was the first plane. That was perfect, I told her, I would put her on it. Here is more ignominy, said North: I rather liked the symmetry of putting Léa on the same flight as Lydia twenty-four hours later, after a night that I thought would be rather agitated.

The call from Lydia came moments after that conversation ended. She was thanking me for those four days and once again predicting the success of my book. I was thanking her. Small wonder if, once again, my voice didn't seem to me to be my own. As always, she worried whether there were provisions in the refrigerator and the pantry for my dinner, or was I planning to go out? This gave me the opening to tell her that it looked to me as though the good weather would probably hold, so I would sail over to Nantucket that evening. With the new moon, every star would be out. I would call her from the yacht club in Nantucket, as soon as I went ashore. Then you've told Richard you are coming? she asked, Richard being my old Nantucket friend. No, I haven't, I said, I don't want him and Susan to start making dinner plans and God knows what, I'd rather surprise them. In fact, I may get some sleep onboard, go out for a sail, and only show up at their door in the evening. This was an idea that had just come into my head. That way she wouldn't call me at the house during the evening or night while Léa was there, or at Richard's to ask whether I had already arrived. When I did call in the morning, I would say I was calling from Nantucket, even though in reality I would be just about to leave.

Had Léa changed? That was the question I asked myself as I examined and reexamined her body, searching for shaming traces of the most recent great love who had so mistreated her and Lord knows how many others whom she might not have wished to mention. There weren't any. The scars had been absorbed into her perfect smooth skin, the marks of bruises had faded, the thighs and buttocks under me, the breasts I pressed as though by brute force I would possess them differently, her mouth–they were no stranger or more familiar than ever. I entered her, and as always it was she who at once set the rhythm of our engagement and its term. I knew I had lost my head. There was no holding back, no remission, and no escape. At least I had not taken her to Lydia's bed. We were in the smaller bedroom upstairs, the one my uncle had used until the end, disliking the larger room that he thought too connubial, in the four-poster bed that nothing could rock, reflected in the Chippendale mirror just over my uncle's chest of drawers. That this fine family antique of which he was so proud someday might give his heir the first opportunity to observe his rod plunge into the buttocks of the French savage astride him and, have it joined, as the pumping continued, by the furious savage's fingers alternating their service between the rod and the orifice that received it–what would he have thought had the image come before his eyes? I don't know; men who live out their lives alone are fundamentally perverse, and he and I were alike in more ways than one. It might have been very much to his taste. There was no doubt about me: I determined before we reached the climax to move that mirror to face the bed Lydia and I shared, to revive the same show with a new leading lady. When we finished, at the point I had become exhausted, I said I had feared she would look like a battered wife, marked on her body, if not her face. She made a little grimace and said, Oh, that guy! He was just a little harder on me than you. He didn't wait for me to offer to do what I knew he wanted, he tried to make me do it. I only told you he was brutal because I know you love me and that would make you pay attention. I couldn't stand him because he was so cheap. He made me pay for my train ticket, and on the Ile de Ré when we all went to a restaurant he would say it was going to be *a la romana,* and split the check with the friend we were staying with. The big deal about *a la romana* was that he split it down the middle, instead of adding up to the last cent the price of each dish any one of us ate. The guy is cheap and rich!

There! said North abruptly. At last you have seen me fuck. I bet you wondered whether I would resist telling. Believe me, I have tried.

I didn't think North expected me to answer. He seemed distracted, lost somewhere in his memories. He shook his head finally, as though he were chasing away a headache, and said: I realized that if I wanted to give her a chance to have a swim I should do it then, before the sun had sunk too low and there was a chill in the air. I asked whether she preferred the pool, which was just beyond the garden, surrounded by a hedge of rhododendron and mountain laurel, or the beach. The beach, she said, she wanted to see my beach, the one that I had talked about so beautifully. I took a wine cooler and a bottle of champagne from the fridge and glasses, four towels so we could wrap ourselves from top to toe after swimming, a sheet to lie on, and some grapes and peaches. We drove to West Beach, the beach that's chained off from the world that I have already described to you. I was completely serene. I looked forward to showing it to Léa so she would know a really fine beach, so unlike the ones she was accustomed to in Europe, overrun by tourists and in so many places with ten-story hotels set practically at water's edge. There wasn't a chance of meeting anyone there at that hour during the week. If I happened to be wrong, I thought I had an answer that would do. This is a French journalist who had the good sense to want to see the island on a September day. I am showing her the best we've got. That was what I was going to say, and there was nothing in it to worry about, because it wasn't the sort of thing that anyone would bother to rush to telephone Lydia about or would remember well enough to bring up in some conversation over drinks when we were next on the island. In fact, I was quite aware that my fear of being seen with Léa was absurd, because there was no one on the Vineyard who was intimate enough with Lydia to undertake such a call. And on our next visit we would surely avoid locals, just as this time.

It had been another very hot day, and despite the hour and the ocean breeze, it was still very warm at the beach. The ocean was an astonishing Prussian blue, with little curly wrinkles crisscrossing it, as in a child's watercolor. As I had expected, we were alone, and, with the pride of an owner showing off his estate, I pointed out to Léa the beauties of the view. She let out a yelp of satisfaction, ran to the water, tested it with her foot, and reported it was perfect. I thought we would swim right away, but she remembered the champagne and said we should drink it while it was still very cold. Besides, she wasn't against giving her tan another half hour in the sun. That was all right with me. I felt good—that sense of physical well-being that sometimes infuses all one's bones, to the tips of one's fingers and toes—and I think I would have been equally content swimming, turning cartwheels on the smooth, hard sand, running along the waterline, or lying immobile with only my head protruding from the sand, as I used to, so many years ago, on this very beach, during the summer when Ellen discovered the ineffable thrill of burying boys and patting down the sand over them and practiced this new art every day on her little brother. I spread out the brick-red sheet, shed my shorts, and worked the cork out of the bottle. Léa had stripped off her bikini the moment we arrived. We began to drink, and soon we were very silly. Léa would fill her mouth with it and spray me; I was washing the sand off the inside of her thighs and the valley between her buttocks and tugging on her hairs sometimes with my fingers and sometimes with my teeth. The bottle was almost empty by the time we made love.

I have told you that I felt exhausted when we finished in the house. She had, indeed, emptied me, and as I kept driving into her on that red sheet I realized that no matter how many times we changed positions, no matter how she used her mouth and hands, no matter what extreme edges of pleasure I reached, so far as I was concerned time stood still. There had once been a beginning to what we were doing but it was so long ago I wasn't able to remember it, and I believed there need not be an end. Perhaps there couldn't be one. At some point she started to shriek: a sort of sustained and unearthly Ahh, ahh, a series of notes that started high and descended, which I heard and did not hear, although I remember stroking her cheek and whispering over and over, It's all right, as though she needed to be consoled, and felt my hand become wet. She was weeping. An end did come, said North. It took me by surprise and shook us. I think we fell asleep almost immediately.

I don't know how long I slept. Léa shook me out of a bad dream, said North. I had been at the point of executing an increasingly difficult maneuver. It was all about the painting by Léa that was hanging in my office. The ceiling of that room had become unreasonably high, and the painting had been moved. It was now at a height on the wall that I could not possibly reach without a ladder, and I had to reach it because Léa for a reason that never became clear wanted me to take it out of the frame and off its stretcher. Fortunately, there was a ladder somewhere about the office, one of those ladders that makes an isosceles triangle when you open it. I brought it into the room and set it up and was about to climb it to get the painting when I realized it was no longer where it had been. It was now on the wall of a building across the street, still considerably higher than the level at which Léa and I stood, and oddly enough my room had become very open with only a sort of parapet between it and the street, so that it seemed that a very long ladder could be leaned against the parapet on my side and against the outside wall of that building on the other side of the street, just below the painting, and I could, if I was careful—particularly if someone steadied the ladder—cross over on all fours and very gently recover the painting. An aluminum extension ladder could also be found in the office. It made a terrible clanking noise as I lugged it into the room. Right away, I started feeding it out over the street. It reached the other side, but it did not seem possible that at the angle that was required the ladder could support the weight of a large man. I thought that when I got out on it I would freeze from fear and be unable to advance or get back. In fact, my forearms were already becoming very weak. I had great difficulty controlling the enormous ladder, which I had made even longer by extending it, and couldn't understand why Léa was totally indifferent to the extreme danger. Still partly within the dream, I waded knee-deep into the ocean, stuck my head in the water, and finally came to.

Let's swim, I said. But she remembered that I had also brought peaches in my cooler. We ate them, sitting up side by side. I was quiet, trying to make sure the nightmare was completely behind me, but as it sometimes happens, I kept returning to it, looking for solutions to the problem I could not solve before. That is when she startled me so that the dream might as well have never happened. All of a sudden, North told me, without any sort of preface, she said, I am so happy I will be living in New York. I have never had a lover like you, I have never had so much pleasure. I took her by the shoulder, North continued, and asked what in the world she was talking about, hadn't she told me just a few hours earlier that she had declined the New York offer and was going back to Paris tomorrow? In reply, she shook her head, and told me I was silly. She had only said that so I wouldn't be furious, so I would be nice to her. And it had worked! She put her face against mine and nuzzled me. Then she looked up and told me, I will be your own whore on Seventy-eighth Street! I will be there whenever you want me. On your way home from your office. If you wake up in the night and are scared and want me. Just make love to me the way you did today. Perhaps because I had just slept, said North, I was quite lucid. I understood that there was nothing to be gained from a discussion. In fact, I thought I could only make the situation worse, because if I complained or threatened, she would laugh, and I couldn't tell what I would do then. So I just said, I see, and sat there waiting.

I suppose she too had slept, because she was again full of energy. You are right, let's swim, she cried out, we should start right now. If I thought she was good in the water in Spetsai, she told me, she would show me how she had improved, practicing every day in the surf on the Ile de Ré, where there were real breakers and not the little wavelets that we seemed to have here. With that she dashed to the water, dove in without looking back, and, doing her beautiful, elongated, totally efficient crawl, set course for the horizon. There was a short while, during which I was unable to decide what to do. Then I followed. By waiting, I had given her—not that she needed it in the least—a good handicap. I thought that I could catch her, if I made a real effort, but I didn't try. There was no point; I had nothing to say to her, no caress to offer. She was swimming extremely fast, sprinting from the start, which is not what I usually do in the open ocean, and I had quite enough to do trying to keep up and perhaps slowly gain on her. I now realized that what I had thought was equanimity in the face of her treachery was in reality a sort of contained rage, filling my lungs to capacity, pouring reserves of strength into legs, shoulders, and arms. I too was swimming well in this race that wasn't one, ready, I thought, to keep on until the last drop of her strength was drained, however long it took. Perhaps my state had mysteriously communicated itself to her—the correct explanation I believe is simpler: Her craziness was the ugly side of the high intelligence and eerie sensitivity that made her able to see through me at a glance—because the longer we swam, never turning away from the horizon, the more our effort resembled an undisguised chase. I don't know how much time had passed, I don't swim with a watch, but the beach had become really quite distant when, looking up, I saw that she was no longer swimming; she was treading water. Without slowing down, I closed in until perhaps fewer than one hundred feet separated us. Thereupon, I too stopped. Almost right away, I heard her cry my name. Not like someone in distress, but loud, wanting to be heard. Here I am, I called back and waved my right arm. Right here. I can't see you, she cried. Please come nearer. Of course, this was like the bay in Spetsai, across from Spetsopoulos. She could not see me, although her face was turned right in my direction and I had kept on waving my arm. All right, I called back, coming! I swam maybe another sixty or seventy feet in her direction and, rising in the water, waved both arms. She still couldn't see me. That meant she was even blinder than I had thought. Here I am, I called again, right beside you. John, she cried, don't make fun of me, I don't know where you are, I don't know where I am, you've got to come close and lead me. All right, I answered, just wait a moment, I have a bad cramp in my foot and I have to get rid of it first.

This was, of course, a lie, said North. I needed to delay because my mind had given birth to a thought of extraordinary hideousness that I thought I must resist. I can tell by the expression on your face that you guessed it at once. You are right; it had become clear to me that all I had to do to purge my life of this demon, to save Lydia and myself from shame and worse, was to get away without another word. I had not enticed her to my lair on the island, I had not tricked her into this mad attempt on the ocean; she had done it all herself. Let her now sink or swim. And I saw with the same clarity that absent some weird mischance no one would know about my involvement in her disappearance. She had stayed at a hotel and she had checked out telling the cashier that she was taking the ferry to New Bedford; who was to say whether she took it or didn't or what happened after she got off the ferry if she ever got on? I could look deeper too, at the permutations of various outcomes, and still see no danger that constrained me to make my way to that monster and nurse her back to shore. Perhaps you think that this was too much thinking to do while I was supposedly massaging the cramp. If you do, you are wrong, all of it and much more was instantly present in my mind. It may be that a plan had been forming while, quickening the pace, stroke by stroke I followed inexorably in Léa's wake. I knew what to do: I filled my lungs, dove, and swam underwater away from the girl, not yet toward the shore but parallel to it. Ever since I was a boy, I have been able to swim underwater longer than anyone I know. When I surfaced and looked toward Léa I saw that now it was she who was waving frantically. If she was still calling my name, I could not hear it. It did not seem necessary to do so, but I dove once again and swam farther along the shore. This time when I came up and looked I could not see her. Were there shapes to be made out where she had been, and one of Léa? I was uncertain. If she had been waving still, I would have seen the white against the water that had turned black, but there was nothing like it.

And suddenly, said North, just as the hideous design had earlier crowded all other thoughts out of my mind, horror at what I had done and pity for this girl, for this body over which I had writhed with pleasure, possessed me equally, and I began to yell her name with all the force I had over and over and over. Then, although I knew it was useless, I began to swim to where I thought I had left her, doing that horribly tiring stroke, which is freestyle with your head out of the water so you can keep looking and looking, and I kept this up until the stars came out burning in the sky but I couldn't find her. I then realized that if I didn't go for the shore while I still thought I knew where it was it would soon be too late. As it was, even if I started immediately, it was not impossible that I too would drown. There was apparently a reserve of strength in me though. I staggered out of the water almost exactly where Léa and I had gone in. Crickets were making an insane noise in the dune. They and the waves were the only sound. There was no other human figure. My teeth were chattering. I dried myself, drank what remained of the champagne, and packed up the stuff. It seemed best to take the bikini with me. I left two towels. If she made it to shore, which I doubted, because fog was coming in, they would be much more useful to her than those two scraps of cloth. Then I went home.

A plan for my next steps was ripening. I would have some bread, sausage, and cheese, and just a little wine. Then I would dress warmly for the night sail, pack my toilet kit and clothes to go ashore in when I got to Nantucket and a bottle of whiskey and some more sausage and cheese, and put the clothes Léa had taken off and her bikini into her suitcase. It seemed to me best to leave the suitcase at home, for the time being. If the improbable had happened, and she survived, it would not help to have it seem that I had tried to get rid of it. The time to do it would come later, after I got back, if she hadn't been heard from. That was giving her a good forty-eight hours to rise from the dead, which in the circumstances was ample. These simple chores finished, I would drive to Vineyard Haven, row myself out to the mooring, and at last board my boat. Immense happiness. Wasn't sailing my boat, being with her alone, whispering my secrets to her, what I really lived for?

The rest, said North, is deplorable. It's like another bad dream, this one of a boy's adventure story gone very wrong. Are you fond of sea adventures? No? Not even Conrad? That's all right. So often he overdoes it. You will hear my seagoing tale, such as I think it is, told very simply, stripped down, without the sonorities of *Typhoon*. I got to the boat. The breeze, as I had expected, had freshened, and the moment I hoisted the mainsail *Cassandra* perked up, ready to go. I did not turn on the running lights—the less chance of creating witnesses to the hour of my departure the better—and cast off the mooring. We began to move in total silence and with total grace. The darkness and the fog that was rolling in from the south and had reached the harbor were nothing to me. I could have sailed there blindfolded. In no time flat, we were out. I turned on the running lights, cranked the jib up the mast, set it, adjusted the main, and set the course for East Chop. I loved the feel of my boat. We rounded the Chop. The wind was from the south, which was usual. On a reach, the boat humming, I headed for Cape Poge. So far it had all been a cinch. It would be another cup of tea when we were past Edgartown and entered waters that are like a goddamn choppy minefield, with shoals all around you. Then the real fun would begin, especially if the breeze stiffened and did not blow away the fog. With visibility rapidly declining to nothing, I judged it prudent to get out my previous year's purchase, a handheld GPS, and verified what I had done. So far, the compass had stood me in good stead. I had not made any mistakes. There was no reason that I shouldn't dig into the food and treat myself to a real drink. *Cassandra* has an open cockpit, as befits a racing boat, and having fastened the jib and the main, I huddled in it, feeling cozy in my oilskins, and concentrated on the wheel and the food and drink. The whiskey was slowly but perceptibly steadying my nerves. Pillows of fog swept over the deck of my boat and I exulted in the challenge. What else was a great sailboat for, if one had been her skipper for as long as I had, and its brave mast and huge sails were in familiarity and function no different from the trunk of your body and arms only vastly stronger and more beautiful? My jitters definitely over, I examined my ghastly deed. That I was guilty, I did not for a moment doubt, the question was, of what? Not murder; I had not killed the girl, I had not planned it. It was a simple truth that I was not ready for it, though doubtless to kill her seemed to be a price I would have paid for keeping her away from Lydia. Not just out of fear for my tranquillity and happiness, but because I would have rather died myself than seen Lydia humiliated. That was the true nature of Léa's threat. But it hadn't yet come to that. The other simple truth was that I had done something unforgivable and vile by leaving the girl in mortal danger when it would have been easy for me to bring her out of it. Was there any excuse? I did not think so. Whereupon, a squeaky little voice piped up on my behalf, reminding me, as though that were needed, that the girl was a phenomenally strong swimmer, a much better swimmer than I. Yes, but blind, my more respectable voice replied, blind as a bat, isn't that how I had put it? Yes, but I would not have left her out there—I was pretty sure—if she had been a weak swimmer, or even just a normally competent swimmer. I certainly wouldn't have set a trap, wouldn't have lured her out way off shore only to abandon her there, I reassured myself. We went back and forth like that, my conscience and I, and it was pretty boring, but nothing changed, or could ever change, I thought, the fundamental fact that I had let a crazy and wicked girl who loved me die a dreadful death. No, it wasn't an assured death; for all I knew, with her stamina, she would wash up on a Vineyard beach naked and only half dead. The dogfish and the crabs would not have made a meal of her. I was not about to turn myself in to the police—as a matter of fact, I wasn't sure what crime I could be accused of, although I supposed one could be found to fit my case. The effect, were I to do such a crazy thing, was bound to be worse for Lydia than anything that Léa might have done. I had to dispose of my case myself. A solution appeared before me: I would roll the dice for life or death. She had had a chance to make it or to drown, and so would I; in any case, I would not go scot-free. The fog had thickened so that I could not make out clearly the bow of my boat, the splendid breeze had turned into a gale whose whistling split my ears. *Cassandra* was rising and falling with waves of a height I had not foreseen. I checked the GPS and the chart again. We were halfway to Cape Poge, heading for the old lightship that is no more. If only, I said to my boat, if only I could do this without hurting you. There was no such way. I tossed the GPS overboard and with my other hand tore out the electrical wires that led to the compass. Its face went black. The last time I had *Cassandra* on a reach like that, heeling like a dinghy, was just two days ago, when we ran back from the Elizabeth Islands, in beautiful sunshine, the sea festive with many colored spinnakers of other ships and, in comparison, tame. We were all alone now and blind. I could make out the cockpit, the deck as far as to the mast, and the waves that washed over it. That was all. Now the only way to stay on the course I had set was to be true to the wind, which I judged to be steady although growing in strength. It turned out that I did not steer badly. The shoal I ran onto was just past the old lightship, so I had strayed very little. Had I been able to free us of the shoal quickly, I would have saved my beautiful *Cassandra,* but before I could manage it the waves filled the cockpit and turned her on her side. Then they broke her up. I survived clinging to the rudder. Since I had determined not to load the dice, I was not wearing a life vest. That gesture in fact loaded the dice against me. It was a miracle or a fluke that I didn't drown. My brother-in-law, Ralph, was the one who started the Coast Guard search. When Lydia told him that I was on my way to Nantucket, right away, on a hunch, he checked the weather. He knew exactly what that squall could do even to a good sailor with navigational instruments.

North fell silent, his head bowed.

For a while, I didn't dare to speak. Then I asked him, What happened later?

What do you mean, he replied.

I mean to Léa, for instance. Have you found out whether she really drowned?

North laughed and shook his head. No, he said, I have not had *de ses nouvelles.* After I was fished out, I was obliged to stay in the hospital longer than I would have imagined. When I got out, I went carefully through the Martha's Vineyard papers, the *New York Times,* obviously, and also three of the Paris dailies, for the two weeks after the wreck, looking for some sort of mention of her disappearance. I never found any. A short time after my discharge, I had to go to the Vineyard to deal with the marine insurance claim. Her little suitcase was exactly where I had left it, in the closet in my uncle's bedroom. I took it with me on the plane to Boston and there I left it at the airport, having first wiped it clean of fingerprints and removed the luggage tag. I suppose it's still at the Lost and Found.

Do you really think she could have survived? I said after a while. I had been lost in thought.

Your guess is as good as mine, was his reply. It was not impossible, but all I can say for sure is that I don't know. She hasn't come near me. I haven't gone near people who know her.

But why, I asked, utterly uncomprehending, if she were alive, why wouldn't she seek you out? How could this be?

That's easy, said North. Wouldn't she be afraid that given another chance I would really kill her?

And you, and Lydia?

Lydia is well. She found it only natural that after the shipwreck and my illness I would need to get away for a while. As for me, you know more about me now than anyone else alive.

SHIPWRECK

A Reader's Guide

LOUIS BEGLEY

A CONVERSATION WITH
LOUIS BEGLEY

Donald Hall has published twenty books of poetry. His short stories are collected in Willow Temple *(2003). Forthcoming is a memoir,* The Best Day the Worst Day, *about his late wife, Jane Kenyon, and a selection of his poetry from 1950 to the present.*

Donald Hall: The first thing to notice, the first thing to astonish, is the form of the novel–John North's monologue over three days to a nameless listener. "I made no comment," the listener tells us. "It seemed best to say nothing." In one of his few references to himself, he speaks of John North as "this man so like me in appearance, in demeanor." Maybe he notes class and education only, but it raises the thought that North is in effect talking to himself. Did you have any such notions?

Louis Begley: It is possible that North is talking to himself. Small pieces of stage business, however, point in the other direction. Occasionally, the mostly silent ostensible narrator says something and bestirs himself to do certain things. He drinks, he eats, he accompanies North to the toilet. More important, he observes North and reports on him. None of this, I agree in advance, is conclusive. It could be that North and I are enjoying a private joke.

A reason to think that North is not alone that I find persuasive is the tension of the narrative. I think it comes from North's always addressing someone who is in fact right across the table from him, rather than speaking to the abstraction called a Reader.

DH: Did the monologue form occasion special difficulties in the writing?

LB: It didn't. I had no hesitation about the form. "The Rime of the Ancient Mariner" was very much in my mind; it could not be dislodged. I wanted the tale to be told by a compulsive talker, one of those obnoxious people whom at first you can't get to shut up, and later would gladly pay if only they kept going.

DH: In the *Paris Review* interview, done while you were writing *Shipwreck,* you talk about beginning a novel with a "clear image of the protagonist and of the protagonist's predicament," and of knowing "how the predicament will resolve itself." Did you know how *Shipwreck* would end?

LB: Yes. As I may have said in the *Paris Review* conversation, I had the ending so clearly in mind that I wrote it out before I started on the beginning. Such changes as I made later in the ending had to do with the geography of Martha's Vineyard, the exact place where North's ship would be wrecked, and, of course, the use of words.

There must have been eight or ten printed drafts with nothing but word changes. And between those printed versions I was constantly changing words on the screen of my laptop. But nothing of substance was altered.

DH: While being interviewed by Léa at the beginning of the novel, John North talks about how a novelist uses "tales and anecdotes told to him by others. When he is dining out, for instance, like Henry James." Was there such a seed for *Shipwreck*? Do you remember how the novel began and how it grew?

With *Loss,* John North "had a pretty good draft"of the last scene in his book "before I started the first chapter." Did you ever do such a thing?

LB: I am sorry to report that I did not get the idea of *Shipwreck* dining out.

Its germ was a thought that came to me in Venice, I believe shortly after I had finished *Schmidt Delivered* and before I started *Mistler's Exit*. I wanted to try to write a thriller about a married young man with children who decides he must get rid of an intrusive mistress who is threatening the tranquility of his family. Of course, he wants to commit a perfect crime so that he can live happily ever after. That aspect of the transaction is not, in his opinion, difficult to work out. The real problem is that he genuinely likes his mistress, and therefore, he wants to make sure that he doesn't frighten her or cause her pain.

I had a solution to that problem as well, but I didn't get around to testing it because I turned instead to *Mistler's Exit*.

But, when *Mistler's Exit* was done, the old thriller idea rose up in a new shape, that of a crime that may not be a crime at all, at the root of which is the very complicated relationship between North and his mistress, Léa.

So it is true that, like North when he was writing *Loss,* I had the last scene in hand when I got to work.

DH: North's monologue takes place at a bar called L'Entre Deux Mondes. The name of the establishment seizes me. I found myself giving *Shipwreck* an alternative title: *Between Two Worlds*. I seem to take the name of the establishment as being descriptive of the novel. Do you see any such possibility?

LB: You are exactly right. Where the narration takes place is a mystery, and I intended it to be such. At one point it occurred to me that L'Entre Deux Mondes could be a quiet corner of an insane asylum.

DH: I do not confuse Louis Begley with John North, but I wonder if your feelings as a novelist jibe with his. He does not want to pick one of his novels as best because "one can't say that sort of thing about a book any more than about children." You say something similar about your own work in a *Paris Review* interview. When John North writes a novel that makes use of memories, he tells us, writing the novel exorcises these memories. Has such a phenomenon happened to you?

LB: North's views about the craft of the novel are ones I find it easy to accept and occasionally to put forward as my own.

I do not agree, however, that using memories in a novel exorcises them. For instance, writing *Wartime Lies* did not have the cathartic or curative effect of relieving me of night-mares about World War II in Poland, or my inability to watch scenes of violence on television or on a motion-picture screen, or my ghastly fear of other humans. I am not particularly afraid of dangers associated with the elements or airplane or auto-mobile accidents or other threats that do not have in them the component of human malice directed at me. By contrast, the thought of what other men may choose to do to me puts me in a state of panic.

DH: John North undergoes an epiphany about his works: "none possessed the literary merit that critical opinion ascribed to them." Does not every good writer undergo such notions? Have you?

LB: I certainly have. But I never reach a secure feeling of satis-faction about my work in the first place. I don't stop question-ing it, even if, when I do a reading from one of my novels, a particular passage strikes me as well written, or amusing, or even engrossing. Indeed, I think it's a miracle when a reader, or a friend, or a reviewer tells me that what I have written is good.

DH: "I don't teach creative writing," says John North. Can you imagine doing such a thing?

LB: I am not sure that it can be done.

Of course, people who want to write fiction can be taught grammar, punctuation, and rudiments of style, by which I mean such matters as that the structure of sentences has to be varied, that one must avoid using the same word over and over when adequate synonyms exist unless the repetition is intentional, and that one must beware of malapropisms and metaphors that are dead on arrival.

And one can be told that one needs to carry the reader along by the strength of the narrative.

But will such precepts do any good to students who do not have an innate love for words and talent for using them? Or the willpower required if one is going to police what one has written?

I doubt it.

But it may be that I have never been taught by a really good teacher of creative writing.

DH: Henry James had a way with proper names. May Bartram is the warmer one, John Marcher considerably cooler. What of John North's name?

LB: Yes, North is a cold name and should be taken as something of a signal.

DH: You and John Updike were members of the same class at Harvard. You were editor of a literary magazine, the *Harvard Advocate,* and he of the humorous *Harvard Lampoon.* I believe that you both took writing courses with Albert Guerard. Did you know each other?

LB: I don't remember John's having been in the class taught by Albert Guerard that I attended. At one time I thought he was already in the more advanced class taught by Archibald MacLeish. However, it turns out that neither of us made it to that summit of creative writing.

John and I did know each other at that time, but I do not

believe that we knew each other well. We became friends about four years later, when he had moved to Ipswich and I was in my first year of Harvard Law School.

DH: In an account of your work as a lawyer, in the *New Yorker* profile of you, you are described as excellently combative, highly successful as a negotiator. Is there a way in which your fiction provides another outlet for, oh, competitiveness?

LB: I am not competitive as a novelist, perhaps because I know that the only writers I would care to take on would knock me out of the ring. They are the usual group: Proust, Tolstoy, Flaubert, Kafka. Given such ambition, it's best that I keep a low profile.

It is in fact possible that writing fiction has liberated me from the need to be at the head of the class.

DH: The *New Yorker* writer, speaking of your fiction after *Wartime Lies,* says that "it's as though Begley had decided to explore every negative possibility of his grown up existence, to see where the wrong turns would have lead." Can you see some of your fictions as counterautobiographical?

LB: Hal Espen's observation is profound, and, perhaps for that reason, I am not sure I understand it completely. To the extent that I do grasp his intention, I would say that I am very hard in my novels on protagonists who could be my doubles but, of course, aren't.

DH: Your second novel came out two years after your first, your third novel one year later. The fourth, fifth, and sixth came two years apart. Only *Shipwreck* occasioned a three-year gap between publications. Was it more difficult? Did it take more drafting? Was the rest of your life getting in the way?

LB: I think that what held me back was the cumulative weight of legal work–I was extraordinarily busy as a lawyer when I was writing *Shipwreck*–and the sort of duties one accumulates as one publishes books, for instance writing articles and essays that some magazine or newspaper has commissioned, giving an occasional speech, correcting translations of novels as they are bought for publication in a language I know, or giving an occasional reading to promote my work and, very important to me, coming in contact with readers. Before one has published a couple of books, one is not asked to do such things. Indeed, one has no opportunity to undertake them.

Of course, every hour spent on these "paraliterary" pursuits is an hour that one hasn't devoted to one's work as a novelist.

DH: You wrote your first novel, *Wartime Lies,* when you received a four-month sabbatical from your law firm. You had written no fiction in the decades after college. At some point, did you expect to? Were you waiting for sufficient time?

LB: Out of modesty or superstitious fear, I did my utmost to keep thoughts of writing fiction out of my head. People occasionally asked why I didn't try to write. I had a stock answer that was on a certain level truthful: I have no time.

There is, of course, another truth: Time can always be found if one wants to write and dares to.

The long delay was fortunate, because evidently I needed to mature in various ways before undertaking to write about my experiences during World War II. I am certain that I would have made a hash of it if I had tried to do it before I was so ready for *Wartime Lies* that the novel could and did force itself on me.

DH: You have said that after you wrote your second novel, you discovered that you liked writing. Is it possible to say what you like about it?

LB: Letting a character grow inside me, and getting to understand him and his dilemma, is great fun. More unbeatable fun comes in telling the character's story and providing the setting for it. The best fun of all is to discover as I write the crowd of observations and jokes stored somewhere in my head that I had not known about before I came to use them.

North says something quite similar in the course of his fateful interview with Lea.

DH: Now that you have largely retired from the law, and writing is no longer a matter for weekends and vacations, do you find yourself changing in your attitude toward writing? I can imagine feeling freed; I can imagine feeling terrified.

The *Paris Review* interviewer asked you about your life after law, when you would be able to devote yourself to writing, and you remarked that it would depend "entirely on whether there is water left in the well." Does there appear to be water left in the well?

LB: How well you understand me!

I think it is fabulous, too good to be true, that I can now take as much time as I like or need to write a novel—a task for which there is no deadline, because I would not dream of getting a contract for a novel I haven't completed to the point of its being ready, in my judgment, to be published. But I am afraid of not being able to put my time to good use, precisely because there is no water left in the well, or, equally possible and even more terrifying, because my intellectual power will flag.

Is there water left in the well? I hope so and will soon find out as I try to make progress on what should be my eighth novel.

READING GROUP QUESTIONS AND TOPICS FOR DISCUSSION

1. John North has been faithful to his wife. Why does he suddenly turn adulterer?

2. Considering John North's obsession with Léa, are you skeptical of his love for his wife?

3. May North's resentment of Lydia's family provide a motive for his betrayal of Lydia? Or does North obsess about Léa because he has decided that his own work is without value?

4. From what you know of John North's parents, can you imagine his upbringing? How has it affected his character?

5. John North will not accompany Lydia to Japan. Why? What is the effect on his marriage?

6. Will John North and Lydia live happily forever after?

7. Despite his conviction that his novels are without literary merit, North works with great concentration on his subsequent novel, *Loss*. Does this give the lie to his self-deprecation?

8. Throughout the book, there are foreshadowings. John North tells a story from *Daniel Deronda*: Gwendolyn does not throw the rope to the drowning Grandcourt, deliberately withholding it. "I cannot tell you the resonance of this scene within me." In another place, he tells Léa that if Lydia finds out, "I believe I will kill you"—and "I will kill you if you come near Lydia." Did you expect something like the conclusion?

9. "I had fallen in love," says John North after his first erotic encounter with Léa. Is he in love?

10. John North has no friends to play squash with. Does he have friends?

11. After John North abandons Léa to the sea, he rolls the dice on his own drowning. Is his gamble in character?

12. Is Léa dead?

13. Will Bunny Frank's "obituary envy" alter John North's feelings about the Frank family?

14. John North tells his listener, in the novel's last line, "You know more about me now than anyone else alive." Does this sentence in effect end the novel?

15. Imagine the rest of John North's life.

16. As a little boy evading Nazis in Poland, Louis Begley had to think ahead, planning every move. His prose style has been called lapidary. Can we associate this quality with the watchfulness and deliberation that he had to practice as a child?

PHOTO: JERRY BAUER

LOUIS BEGLEY lives in New York City. His previous novels are *Schmidt Delivered, Wartime Lies, The Man Who Was Late, As Max Saw It, About Schmidt*, and *Mistler's Exit*. His website is www.louisbegley.com.